BEFORE ALL THE WORLD

ALSO BY MORIEL ROTHMAN-ZECHER

Sadness Is a White Bird

BEFORE ALL THE WORLD

Moriel Rothman-Zecher

FARRAR, STRAUS AND GIROUX
NEW YORK

For Nahar, and for Kayla

For Esther, and for her youngest sibling, Leonore

Farrar, Straus and Giroux
120 Broadway, New York 10271

Printed in the United States of America
First edition, 2022

Library of Congress Cataloging-in-Publication Data
Names: Rothman-Zecher, Moriel, author.
Title: Before all the world / Moriel Rothman-Zecher.
Description: First edition. | New York : Farrar, Straus and Giroux, 2022.
Identifiers: LCCN 2022023657 | ISBN 9780374231668 (hardcover)
Subjects: LCGFT: Novels.
Classification: LCC PR9510.9.R69 B44 2022 | DDC 823/.92—dc23
LC record available at https://lccn.loc.gov/2022023657

Designed by Gretchen Achilles

1 3 5 7 9 10 8 6 4 2

'kh'kush dikh, farkoltent yiddish leben /

I kiss you, disheveled Jewish life

—YANKEV GLATSHTEYN / RUTH WHITMAN

a mayseh

By Gittl Khayeles

Translated by

Charles Patterson (Roses)

Contents

dustvillage

philadelphiye

Translator's Note

How about Zatelsk?

What?

Should Zatelsk be capitalized in american?

yoh.

Why?

Gittl shrugged. Maybe a dustvillage is more like a person than a god.

How about philadelphia, then?

You decide. Is your philadelphiye more like a person or a god?

Well, what's a god, Comradess?

A falsehope.

I'll drink to that. And a person?

A thing made from maysehs and tayve and the small choices of each moment.

In the year and a half since this exchange with the author, I have spent many mornings translating the following pages, at times adhering to the rules which the author and I established, as above, and at others inventing rules of my own; striving at many junctures to be faithful to the Yiddish source, while also straying deliberately from its bounds at others, adding, altering, inventing: obeying the urge and mutterings of history to tell a truthsome story, in conversation with the original mayseh.

It is my hope that this translation will find favor in the author's eyes, and in Reyza's, and in other readers' as well. For even as I feel everything closing around me, once again, I too still choose to believe that all the world is not darkness.

CHARLES PATTERSON (ROSES)
Moscow, May 1936

dustvillage

a mayseh

Once there was a child what was called Reyza.
di mayseh iz avek.[1]

1 Literally: "The story is gone, or, away." Idiomatically: "The end."

a beforemayseh

Once there was a jew what was called Gittl, and Gittl sat amidst a pile of her siblings what were called Anshl and Hendl and Zimml and Reyza. When the clan of death came, they took everyone to the forest except for Gittl and one other jew. The other jew was called Leyb.

Hawkchicken
(an aftermayseh)

And so yoh, Cricket's.

On his first time at Cricket's, Leyb stood only at the edges of the room, overwatching the men what inpiled there every shabbes evening in philadelphiye, and what seemed to Leyb not so much amerikanish or even men, but rather as a single sunwarmed river, yoh, and Leyb imagined submerging into this evermoving clamor of bodies, and finding there only quiet, and he felt the surges of his tayve,[2] and wanted for his tayve to merge into one of the many mouths of the Cricket's river of grasping and stroking and drinking and howling and gasping and trumpets and smoke, but he found no such opening and so remained cornersome and dryish and he waited until Cricket's began to fold into itself and become, in preparation for the six days of the week

2 "Urge and urge and urge," as Walt would have it.

what followed, once again a place of nothingness, an emptyish building, yoh, or perhaps a sockshop, and then Leyb tohomewent alone.

On his second time at Cricket's, a part of the river offtrickled to shtip[3] Leyb in the backroom and the gold band on the ring finger of this man's hand was cold against the skin near Leyb's opening as this man, what was really only made from water, readied to inslide into Leyb, and Leyb was for a gathering of moments become gebensht[4] with elektrish amerikanish upfilledness and an awayfeeling and, yoh, quiet.

On his third time at Cricket's, Leyb met Charles.[5]

ikh gleyb nit az di gantze velt iz kheyshekh,[6] Leyb quieted to himself after passing under the door's lintel, not recalling from where precisely came this phrase, feeling only the way it slightly settled the dust what rose in him with each breath.

And a good evening to you, naye feygele, said a man what had inwalked just after Leyb, and was updraping his coat on the coatrack. He offtook his hat and towardtipped it to Leyb.

Despite having by this point passed most of his years

---

3 "Fuck."

4 "Blessed."

5 zeyer ayngenem, baby.

6 "I do not believe that all the world is darkness."

in the belly of the goldene medineh, Leyb remained eternally greenbeast newcome, and so had failed to develop a fluent comprehension of modernishe amerikanishe eugenics. Leyb knew only to sense jew or goy by just opening his nostrils, and so, nostrils flared, Leyb did right away sense that the man what had inwalked just behind him was not a jew, lacking, as his scent was, in that particular underhum of mashed sevenfish.

You're knowing to speak jewish? Leyb said in american.

Don't look so farvundert, said the man.

I'm not surprised from anything, Leyb said. Only I wanted to tell you that feygele just is meaning bird.

You don't say, said the man, upraising only one of his eyebrows.

Leyb searched the drawers of his chest for a shtikl of unjewsome american what he might place on his tongue.

I do say? Leyb said.

Alright, newbird, the man said, placing his hat among the sixteen or twenty other hats. How about you buy me a drink to make up for any potential iniquities? A big pinecone like you must have a few extra rubles. The man touched a hand to his belly. And I ought to be able to scrounge up a pound of flesh, just in case.

Leyb did not laugh. He was then only looking upon this man's fingers, what were stained with ink, and what were neatly upscrolling the sleeves of his shirt, and at the softdance of tendons in the man's nakedbecoming forearms, and inside Leyb, his tayve stretched and scratched at the back of his eyes. Somewhere else in the mainroom of Cricket's, someone screamed, maybe with laughter, maybe without.

Lighten up, kid, the man said, searching for Leyb's eyes with his eyes.

Leyb nodded, looked at the man's eyes, looked away.

I should introduce myself more properly. I'm Charles, Charles said, outstretching his hand. Fellow traveler of Red Emma, stuck in the tower of our very own city hall, which is to say, newboy: I'm on your side if you're on mine.

Leyb removed his hand from his pocket, leaving a film of moisture on the coins therein, wet beading on the metal like dew on the rebbe's irongate in the mornings of Zatelsk's latesummer,

yoh but the gates can rot and the hairs from the longest rebbebeard outfall

next to the way what dewdrops clung to the fingers of pine remember Leyb'ele

and grasped Charles's hand with his hand. Charles's palm was dry and warm, and Leyb ran his mind over the feeling of Charles's hand overbrushing his cheek and then grasping the back of his neck and sliding down his back and towardpulling him inward to where there would be softness and hardness alike and then the mustful bar, what was not really a bar, what was really just a den of tin and furnace smoke and coagulated dreams, began to feel once more unto Leyb as a river.

On that note, did you hear that Comrade Goldman might be allowed back for a second crack at the city of brotherly love later this year?

Oh, Leyb said, not much caring this way or that from the second coming of Emke Goldman or from brothersome fissures in the city of love.

Anyhow, Charles said. How about that drink?

Leyb had heard the Halpers saying that the blacks[7] were very much poor, more even than the poorjews of philadelphiye, so he took his dewy rubles, what he had actually very few, and moved toward the barman, what had around his neck a horizonglowish tie and hair what was painted strawish. Behind him perched a squat row of bottles, mauve, dim, taupe, dapple, jasmine, aquamarine, reddish, clear. Charles put his fingertips on Leyb's shoulder, and said something to the pretty barman in

---

7 Orig.: "shvartze." Much as I would like to take Leyb and Gittl at their word regarding their overheard suggestion that this term might be deployed without malice, both lived experience and literary exploration serve to undermine said claim. Even if "shvartze" is not identical to the word upon which america was founded, and which it continues to wield in order to undergird the brutalization, exploitation, and racialized class stratification requisite to sate its various capitalistic and cannibalistic appetites, the term is grotesque and hateful enough in its own right.

rhymesome american.[8] The barman blinked with one of his eyes and shook his head at Leyb's palmful of coins and passed two glasses of blood
it's wine Leyb'ele
it's just wine
across the bar and Charles took them without giving to the barman any money soever. Leyb inbreathed one breath through his nose, awaytook one glass from Charles's hand, downdrank half its contents in one zhlyuk. Around them the night was savage, was soft, was a strumming slipping between alternately steady and swaying sweating forms, was streaks of silver threaded through earlobes, was the stab of fishhooks coddled into jowls, was outjutting sexes, was lost, was startling itself, was just another shabbes evening at Cricket's.

Drinks have gotten so goddamn expensive, Charles said.

Leyb tried to raise one eyebrow unto Charles, but could not aloneraise each of his two brows as could his interlocutor, and so got stuck looking more rye than wry.

Charles drew from his own pocket a metal case and from the case two paperwrapped bonefingers of tobacco.

Things were better, in a sense, Charles said, before america's noble experiment expired, the hooch's taste

---

8 "Tabulate it, Nate."

notwithstanding. Most of the erstwhile blind tigers seem to have had no trouble finding their eyes in this new era, and even though we're still underground, Cricket's has been upping its rates to keep pace, but I suppose so go the workings of capital, hey?

I suppose, Leyb said, and took a cigarette from Charles and placed it between his teeth, feeling his tayve rushing within him as Charles placed a hand over Leyb's hand and lit Leyb's cigarette with another metal box, this one smaller and towardpointing a steady finger of fire to the ceiling, what could not be seen for all the smoke filling the room but what Leyb believed to be there nevertheless.

Charles lit his own cigarette, blew out a pillar of smoke, and spoke. Did you ever make it to a blind tiger, newboy?

Leyb nodded, then shook his head, then tilted his head to the side.

A speakeasy.

Leyb, what didn't know from speaking easy, certainish notly in american, shrugged, his teeth resting on the cigarette's end.

The thing is, Charles said, those speakeasy kittens weren't concerned in the least with who was fucking whom, giving that we were all fucking america together, as it were. Suddenly, though, the bulk of the populace seems to have worked itself up into such a state of confusion regarding our so-called sodomitical sodality, which they seem to have deemed somehow both nonexistent and supremely threa— Watch it with that thing, baby.

Leyb's tongue had been circling the end of his cigarette, and its ashen beginning had grown longer and flimsier, the various embers attached by only the faintest threads of paper and dried plant.

Ashtray, Nathaniel? Charles said to the barman, who withdrew from the underbar a ridged and hollow thing, what could not have been the shell of a smallish turtle but what looked to Leyb to be, and Charles held it out for Leyb and Leyb rimtapped his cigarette and half of it fell into the empty shell where it glowed reddish and lonesome, and all three men watched it until it receded fully into darkness and Charles replaced the shell on the bar and coughed, and the barman resumed his ritual of rummage and rustle, and Leyb chewed the flesh on the inside of his cheek.

Don't worry though, Charles said. They haven't raided Cricket's yet, and we're already—what is it now—a couple of weeks into this new era, so I figure we're alright here until we're not.

Leyb nodded, had not been so much listening to what Charles was saying, had been instead coaxing his tayve to continue its prowl of his skin, his nape, his sex, his memories, his eyes, as Charles awaywent into his own wordsworld.

Leyb downdrank another zhlyuk.

So, vi heystu anyway, kid?

Leyb.

Leyb, Charles said. Lion, yes?

It's meaning lion, yes, Leyb said, drinking more, and wiping his wrist on his mouth's edges, feeling his lips overbrush his own arm and wanting then to overbrush his lips on Charles's arm, wanting for Charles's lips to overbrush his face, wanting another moment of quiet and breath.

Would it be alright if I call you Lion?

It's alright, Leyb said.

Alright then, l'khayim, Lion, Charles said, and he moved his glass toward Leyb's but stopped short, and Leyb saw that his own glass was empty, and he watched as Charles signaled to the barman and downdrank the rest of his own blood and then suffocated the remainder of his cigarette in the burgundy droplets congregated at the bottom of the glass, placed the soggish remnant in the barresting ashturtle, retrieved the two drinks from the barman with an eyeblink of his own, and then handed a second glass to Leyb, their fingers touching, oh soarish oh stay.

Let's try that again? Charles said. Toward strength, Leyb.

Glass clinked against glass amidst the smoke. Leyb's own cigarette had burned down into a single ball of fire what was dancing a frantic yontiff[9] dance near his fingertips and Charles licked his own forefinger and his centerfinger and also his thumb and towardreached to Leyb's mouth and clamped his wettened inkstained fingers around the fire and it sizzled and was gone and Charles's body was now close to Leyb's and somewhere else in Cricket's someone howled again, and Leyb stillstayed and then forwardswayed slightly as Charles retreated one halfstep.

How old are you, Lion?

Twenty almost.

Well, Charles said. I guess if I'm any sort of bird, that makes me a chickenhawk.

A what?

Don't worry about it.

How old are you.

I'll be thirty-three in April, Charles said.

just how old Mameshi was

yoh the best chessplayer in all of Zatelsk

You okay, Lion?

Why should I not be, because you're a hawkchicken?

Charles laughed. Leyb put his glass to his lips and drank again, hardish, longish, longing for the beforemoment of tayve to return and to banish the moments of his mameshi and Zanvl and Shprintzl, what

9 "Redletterday."

moments he did not wish to hold or be held by now or again ever.
yoh but that's not true Leyb
cannot be true Leyb'ele ours

Hey, Charles said, upbringing his fingertips to Leyb's cheek. I didn't mean to laugh at you, Lion. Tell if you want me to go and I'll go. You'll have your pick of the litter in here tonight, I'm sure of it, with big sad eyes like those.

Leyb was silent.

Well, Charles said. I was glad to make your acquaintance, zeyer ayngenem, baby, and thanks for getting me these drinks.

No, Leyb said, pushing the word past the desiccated grapes coating the tunnel of his throat, through the breath upfilling his body.

Charles looked at Leyb, one eyebrow upraised.

I have not got for you the drinks, Leyb said. You have got for me.

You've got a point there, Lion, Charles said, his eyes aroundsearching Leyb's eyes. One more?

Leyb nodded, waiting now at the edge of the forest, surrounded by tall grasses and a band of hedgehogs and fireants, and there was the sound of a river and the smell of burning small trees and the smell of charred pages and smoked whitefish and the sound of the wind and strumming and singing
tum bala tum bala

and then Charles returned, once more holding two glasses, and said, To the procreant urge of the world, as it were.

As it were?

Whitman, baby. Don't get too hung up on the procreant part, if that's what's got you looking so farzorgt. Walt would've been one of the city of brotherly love's most famous feygeles, except that folks were less obsessed with feygelizing back then . . .

Aha, Leyb said. So we're come back to talking about birds.

So it seems. Will you spread your wings and trip the light fantastic with me, Lion?

Charles towardleaned his head to the backroom door, from behind what bemuffled trumpetsounds strained to escape. Leyb nodded, and followed Charles into the backroom, and Charles closed the door behind them and faced Leyb, and then put one hand around his waist and then the other and Leyb realized only then that they would in truth dance, and he put his arms through Charles's arms and behind Charles's back and Charles pulled Leyb toward him and Leyb let himself forwardfall and they moved together back and forth and were surrounded by other men rocking and drinksloshing and tripping fantastish in the smokedark graylight and laughing and kneeling and whispering into one another in the almostsafe almostsilence that undersat the music, in scrawny and tubbish and reaching states of dress and gentle undress. Leyb pressed himself forward and one of Charles's palms slipped up Leyb's fabricoated spine, and his fingers brushed the hairs on the back of Leyb's neck, and Leyb, what had never been happy, even before the forest, felt something lightsome wing between his ribcage and he pressed his lips down onto Charles's neck and did not awaytake them from there for a long time.

After this long time had passed, Charles moved his hand from Leyb's nape and onto the side of his face, and moved his own face downward and then kissed Leyb on his mouth, and behind the soft and sharp of Charles's kiss, Leyb's mouth contorted into a dustvillage shape what, if it were not obscured by the lips of this other man and the cloudpillar of smoke and hopes inside Cricket's and could be freely gazed upon by humanish eyes, might have been mistaken for an american smile.

Then Leyb decided to leave, thinking to himself that Yutke might grow fearfilled if he didn't return to sleep at the Halperhome. Odd and of course false though this thoughtseed was, Leyb let it rest in the soil of his mind, let it nibble with its roots on the maysehs buried therein, and anyway Leyb felt like he might become sick from approximating for longer than he was used to a sort of smile under the press of Charles's lips and the prickle of his mustache, and so he removed his lips from Charles's lips.

I will go home, Leyb said, and Charles quickly offtook his hands from Leyb, and across his eyes in the dark there was a quickflicker of hurt before the guardedness of thickets could be backpulled, but Leyb reached out his hands and caught one of Charles's awayflying hands, and he pulled it to his mouth, and wanted to kiss Charles's palm but Charles's hands were now clenched so he kissed instead Charles's knuckle and then downbit on Charles's knuckle not too hardish[10] and looked up at Charles's eyes, and Charles withdrew his hand from Leyb's mouth and closed his eyes and opened them and leaned forward and kissed Leyb on his forehead.

Alright then. It was good to meet you, Lion, Charles said.

Leyb nodded.

Will you come back next week? Charles said.

I will come back, Leyb said.

yoh and we also
we hoped that he would

And he did.

---

10 Though not too lightsome either, Lion.

yoh but
there is
always
before

a mayseh fin Zatelsk

And so yoh, Leyb was the youngest of three children, after Zanvl and Shprintzl, born to Mirele and Shulem Usherl in the dustvillage what was known as Zatelsk. Zatelsk was bifurcated by a murkish river of melted snow and weeds what looked like clumps of hair, and boasted a resplendent graveyard filled with dozens of anxious dead, almost all of what died on their very own days. Each evening in Zatelsk, as the sun crept into the swollen night, Khayele the mousemaker would walk to the edge of the forest, tonguepouch in hand and handy incantations on tongue, and would lead a portion of Zatelsk's population in negotiations with the death-malekh what is made from only eyes, the veinish stalks of what are togetherbraided like lumpen coils of un-cooked eggdrippish shabbesdough, yoh, and they were fierce and slippery, the eyestalks and the negotiations, but Khayele and the other jews knew from haggling, knew from planting tongues inside the earth at the edge of the forest, such that the multitudinous eyes what opened wider as the night slermed inward unto Zatelsk might be distracted by the gray and pink squiggles of flesh outpoking between pinefingers and lolling about in patches of sorrel, mint and sorrel, mint and sorrel and wild horseradish, wild horseradish and severed tongues, look at the tongues, look at the tongues and away from us, omeyn, and in this way, most of the people in Zatelsk could remain living and safe like a squirmish fatbrown hebrew baby jammed into a barely leaking swaddle of reeds, slurring about in the winter nile, pirannish and crocodilish and humanish nibblings below be goddamned.

Most mornings in Zatelsk, most people would wake with crumbles of sleep in their eyes, alive, awake, omeyn, and then would either go davn the dawnprayers or snuggle under the blankets for a feathery shtip, depending, of course, on the density of the icicles lilting outside the windows like puffy translucent tongues not of chickens, in this case, but of albino weedsnakes, and on the badness of dreams dreamed the night before about leprous limbless lizards and other subjects, and on whether these dreams called out to be strengthened and fortified and whispered into the field of your lover's eardrum, or if they needed healing and for the lordlet what turned Bilom's curse from a curse to a blessing to do the same for the dreamer's dream, to make swords into sewing needles, and to make czars and pharaohs into toads, their edicts into toadstools, their men into toadstools, their rifles into toadstools, their nooses into sphygmomanometers, what the people of Zatelsk knew from, for the people of Zatelsk were not dumb of modernity, yoh, the people of Zatelsk knew the usefulness of such scientifish tools what might peep their steelish heads into a jew's privatemost spleens and livers, knew also that being hanged was not generally good for a jew's health.

The morning activities also depended of course on the collaborators the denizens of Zatelsk found in their various cousins or friends or palms or fingertips or gods. Most, on most mornings, as the light bled into the rooms, would of course prefer to flop or waltz or glide, as each case may be, for the methods and manners of shtipping were as varied in the village of Zatelsk as in any bohemiyesh metropolis, and perhaps more so, given that a good measure of creativity was required in a village of 312, where even the faithless fornicators like Gittl the slaughterer's daughter and rabbiteyed Itzl the orphaned porter ran out of options before half a single headmonth could pass and found themselves in each other's goosepimpled arms more milkish mornings than not. Of course, preferences notwithstanding, for as any halfwit what has done at least a bissl of learning knows, only a malekh gets to shtip as often as they want, yoh, most mornings, most of the men made their way to Zatelsk's only shil,[11] where they would shokl[12] their hips toward jerusalem, and most of the women, finding no deep delight in the act of staring at the backs of the men's necks from the crevice of the shil's posterior, would make as if to start the day in tandem with their husbands, pretend to busy themselves with some task or other, tasks what were anyway more foreign than desertscrubbed targimloshn[13] unto the men, until they, the men, left, their prayershawls smelling of mold and lilacs in their hands, their dawnemboldened putzes slowly wilting in their trousers, and then many of the women of Zatelsk would backcrawl to one wheatish bedmat or another, alone or with company, and so it came to pass that the women of Zatelsk, in fact, found methods and means to shtip, in one sense or another, far more frequently than did the men. In this way, perhaps, Zatelsk was unique. Or perhaps not. Before the morning prayers were over, and after the morn-

---

11 "Godhouse."

12 "Forwardthrust."

13 Lit.: "translationtongue," i.e., Aramaic; the construction of this word mirrors that of the superlatively familiar "mamaloshn," or, "mamatongue," i.e., Yiddish, suggesting, perhaps, both a parallel and a chasm between the translational and the familial. (One of my hopes with this translation, it might be noted, is to bridge that chasm.)

ing shtipping had finished, many of the women would spark a fire and let dance in the pan just a few pinches of sorrel and a snippet of thyme or two, and the room would smell appetizing for when the men returned, allowing said men to make the belief that their various valorwifes held their gastronomish wellbeing as sacrosanct, and this way, the people of Zatelsk were happy.

Of course, no one in Zatelsk was happy, happiness being a modernish blasphemish ambition. But content. The people of Zatelsk were content. Even young Leyb had been content enough in his misery. Unlike the other boys in kheyder, he didn't care to talk about amerike's feelings, or her headsized globulent jugs of money. Nor did he care to discourse about the smaller, more proportional teats of the meydeles of Zatelsk, nor would he have cared to do so at a later stage of his boytimes, even if he had reached those times in Zatelsk, yoh, Leyb was not even interested in the classical afterkheyder method of profiteering, in what a bukher[14] would offer Burikh Bendet Asnes a sweep of his workshop for next to nothing, with the knowledge that Burikh Bendet was usually too drunk to recall if he'd already paid said enterprisish bukher and thus could be convinced to twicepay the agreed upon sum, yoh, or four times,

14 "Boychik."

or, as in the famous case of an impish jewlet what was called Shmerl, fourteen times for the very same sweep, you may believe it or don't.[15]

But so yoh, Leyb was gloomishly content to wander the fields with his friends, the hedgehogs and fireants of Zatelsk, sitting down with them by the northbanks of the splendid Zatelsker river for a breakfast of berries and smoked herring, pondering with them about the ways of the world, dreaming about joyish boys, sprinkling on their variously spikesome and poddish heads a fistful of raisins with almonds each time the critters would unravel a difficulty, all the while staying clear of the forest what allsided Zatelsk, knowing like any jew knew that this was where the deathmalekh made from only eyes waited, and also wild beasts like lynxes and bears, but of course not knowing what would happen when the clan of death came.

---

15 Orig.: ir megt dos gleybn oder neyn. Possible nod to the shmaltzy Yiddish theater song which bears almost the same name, and of which the author once did a rendition—an astonishing moment, in truth: the only time I recall ever hearing Gittl sing.

Coffinbird

And yoh so then the next shabbes Leyb arrived at Cricket's with his tayve streaming through his body, aroundlooking through the riversome crowd for Charles, what he was not anywhere finding, not in the front-room or the backroom. Leyb went then to buy a drink and passed his coins across the bar, and his money was not rejected but accepted, and Leyb thought to maybe ask the barman if he had seen Charles, but he did not ask, and so Leyb downdrawnk the glasscontents and passed to the barman more coins and poured a second glass directly into the gurgle of his stomach and the ache of his loins and the suremost knowledge that Charles wasn't of course caring if Leyb backcame or didn't. So too a third glass. Then he had to pish and walked to the watercloset. He opened the door but there was in there another man what was just standing by the sink.

Sorry, Leyb said, but the man circled his hand in the air.

It's alright, the man said. You can come in.

The man was wearing a white shirt and had crystalline eyes what were glancing at Leyb's face as he entered, and so Leyb looked upon him for a moment and then awaylooked, stepped, stillstood, released his bodycontents of rustish yellow into the bowl. When he finished pishing, the man was still there. Now, though, the man's eyes were facing toward the ground and his cheeks were filled with firereds and humblesome pinks and his sex was outsprung from his trousers and held hardened within his hand.

Hey, the man said, glancing shyishly up at Leyb, his voice like a bag of pebbles.

Leyb looked at him, looked around the small watercloset to see if maybe this man was speaking to someone else, but of course no one else was in there.

C'mere, the man said.

Leyb glanced at the man's sex, what was long and tiltish to the left and was goyishly uncut and darkred like a beet, with hair around its base like outearthed tangles of roots and Leyb felt his own tayve swelling against the banks of his ribcage from the smooth of the man's sex and the thrill of its tilt and the slide of the man's hand down and then up, pulling the skin back, straining slightly his hips toward Leyb as if in prayer, and his eyes still so shyish and castdown, and Leyb selftold that anyway Charles hadn't meant the kiss on his forehead any more than did Gittl, that there was no one actually caring from him much that way or this,

that longhope was poison, that the best he could place his hope was upon short bursts of submersion within rivers like the river proferred before him in this man's outsprung sex and his downcast eyes and so Leyb? He nodded his head and his tayve lapped within him and he stepped forward inside the small room
Leyb
Leyb'ele
and he took hold of the man's sex, and felt it swell bigger in his hand, waited then with inheld breath for the man to place his hands onto him, onto his back or onto his own sex or perhaps onto his cheek but instead? Leyb felt something crashing into his nose and thought for one moment that he had drinkishly slipped and lost his foothold on the coldtile ground and bumped faceward into the sink. He tasted thickish wine
it's blood Leyb'ele
it's just blood
leaking into his mouth and then felt a musclehard arm weedsnake around his neck and the man was now yelling, no more softstones in his voice, Goddamned pervert! Get your disgusting hands off of me!

And Leyb understood the words but did not understand, because his hands were off the man, were now flapping in the air like smallsome wings, but the arm was still snaketight fleshful strict around his neck and Leyb felt himself being dragged then into the forest and so he started flailing like a carpfish, tried to dig his fins into the bark of the man's torso, to sink his pharyngeal teeth into the man's swaying limbs, to flick his tail back into the trunks of the man's shins, and everywhere there was dirt and flies and torn pages and pine needles and prayerbooks and sweet carobs and shabbes spices and candles made from teeth and sunflakes and corpses of vultures drenched in wax and wind and measured portions of stones and ink on skinscrolls and at the man's feet, hedgehogs swarmed and bit into his ankles with all the strength they had stored in their tiny nervous jaws and a trail of fireants crawled into the man's eyesockets and lit him from within on fire, but for what? Not enough hedgehogs, not enough strength, not enough ants, and not enough fire, for in this new sort of Cricket's dance, Leyb was firstly crumpled down onto the floor, his cheek pressed against chill and outsplashed urine, and he tried again to kick with his feet but it was nothing more than the flip of a carpfin, and then he felt a hammer crash into his face under his eye, only it wasn't a hammer, just a shoe, and it wasn't such a hardkick just a halfhearted footflick and the shoe had such thickrich dirt shimmied between its ridges and even one or two earthworms and smelled like warm fecund earth

Leyb sibling mine

Leyb'ele ours

and then Leyb's older brother Zanvl?

He was downpressed on top of him, then Gittl

came and pulled him, her arm wrapped around his neck, and Leyb tried to say to Gittl that he couldn't so much breathe, that she should please just be letting go, that he didn't understand what was happening, that he was very much confused. But Leyb? He'd forgotten all of his american and Gittl wasn't listening to his jewish and he'd forgotten how even to davn in anytongue so-ever and so only snowbanks fell from his open mouth, only cornercurls sprouted from his nostrils, fully grown. He was pulled upward, his body slackish, but his betraysome feet complied with the marching motion, yoh, his feet moved to help the man what was not Gittl at all, they helped to walk Leyb toward the forest, even as hedgehogs tried to backhold him and also fireants, and Leyb then did pull remnants of hummish prayers from the drawers in his chest, yoh, and he was drooling spices and dribbling rain and leaking flames.

All around Zatelsk now, they were coming
yoh it was morning
it was morning in Zatelsk
and they began grabbing at the men what were just before this praying
yoh the men they were walking from the shil
taleysim neatly folded after dawntimeprayer
together in the backroom of smoke and hope
yoh the men they had been shokling their hips

as elsewhere in Zatelsk the women also were
what were just before this laughing and leaning into one another's necks
yoh they were singing
they were all singing
what were singing to each other on the back of the music and they said to everyone
yoh they said to gather together back inside the shil
they went from house to house to say it
Perverts! Goddamn inverts! And everyone began to run and also to wail
yoh but no one was running though all could see their tusks jutting from their bellies
could taste the specific way the clan of death sang as they walked throughout Zatelsk
and the men what came inside stood still and watched as the prayershawls slid from the bared shoulders of all the men what had already been inside and all this fabric curled up there on the ground and wilted, and as the worshipers ran by them, the men what had come inside grabbed for them
yoh and they placed their hands on the men in the shil
they led the first group
and pulled them into the forest
yoh into forest
they pulled everyone into the forest
and everywhere there was dust.

Everyone ran toward the door what was the only out-way from Cricket's, and each was for himself and no one soever of course was coming to help Leyb, just like his tateshi didn't, his tateshi what didn't even raise a hand, what just solemned prayers like rotten pears and perished, and Leyb wondered if of course it was he himself what had brought the clan of death with him, what had dragged all the men away from Cricket's and out altogether from philadelphiye and directly into Zatelsk what was allsided by the forest, and if after all Gittl should have left him to be like dead among the dead until he was actually dead.

And then Leyb heard his name in a voice too low to be Gittl's.

Leyb?

Leyb

Leyb

And then again.

Leyb!

Leyb beheld then from his downheld angle Charles fastwalking toward him, and he wondered if Charles maybe had meant after all the kiss what Leyb had held between the creases of his forehead for one week, and then Leyb? He felt so sorry for everything.

What are you doing? Charles said, and his voice

was not the same voice what Leyb remembered, and Leyb wanted to tell Charles something, but Leyb? He could not find the words to say anything but omeyn, so Leyb did not say anything at all.

Shut your ignorant mouth, boy, not another goddamn word, the onholding man said, and with his voice rising, the tightness around Leyb's neck was become also risen, but Leyb was again confused because in truth, yoh, Leyb was only a boy he was not yet twenty but from his mouth were coming no words soever, only he was trying then to breathe.

I am the law, the man said, and the weedsnake grew stricter still around Leyb.

Take it easy now, sir, Charles said. He's just a kid. He's new here, sir. Why don't you ease up a bit? Leyb saw on Charles's face the smile of a man what laughs with leeches,[16] and then Charles glanced at Leyb, and the smile was whisked away from his face and he said in a softvoice what was the same voice what Leyb remembered, Keep calm, Lion, you're going to be just—

And then the fleshpressure was gone from around Leyb's neck and Leyb dropped his hands to his knees and inbreathed so much air it was scraping his throat and his gills from inside but then softer after some more

---

16 Orig: lakht mit yasherkes. Idiomatically, this can mean "one who laughs because he is forced to laugh," or "one who laughs to mask the screaming of his soul."

breaths, and Leyb looked up and saw that the man's two hands were rummaging into Charles's chest, and there they had grabbed hold of his coat just by his heart and Leyb saw one of the buttons offsplit and Charles stumbled backward and the man still held on to his coat and shrieked in american, Goddamn it listen to me, boy, we've got to follow some sort of protocol with this squirming invert, but who the hell do you think you are to backtalk me, have you looked in the mirror recently boy, rope is your protocol you ignorant boy, you goddamn pervert boy, who the hell, one more word from your ugly mouth and I swear to christ, and the man leaned his face closer to Charles's face and spit onto Charles's face and Charles's head backswung as though fiststruck, and then his hand moved forward and pushed upon the man's mouth, and the man let go of Charles's shirt and backstepped but not from the force of any Charlesome blow soever, for he backstepped steadily, and there was a calm coursing from his body, and he pulled from behind his back something what glowed dull in the smoke of Cricket's mainroom and Leyb?

Leyb

Leyb

Leyb watched,

Leyb

zis'ele

he watched and understood that this dullglow was of a small gun

Leyb'ele
sibling ours
and then Leyb opened his mouth and no sound came from his mouth
Leyb'ele
Leyb'ele
and then, you may believe it or don't, from Leyb's open mouth came a song
tum bala tum bala tum balalaike
tum bala tum bala tum balalaike
and everyone in Zatelsk turned to look unto Leyb and Leyb's face burned for he did not have a beautiful songvoice like Shprintzl but anyway the song continued and the man turned to look and when the man backturned to find Charles, Charles was not there for to find
tum balalaike
play balalaike
and the lawman sniffed and licked his lips and awayput his weapon and scratched his cheek and replaced his snakearm around Leyb's neck and said, Alright invert shut your goddamn mouth,
tum balalaike
happy may we be
and Leyb closed his mouth and the singing ceased and then Leyb? He was dragged by his neck by the man out from Cricket's, and another man came to help, not to

help Leyb, but to help the man what was offdragging Leyb into the forest of philadelphiye along with the other worshipers what they had caught.[17]

---

17 And elsewhere in the dimming night, Charles, who had been swept up in the panicked-animal midst of the crowd stampeding out from Cricket's, stopped running, tried to catch his breath beneath a sky spitting waters; and he thought about young Lion, and told himself that he would be fine, that the purveyors of america's law would go easy on him, that by leaving Leyb there alone, by removing himself from the scene, Charles had lessened the danger to them both (Was there truth to this, or was this only cowardice in elaborate garments? Hard to say, as it were, fingers pressed against the translator's right temple like the barrel of a ghostly gun); and in the meantime, the waters were rising around him, but also seemingly within him, as though they had coated the insides of his lungs; he stood there, for a moment, waiting for his breathing to ease, water dripping down his face and torso, for his hat had been knocked from his head and onto the floor of Cricket's, and his good overcoat, missing its top button, now struggled to guard his body from the rain; he hunched his shoulders, gripped each hand inside the other, pressed the ball of his hands into his belly, held his breath inside his chest to try to staunch the waters rising therein, but the waters continued to rise, and his breath did not return to normal and the night was closing all around him, everything was closing around him, and Charles began to move, again, and he found himself singing, once again, "Better keep walking, Zachariah Walker," and he clamped his mouth shut over the words, but the melody continued to reverberate against the walls of Charles's mind as he walked in the direction of home.

And yoh there was still for Leyb the still small strum of a balalaike, yoh, the scent of aftershabbes, yoh, wine and candlewax and spiced dirt, and also strumming, yoh

all we could do

all we could do

and then he was awaytaken from Cricket's.

yoh and before that
but before that
before that
o wa

a mayseh fin avekgeyn[18]

Gittl.

Leyb's voice struggled to gain purchase in his throat, in the air around him, but yoh, he had now to speak.

What is it, Leyb'ele?

Gittl!

What is it?

You're coming also, not so? Gittl?

Me? No. Not so.

water lapping around Leyb's ankles
omeyn and omeyn

But I don't know to swim, Gittl.

It's okay, Leyb'ele. You know to sing, not so?

Stands a boy, stands and thinks.

yoh trakht un trakht
a gantze nakht

So, nu. You see? You don't need to know to swim.

---

18 "A story of awaygoing."

You sing, you just sing, and there will be all manner of mammals what will come to help a jew what cannot swim.

How do you know this, Gittl? It's written?

I know it.

It will help?

It will help.

Gittl.

What?

Gittl!

What is it, Leyb?

I want that you should come also.

I cannot, Leyb'ele. I have to stay near my siblings, in case they need me.

Oh.

humlick of the water tumblecracking on itself
would drink itself but for the salt

Don't be frightened, Leyb. Look upon me.

Can I stay also?

No. You have only to walk, Leyb'ele. And to sing, Leyb'ele. You have a beautiful voice.

what is louder than the trees
what is cleverer than the breeze

Gittl.

What is it?

Gittl, you see? I'm not crying, like you told me. You see? Can I stay also?

I see, Leyb'ele. Say after me, I do not believe that all the world is darkness.

Can I stay also?

I see, Leyb.

Gittl?

You have to go now.

Gittl! You see?

I see, Leyb'ele. You have to go now.

And then Gittl went to wander around the edges of the forest, where her siblings caught dreamlets and learned to speak, where she had alone gentled into the earth an entire dustvillage, but for one other jew, what Gittl had heard, and outpulled, and wiped the stink from his eyes with her thumbs and made him stand, and then pushed him into the ocean, and told him to walk, and so yoh, this one other jew went alone into amerike.

Awayflight

And so it came to pass that a hideous screeching music rushed forth and filled the emptied alley, yea, the openmouthed valley, and lo, the two parts of the law what just moments before had been discoursing about the enormish stature and beastly bulgesome muscles of the boy what one of them had so bravely offfought and subdued and awaychased into the darksome night without even withdrawing his weapon, grew afeard, for the sound came as though from the jew's body but it was not a human sound, and so four palms crawled to cover his mouth and twenty fingers alongscrabbled his face but the sound did not subside, and the whole valley was become upfilled with the smell of salted water and clouds and also dew and rain and also sputum and retch, yea, and the sound grew louder and shriller and the four hands then awayflew from the jew for to cover the four pinkish ears of these two poor finkish men.

Goddamn it! Shut this invert up.

You shut him up, this one's yours.

And lo, the brave lawpart then moved to strike a blow unto the cunning jew's ugly face.

And lo, Goddamn it, he bellowed, for lo, it was not so, lo, not so, yoh, for the sound became the sight and the sight became the song and there before the upraised fist of the law stood jew after jew after jew, holding jugs of ink and water, gripping baskets of herring and torn pages and laughing, yoh, dancing, even the smallest of them, yoh, laughing and dancing, and the lawpart took a step away from the jewslaughter, and was tripped, verily, he was tripped, not by any jew, of course, but by his brave lawpartner, what had become limbtangled in the thicket of a hydrant, oy, who had put this hydrant there was it got'ele above in the spitting heavens?

feh was it got'ele

nope it was not

Verily it was the city of very brotherly love what had first of all put it there in case of fires, yoh, and now amerike's law stumbled upon it and the lawparts were all upon each other, got'ele forbid, all touching warm and tender amidst the wet, and quickly they righted themselves, and turned again to face the jew, but then, just then, yoh, there was a growlish sound come from the mouth of a ram what was caught also after all in the thicket by its horns, and one lawpart then aimed his foot for to kick the mammal and he struck it, lo, and there was the dullish sound of cracking bone beneath fat and fur and flesh, but then, just then, the thicket burst into flames, only of course it was not a thicket but a hydrant, it was of course not flames but only waters, waters what soaked the lawparts to their intact bones, even as from the jew's mouth hideous sounds continued to emerge, yoh, everplaying, and all around him there was jewful dancing and silenced mirth, and the mammal was now both growlish and whimpersome at once, and these parts of amerike's law?

yoh what do you intend to do
before all the world

We intend in truth to leave this jew alone, for this jew gives us the heebie-jeebies, gee whiz, and we do have our families to think of and all, we intend to get out of here, to leave this godforsaken place.

so yoh
leave

They left, yoh, they ran from the ram and hydrant and from the jew surrounded by three hundred jews what he, the one jew, could neither hold nor behold
yoh we're sorry for this zis'ele
would that otherwise it was
and then the law was gone and the ram was panting, its brittle body broken from the foot of amerike's law dug into it, blood falling from around its tongue, warm and shining in the night like melted sun on the coldish

ground. And the jew? He reached toward the mammal for to stroke it but it shied from his outstretched hand, yoh, and it awaymoved from him until it was gone, and the jew? The jew what was once called child of Mirele, what was later renamed in amerike Halper, what was later renamed in Cricket's Lion? The remnant of a dustvillage what was called Zatelsk?

He closed his eyes and felt smallish spears overbrush his body, he felt embers of tinytap antennae on his skin, he opened his mouth, just a bit, and his friends united in their efforts and together nuzzled three boysenberries onto his tongue, and he sucked on the fruits until their skin came away, and their insides coated his gums, and only then did his deyfek[19] slow, and he lay there, dancing and laughing and not moving and weeping silently amidst the mighty winter waters and overleft mammal scent of philadelphiye's utmost puddles: Leyb, alone, alone, alone.

---

19 "Heartbeat."

yoh but Leyb
remnant of Zatelsk
was not all alone
o wa so before that

a mayseh fin Gittl

Zatelsk, jewish for a mound of upground carp, jewish for an endless circle, jewish for the feeling of a jew's being an awaycast crust of blackbread in a vastish sea, when said jew has never seen the sea, nor would said jew ever awaycast a crust of bread into the neverseen sea unless it was smaller than an olive, what said jew had also never seen, and what this one, this particular crust of bread, was not.

Morning in Zatelsk. Before dawnprayertime, early, early, but Gittl was very much awake. Gittl had dreamed of the lustish spiketaste of pomegranates and the seep of coffee wifting into her nostrils from a percolator, while on the carpet, an earless mammal lay kicking its legs and whinging, dreaming its own dream of giving chase to and catching and also consuming smaller mammals amidst a bed of ferns. Gittl had in her life never tasted a pomegranate, and in the afterdawnprayer morning Mameshi was always lighting the samovar, yoh, but only for chicory for while Tateshi might have been able to procure coffee at almost any fair, a beautiful thanks to all the feathered throats what he slit, and from what he routinely extracted the tongues on behalf of his valor-wife, complaining only always, but Fishl the slaughterer believed coffee to be only for fanciful rebbes, what was another of Zatelsk's wideheld vegetarianish superstitions, as it is written, he what drinketh coffee and is not a fanciful rebbe will surely have all the hairs from his upper and lower beards fall out (3 Kings 3:11), and of course no one in Zatelsk but the clerk and the priest was allowed to keep dogs, and even Phonye the clerk and Phonye the priest wouldn't let their dogs sleep inside, yoh, but anyway no one in Zatelsk had carpets, let alone pomegranates, and so Gittl knew that it was recommended that she recite the dreamer's prayer, to remind the dreamful jew that said jew didn't know a thing from a thing and to ask anyway for blessings to be put upon them, o wa, but instead, Gittl lay still and silent upon the crinklemat on the floor with her four younger siblings, alltogethersqueezed in a pile under a single neverendish blanket, bulbous reddish heads and skinny pale bodies like a book of matches. Then Gittl had a thought, more strange even than her dream:

ikh gleyb nit az di gantze velt iz kheyshekh.[20]

Gittl upsat. A strand of her hair had been under-

20 "I do not believe that all the world is darkness."

wedged beneath sleeping Hendl's head, and Hendl was halfawakebecome with Gittl's upsitting, what served her almost right for the way she had murmured in her sleep nearly the whole night, as in almost every and each night, spooling and unspooling phantasmagoric psalms as the moon glimpted over the dustvillage, trying vainishly to plug its earholes, yoh, but it could not for it was as though the moon's hands, wrought from stretches of nightsky, were tightfastened under a blanket of darkness, its starsiblings murmursome and blithely snorish all around it, no bowing or prostrating soever, and this is a good kind of badfeeling, how it is to be pinned by one's siblings' snortbreathing and sleepspeaking, so neither the moon nor Gittl fully felt that Hendl deserved to be awakepulled, and both were glad when Hendl only groaned and overrolled and resumed her ritual of spooling and murmuring. Gittl rubbed her eyes and closed them and recited finally the dreamer's prayer—yoh, so listen, got'ele, I have dreamed a dream and I don't know from what it is, but so you what made falltongued Meyshe'le upfilled with strength, and what flipped Bilom's curse from a curse to a blessing, make sure to flip all of my dreams into good unto me and want me and guard me and put a blessing on me? omeyn—in order to asidemove the strangeness of her dream, and the thought what aftertrailed it like a bit of puffcloud alongpulled by a thunderhead, but then it came again, the thought, entirely after Gittl had finished the prayer.

Gittl could almost see it, as if it were written in inkish letters on the mammalskin parchment of Zatelsk's predawn.

I do not believe that all the world is darkness.

Was this maybe oversat from a prayer? Definitely not so. It felt blasphemish not prayerful, Shpinozish[21] not sheepful, and Gittl felt a current of swirl in the back of her scalp. She wondered if she would tell Itzl about this thought. Probably not, sweet, rabbiteyed Itzl, beautiful, yoh, but not the brightest. But yoh, beautiful. Gittl thought of the hardness of his chest, of goosepimpled skin pulled tightly over his portermuscles, the way she liked to pull her tongue over his small nipples what jabbed forward like two gemstones amidst the sparsetangle of hair. Although this thought, in turn, brought Gittl facetoface, or tonguetotongue, with Itzl's own tongue, what was stubbish and hesitant and kept him from talking so well and also more importantishly made his kisses wilt in Gittl's mouth, made her own tongue wander the studded corridors of his teeth, searching for something more, oy, the tribulations of dwelling in Zatelsk, jewish for lack of options. If Gittl were instead a denizen of a city, even just a pinsk or a lutsk, to speak not from varshe and vilne, she could with ease, she knew, find for herself a whole quorum of men mit mus-

---

21 Hat-tip to Tovarisch Baruch, as it were.

cles and also mit wit and with tongues what danced and wrestled in elegantish dawns and feversome evenings, o wa.

Gittl outclimbed from amidst her siblings, as Hendl murmured a recipe for the leviathan's belly, a sakh fin khreyn un zaltz, she spooled, un a bissl fin zamd.[22] On the other side of Hendl, Gittl only stepped lightly on her brother Anshl, what growled and darted his hand out like a sharpsome crayfish and poinched her very ankle, and so Gittl may have slightbrought the toes of her other foot forward rather than upward, inpoking them directly where Anshl's Adamish boyrib was not, and causing him to meowl and then to growl again but his hand went not for a second treyfish poinch, and instead he overflipped onto his face, in turn slightly squishing Zimml, and chubbish Zimml squealed and then recommenced his sleepsome snorfling, and Gittl stepped over Zimml and then downcrouched next to sleepingest Reyza, curled contentedly in her corner, yoh, and Gittl brushed a feather of hair from Reyza's face, and smoothed her brow, what was always so furrowed, except when she laughed, especially when she slept. Reyza did not wake.

Freed from the bondage of her siblingpile, Gittl stood, plucked the large metal bucket from beside the

---

22 "A lot of horseradish and salt, and a bit of sand."

door, and picked her tateshi's furless feltcoat from the coattree, pulled it over her sleepdress, outwalked, inholding her breath, as usual, as she bypassed the shack what stood outside the back of the house and inside what the tenderish Fishl carried out his fowlwork every and each day excepting hoary shabbes and frantic yontiff in Zatelsk. Some paces away, Gittl outbreathed, then downcrouched amidst a tangle of grasses and the mutter of various bugs, and as the pish stored overnight in her body released onto the grasses and into the ground and joined the morningsong along with the insects, again came the thought:

I do not believe that all the world is darkness.

Gittl stood and pushed with two fingers on her temple. She knew from reading Tateshi's pseudepigraphal book of Yeysef's wisdoms, widely held to have been authored by the Savant of plontsk two and a half centuries prior, that a jew may get rid of almost any thought by pressing hard enough on her right temple, and may preserve almost any thought by pressing hard enough on the left one. So yoh but on this morning, was Gittl pressing on the left temple or the right one?

Hard to say.

Gittl walked some more paces down toward the great Zatelsker river, what was made mostly of wayward hairweeds, and what was rumored to outspit fully formed shtraymls into the workshops of Furkapsk, just downriver from Zatelsk, and pious kneebearded jews from the world over were said to venture to Furkapsk for to purchase for the honor of shabbes and yontiff alone, surely, and not for any inclination toward peltish boastfulness, these excellent and miraculous sable hats, and not for cheap, poor Zatelsk, wherein the magnificent Zatelsker river outspit only hairy dampish tangles onto the banks, and wherein the workshops contained no hats soever, only terrible shoes, o wa. Gittl found a largely bald opening in the water, downcrouched again, now indipping her bucket, then updrinking right from its giant mouth the coolish sweetish waters, then outspitting only one very small weedish hairball, then looking toward the northbanks, where she watched as a group of dustmotes and springmoths fought each other for space within the amber light cast through the smoke rising from the leaves of the Zatelsker shrubs on the northside of the river.

These particular shrubs, like all Zatelsker shrubs, were burning in perpetuity. No one took their shoes off. Everyone in Zatelsk had too many pairs of shoes. There were a total of 99 jews in Zatelsk what were gleaning the bulk of their parnusseh from cobbling, and 213 other residents, so 425 noncobbler feet to be shod, Rokhl Altes having been born with only a left foot, due, the people of Zatelsk whispered not so quietishly, to Alte's having failed to light the shabbeslights once around peysekh of 5669, one evening, Gittl knew from her own mameshi, in what Alte was caretaking for her alwaysfalldownnik husband, Yarml, what had contracted an unnameable ailment from too much mushroomrustling at the edges of the forest, o wa, but merciless were the whisperers of Zatelsk, and miserable were its cobblers, for even the slowest among them, like narisher Zele Leml Pesls, could make at least two pairs a year, and no one from outside Zatelsk would ever dream of purchasing a pair of shoes from one of the cobblers of Zatelsk, given how the knowledge of their astonishingly low quality of work spread through the neighboring villages like a carefree flush of tuberculosis, to the extent that even the goyim knew to shop for shodding elsewhere, and Zatelsk's local goyim, Phonye the clerk and Phonye'te the clerkwife and Phonye the priest, did all they could to support and sabotage the cobblers of Zatelsk, respectively, buying between four and nine pairs for each of their seven children and spreading hideous rumors through neighboring parishes about the sourcing of the leather, respectively, and anyway, yoh, while the overshodden people of Zatelsk possessed their share of oldfashioned beliefs, even they knew that talking to shrubs, burning or notburning, was about as likely to bring about their liberation as a lump of gefilte was likely to stand, reassemble itself into an approximation of one of the fifteen or so fish'eles from what it had been formed, hop finfully into a luxurious chaise, ride on wooden roads all the way to the czar's recently abandoned golden toothpalace in the center of the capitol, and request a position as the chief accordionist for an entire bolshevik regiment in order to harmoniously accompany the meting out of severemost decapitational punishments unto any man or ataman what even so much as glared at a hapless jew, just as Trotsky's just so angled justicemustache had just promised, and be granted the position, even without having any fingers or foreskin or having held a job in any factory soever and indeed having once owned its very own puddle where it had reportedly employed under very deplorable conditions an entire extended family of toads.[23]

yoh.

Undead kulak gefilte bard golems aside, the jews of Zatelsk had the lord'ele to protect them from the clans of death skittering between the swollen evenings and moaning pines and had the mousemaker to protect them with her tonguepouch from the malekh made from eyes and had nearly one hundred cobblers to protect their soles from splinters, and one tuftish rebbe and his valorwife to protect their souls from shades, and one hirsute weedriver to protect their throats from draught, and so, like a baby in a barely leaking swaddle of reeds, et cetera.

Most days, Zatelsk seemed to Gittl slunkish and

---

23 "They want to go to the commune! They want to make boots with their hands!"

gray like cowscud, yoh, but this morning, this thought-strange morning, Gittl inbreathed deeply through her nose, oxygen being oxygen, more or less, and understood Zatelsk to be jewish for a place filled with springish lovely searing greens and aquamarines and goldwhispering fields and clever shoes and groaning pines and clouds of jasmine and lilac and hyacinth and sorrel and running water and grass and dirt and air, o wa! Or at least a place in what a jew could breathe for herself a normal breath of oxygen.

I do not believe that all the world is darkness.

Gittl thought this thought somewhere inside her Gittlish head, what had upon it darkish hair and in its front greenish eyes and on its nose some freckles and in its mouth some diagonal teeth, et cetera. About how she was comely, Gittl had grown somewhat tired of hearing, for this Gittlish head had, more impressively than some accident of a got'ele what is anyway avek,[24] alonehoned both forks of her holytongue in order to surreptitiously consume the contents of a full tractate of her tateshi's gemoreh, yoh, for it was said that teyreh iz di beste skheyreh,[25] but to be honest she was only

24 Lit.: "Away, gone." Idiomatically, it may be used similarly to the way it functions in Tovarisch L. Hughes's well-known poem, "I loved my friend / He went away from me," i.e., as a stand in for dead.

25 "The Torah is the finest of wares."

somewhat whelmed, and so this Gittlish head also consumed burnish poems and smartsome scientifish articles in jewish and russian from copies of worldsome newspapers what Kisl Mariyashls insnuck and shared with Gittl, and also Gittl had taken from Kisl's underbed a copy of azey hot geredt Tzarathustra in jewish and so knew herself to be an arrow of longing for the other shore, et cetera, though she did think that Nietzsche'le must have lost track of his mind somewhere within his mustache when he wrote that it is not good to live in cities, and also yoh, that all his stupid teeth should rot beneath the shade of this mustache for writing that woman is still not capable of friendship,[26] but Gittl did consider every day lost in what she did not waltz, or glide, or flop, as each case may be, so at least on that she and the talking overmustache were eyetoeyeish, and it was for that reason precisely that she continued to walk, just then, toward Itzl's, though she did decide, as she reached the bridge what was made from shabbesribbons and ashplants and what led directly into a denseful stand of barkpeeling pines, that she would not linger any longer than necessary at Itzl's, pleasant though a second shtip might be, muscles and nipples

---

26 Orig.: nokh iz di froi nit fehig tzu der frayndshaft.

This line is drawn directly from R. Rocker's 1910 Yiddish translation of *Zarathustra*.

and tangles of hair, yoh, but she had too many thoughts to think and not so much time to think them before everyman returned from prayer and Gittl's mameshi finished her own morning endeavors and Gittl would be compelled to cull potatoes and scrub all about the house and would not be having even one finger available to press onto her temples, o wa.

Gittl walked across the northsouth bridge, across the marvelous Zatelsker river, toward Itzl's house, in what he alonelived after his parents died, being nineteen and so old enough to marry, and so on, and what sat all the way on the otherside of the stand of trees what, while being wholly distinct from the forest what hummed and chickled and lecked around Zatelsk, was, while a jew was in it, still dense and overhangful and a little frightish in its own right, if a jew was honest with herself, and some mornings, Gittl wondered about the wisdom of throughgoing all of this in order to see and feel Itzl, but this morning, Gittl didn't wonder so, she just walked.

Just after crossing the bridge, and just before entering the stand of trees, she saw a boy sitting droopishly and sweating under a Zatelsker shrub. After a moment, Gittl recognized him as chessplaying Mirele's youngest, but she could not remember, amidst the thoughts of this morning, how he was called. He seemed to be talking to himself, but not in prayer.

shulem aleykhem,[27] Gittl said.

aleykhem shulem? the boy uplooked.

Don't worry so, my young friend, Gittl said, listen again to my greeting in your mind, not a cossack or a wolfsack, sweetling, neither of what know to speak jewish, not so? Gittl outreached her hand and upruffled the boy's already frowzy hair. Not any scoldsome mameshi either, thanks be to the what in heaven, no evil eye, it's just a Gittl, bypassing.

Oh. The boy outheld his hand to Gittl. In his palm there was a shinish roundsome fruit.

I couldn't take this, Gittl said, downputting her bucket and taking the boysenberry from the boy, holding it between her fingers, inspecting the color swelling beneath its skin. She moved to hand it back to the boy but he closed his small fist and shook his head.

I have many, the boy said.

Gittl nodded. Forgive me, tell me again how you're called, my young friend? Mirele's youngest, not so? Your sister Shprintzl, yoh, now there is a songvoice, o wa.

I'm called Leyb. I'm soon going to go to shil with my tateshi and my brother Zanvl . . . Leyb looked down, and Gittl followed his gaze and saw that finely sticksketched pawprints and tiny antsome mountains decorated the dust around him.

---

27 "Peace upon you."

That's good, I suppose, Gittl said. Well, a beautiful thanks to you, reb Leyb, for this gift. Be healthy for me. Gittl placed the berry very gentlish on her tongue and waved a farewell to the strange little fellow. Gittl backrolled the fruit toward her right molars and bit down, a yontiff of sourness erupting upon her tongue as she stepped into the stand of trees, onto the welcome of fallen pinefingers and crinchling leaves, and Gittl thought: the world is not only darkness, and I am not only myself. I am also a slimish maggotl, and the soaringmost kestrel, and kin to if not one and the same as any scrapehanded scrubwoman in pinsk or minsk or even amerike, or any barleylipped Phonye three towns south, or the stone what stands still by our river of hair. I will not depart when my body departs, o wa, I will become soil, then digested by a hoglet, then expelled through this hoglet and grown into a birch tree, then fallen as a leaf until I turn into a seed what becomes a stuttering puddlish ironworker, then through an embrace with dust I will become an old woman flickering in the early morninglight with eyes what see just as mine see, only filmish and worn, but still wakeful, and I will see then, as now, trees, grasses, air, sourness, water, scent, broken light, life, holy!

Holy?

Can there be holy in this world without an overseeing mastergod, Gittl wondered, having nearly certained by now that there was no such mastergod. Or perhaps,

Gittl thought, this lack of mastergod is the only way there can be holy. Gittl arrived at Iztl's almost singing.

Good morning, good year, Gittl almost sang, only now removing her shoes. What do you make?

Not terrible, Itzl said, shyish still somehow after all these milkish mornings, stretching his firm arms in a pretrickle of sunlight, long since awakened from his nightly porter's two and three quarters hours of sleep. Gittl touched her fingers to his mouth, moved her face forward, licked the side of his neck, tasted salt, felt ripples on her tongue. Itzl kneeled then and openpulled Gittl's tateshi's coat and forwardpushed his head to rub over Gittl's breasts through the fabric of her nightdress, but this felt scratchsome and pestishly irritating unto Gittl so she awaypushed his head. Itzl backleaned and uplooked toward her, waiting for a sign as to where he should next place his mighty hands, his lisping tongue, et cetera.

If this world were all done by design? Gittl said, not being able to not say it. If it were all made purposefully?

Itzl blinked.

I think then we should strangle the mastergod with his own beard, not so? Pluck out his eyeballs with a spoon?

Itzl coughed and his very symmetrish face flushed beneath his curlish hair, the two cornercurls of what he kept eartucked like Gittl liked.

I don't know much about books, Gittl, he said, what

was a dumbfish way of pretending he was more of a nar than he was, that he didn't know from the type of blasphemy being blasphemed right there in his very fornicational home.

But I think it's not, Itzl, Gittl said. I think there is no mastergod, and because of this, I think, there can still be holy.

Itzl, still kneeling, blinked again and downlooked at the floor. Gittl downclimbed onto his slopish lap and pressed her body forward onto his, and put her hands behind his neck to selfsteady. She ran her tongue over his lips, the wicks of his beard scratching as she licked, but then pulled her head backward as his tongue outstretched to search for hers, and instead she moved her mouth to his ear. Don't overthink it, Itzl, she said, and she pushed her tongue deep inside, tasting bitterwax, and pushed her sex down harder onto his hardened sex uppushing through his trousers. Gittl bit softly on his earlobe, and then less softly, and reached between them to downpull on his trousers, but they were firmishly buttoned and the angle was not good and so Itzl moved his own hands between them to debutton and Gittl stood from him and lost some of her balance as she did and she backstepped and halflaughed and then waited for him to disrobe, and watched as his sex moved free from its pantish home. Gittl then turned away from Itzl and walked two paces to remove the single fork and single plate and the cloth from the stable table what Itzl himself had built, and she placed the fork and plate on a chair beside it and draped the cloth over its back and removed her undergarments and placed them also on the chair, and then lay backward still mostly dressed there upon the undressed table, feeling its wood against-pressing her back and listening to the salivish mnapt as Itzl's ineptish tongue khept over his palm once and then again and the squiltsh as he rubbed his palm up and down around his sex, and then up and down, and then up and down, and Gittl growled, nu, Itzl, and Itzl startled, and made a sound, hinf, and waddled quickishly toward where Gittl lay, his pants still aboutgrasping his legs, and Itzl then upscrolled Gittl's nightdress and fervented into her, o wa, but too quickish and with not such a good angle, and Gittl downbit her jaw and shutsqueezed her eyes for the thrustish discomfort to dissipate, but then Itzl slid outward slower and again in and Gittl wrapped her legs behind his back and felt the muscles therein moving, and she began with her legs to forth and back Itzl at a pace what started to feel smoothsome, but after only six or eight times of out and in, Itzl pulled himself out from her entirely and wriggled free from her legs and overstumbled, sex in hand, to overspill all his seedlets into the table's cloth, conscientious as always not to make Gittl into any sort of mameshi, no evil eye, and Gittl sighed inwardly and outwardly, and Itzl uplifted his pants and downsat in the second chair and faithwaited, oh motionless oh dull, like some clayish shtipgolem for Gittl on her own to flicker her finger side to side over her sex, but this morning she did not do so, no, she only stood from the table and kissed the seated orphan porter on his head.

Be healthy for me, my friend, Gittl said.

You too, Itzl said. A beautiful thanks, Gittl.

When anyway will you get married, Gittl said, untangling her undergarments from Itzl's fork and plate placed upon the first chair, avoidsome now from the cloth still overdraped thereupon.

god willing not before tomorrow, Itzl said, and by then maybe the daughter of the slaughterer will change her hardened heart, and consider me more favorably?

You stay away from Hendl, Gittl said, and Itzl quarterlaughed, and Gittl insidely shuddered at the khasenegedank[28] what she had deflected, not for any particular aversion to an orphanish cemetery wedding, et cetera, but to a wedding soever, o wa.

Will you eat something? Or . . . Itzl ran his hand over Gittl's leg, already revivish, yoh, he was quicksome in multiple senses, Gittl had to acknowledge.

Be healthy, Itzl, Gittl shook her head. You should get ready, you'll latearrive for dawnprayer.

The sun was almost fully overpeeking the horizon, and Gittl was thinking again that she had too many

---

28 "Nuptialnudge."

thoughts to think, so she could not linger at Itzl's for anything additional, and she walked out into the predawn and the stand of trees and earlyflowers reaching for her feet and thought first of mountains. She thought of dark peaks upbundled in snipclouds, heavy rockpiles outsliding from the earth in glorious accident, glistering in sunlight and moonlight, o wa. Gittl wanted to take a bite from these mountains, to put her teeth around them, to belch a craggish howl into the crispsome air. Of course, Gittl had never seen mountains. All there was being in Zatelsk were bumps of earth in what the people of Zatelsk were buried, like her own bobeshi eleven and a half months earlier, dead from one of Zatelsk's many jewailments, whose burial had been a briskish affair, she was old anyway, fifty-seven, they told themselves, yisgadal v'yiskadash, and when the wailing of Dveyrl and Alte and also young Shprintzl Mireles what was being trained still as a zugerte[29] had subsided, Gittl's tateshi was too much weeping to speak, so Gittl's mameshi said a prayer for her husband's mameshi, yoh, she said, nu, godlet of the universe, what placed upon your jews only a few more sorrows than we can bear, take care of the jew what you have upyanked into your army of armies, and remember that though

29 "Paidmourner."

our houses of dust and mashedfish are not beautiful, yoh, and though we may blaspheme and bicker, we are trying, somewhat, most of us are, yoh, to find favor by you, but we are busy also, and so maybe you could spare us for a few more afternoons, give us maybe some more time, but of course if you will it different, then so be your will? Then she wept and spit softly to the side and everyone said omeyn, and began to walk toward their dustish sweetly fishhomes quickly, careful not to stay outside so near sunfall for it was nearly peysekh and many things could be thus lurkish in the forest, and Gittl held onto Hendl's hand and Reyza's, and thought then about how everything bad what might happen will happen if the mastergod wills it, according to Mameshi and to everyone, yoh.

But now, mountains and flowers aboutlicking her bare ankles and cracking between her mind's molars, Gittl thought, If there is no mastergod, then maybe everything bad what might happen might happen, but also maybe it won't, o wa. I do not believe that all the world is darkness.

Gittl's belly rumbled as she caught sight of the south-north bridge back over the river, and as she crossed it, she imagined walking home with her new thought cupped in her palms like a small birdlet, and she imagined the delicious taste of all the potatoes what would be awaiting upon Fishl the slaughterer's meatless tish, upon what the family ate only potatoes and fish, potatoes what she would herself have to prepare in order for them to be waiting, but it's what?

Good morning, good year, Gittl could almost hear herself saying, bursting through the door, finding Hendl amidst her own morningscrubbing, and Reyza still curled in her bedcorner, and Mameshi returned home from her endeavors, and Tateshi and Anshl and Zimml soon backcoming from shil. What are we eating for breakfast, all? Gittl would say, and she would selfanswer: You have guessed it, my sweet ones, it's potatoes, and you will not believe how I will prepare these potatoes, something delicious like you have never tasted, all the world is not darkness!

Four astonished eyes would fall upon Gittl, surely.

Gittl, are you drunk? would say Hendl.

Mameshi would give Hendl a patch'ele on the back of her head and Hendl would outyelp and Reyza would awake from the sound and begin to cry.

Look at this, Gittl. Look what you've done. You've come home drunk and made your poor sister Reyza cry, would say Mameshi.

Not drunk, Mameshi mine, Hendl beloved, just happy. And Gittl would go then to Reyza and kiss her sleepingest head and kiss her face and her nose until she was only laughing and Hendl would begin to recite a parable about the dangers of happiness according to the prophet Shmariyahu, and Gittl would whisper to Reyza that their shared sister is such a scholar, o wa.

And then, just then, Anshl and Tateshi would income from shil, Tateshi perhaps coldish and wondering how he had once again misplaced his coat, Zimml trailing right behind, and everyone would be there, yoh, they would all beforewash their hands in preparation for Gittl's promised potatomeal, using the water what Gittl had fetched from the river like every morning with her bucket—

Her bucket. Gittl remembered with a jolt that she had forgotten her bucket. Had forgotten it where? At Itzl's? No! Had downput it near where she'd spoken with the frowzy berrychild of Mirele's, oh catastrophish, Gittl spit, and then turned and backwent over the bridge to search for the bucket, her heart fallen from its place on high, How did I forget the stupidsome bucket, Gittl grimbled to herself, o wa, everything bad what might happen does happen, oh my poor bucket, and then she laughed a bit, but still was grimacing, and still was grimbling, and still was looking and looking more and yet was not finding her bucket, and it was then that she heard the clan of death singing their song inside the forest.

And the words of their song were not so clear to Gittl, only what followed was thuds, was screaming.

And Gittl was at the edge of the stand of trees, and

her feet told her to run back toward her home, but then
she heard it
like Anshl
like Hendl
like Zimml
like Reyza:
stay where you are
Gittl sister of ours
stay there Gittl
we love you o wa
and so Gittl remained there, within the stand of trees, and all the people of Zatelsk were taken to the forest, and almost every jew what had been alive wasn't alive anymore, only of course they were not all taken to the forest, some were just outside the shil, some were down on the footpaths of Zatelsk, some were lain by the northbanks of the river, some by the southbanks, yoh, and some were still inside of their very homes
yoh and we
we were still inside
of our very home
o wa
and when there was darkness all around her, and there was no more singing from the forest, Gittl walked from the stand of trees back into Zatelsk, first to her house where she found her mameshi and tateshi and all of her siblings, and then Gittl walked back over the footpaths and then to the southbank of the river and the

northbank, where there were still flowers and grasses, just as there had been in the morning, and to the pile of people outside the shil, and it was there that she heard gurgling and outpulled Leyb Mireles, and Leyb was not hurt, but could not stand, and Gittl put her arms under his arms and held him until he could, and then she wiped the stink from his eyes with her thumbs, and kissed him on his little glass forehead, and sent him to walk alone across the ocean.

Tormenta

And then Leyb stood. The singing had silenced. All the animals of the dustvillage had awaygone. The law was no more. The rain had stopped. Leyb was alone, yoh, but Leyb was grown. Leyb was almost twenty. Leyb knew to walk, and so he backwalked toward one Halperhome, what was a nicesome home, thanks to Morris Halper's steadyish socksales, the fine textile of what persisted in coddling amerike's bunions and corns even as its stalks and its stocks withered and turned to dust, yoh, this nicesome amerikehearthome of the Halpers, in what Leyb had spent almost all of his nights for seven and then seven years, but in what still Leyb spoke only jewish with Yutke and Morris, whose own springoffs Peter and Joan were making always crampghoul faces, mocking the jewsounds as though they themselves were two uppuffed goyfish
nu so may young christ'ele bless them and keep them
and decircumsize Pete's perfidious putz
rather than the springoffs of two mousesome jews, two

adultish mousesome Halperjews what didn't once reprimand their Peterful and Joanish springoffs with even a single patch'ele, what instead just shuffled from the kitchen, oh shrugful oh glumfish, leaving Leyb there alone with his nonsiblings' laughter and his tongue all coated in jew.

The door was to the Halperhome locked. Leyb knocked.

tuk tuk tuk.

It was late and the night was amphibiash cold and scaly, but opened the door Yutke, what usually sleepwent in the smallmorning anyway. Leyb beheld her beholding his face, yoh, and when she asked him vos iz mit dir geshen,[30] Leyb grabbed hold of a glimmer of softplant in her eyes, familiar even if not familial, and so Leyb? What didn't speak much in american or in jewish? He felt an overpouring rising in his belly
talk Leyb'ele
just talk
and therestanding he spoke in a rush of dustjewish, and to Yutke, he told everything. For what, asks a jew, did this youngerjew so do?

For what else was he to do.

He told Yutke of Cricket's and of the man what downtipped his hat to Leyb and held him and kissed

---

30 "What happened to you?"

his face as they tripped fantastishly the light and of the man what downtripped Leyb so that his face was inpressed right into the wet and cold and thereheld, yoh, and of the snaketight of the law's arm and of the nightstream of the crowd

and yoh when they came
they took everyone to the forest

and the emptied alley, yoh, the openmouthed valley, and the strumming, and Yutke? What once every year or so would ask everyjew to call her Judith, but what lapsed from this asking because what sort of a fish is a Judith? Yutke what once told Leyb that he was efsher a kluger bokher[31] after all when she happenstanced to downglance at a paper what Leyb had inkfilled for school with stacks of neutrons or quatrains or some such, yoh, Leyb did not recall the papercontents only Yutke's words?

Certainishly she hugged Leyb in her arms! And told him that he was like a son to her! And a sibling to Peter and Joan! So cherished was he, this Leyb, it mattered not how or by what he was tripped or inslipped unto or

---

31 "Perhaps a bright boychik."

(A note on transliteration: I chose, throughout the text, to transliterate in accordance with each speaker's dialectal pronunciation, to the extent possible, such that here, for example, it is Yutke Halper's Litvish "kluger bokher," rather than the Volhynian-Zatelskish "kliger bukher.")

by what persons he was wanted or chastened or chased! Oh helpful oh lovesome, Yutke like a mameshi to Leyb was become in this moment!

And yoh of course false was this hopesprout.

Only in Leyb's mind did such a thing transpire

yoh and also

in ours

for verily in the toothful version of this mayseh, what unraveled in the cold under the lintel of a Halperhome in the midst of old helpsome amerike, Yutke stood in front of the door and told him in dullish spitridden jewish that he was not welcomed to keepsleeping under her very roof, that she and her family had enoughdone, and now he was backpaying them with this.

Disgusting, said Yutke to the night. He tells me this and wants that I should have pity upon him, in what world does he think, a laywithman'er,[32] feh.

yoh feh to you Yutke

just because you are so disgustfish from your fusnoglish endeavors not everyone

To where should I go, Leyb quieted.

To think that I should care, Yutke said, not eyelooking upon this very shiverful Leyb.

Leyb did not right away move.

---

32 Orig.: mishkovzokhernik. Here, the Slavic -nik suffix is tacked on to a Biblical Hebrew–derived agent noun (mishkav zakhar: Leviticus, abomination, shall be put to death, et cetera).

gey avek, Yutke said, and then turned, inclosing the door behind her.

And so Leyb?

Awaywent back into the street and the drippish philadelphiye night, alone, alone, alone.

walk Leyb'ele
just walk

And so he walked by foot over the schuylkill river toward the citypart in what he knew lived mostly blacks and he passed by underawnish gathersome crowds, not liking to speak to many at once in american or at all, until he beheld two yingelakh[33] what were his own age or more young even ledgesitting and smoking near the rain and one was bladescraping the edges of an apple what were freefalling into a pile on the wetness below and the other said something and both laughed and so Leyb did not stop to ask them anything, yoh, he just headbent and onwalked and there were no streetlights and no sidewalks and the streets were puddlish and around the puddles Leyb beheld walking an altishke[34] dressed in nicely clothes and umbrellagrasping and she was moving directionishly toward him, so Leyb? He upsummoned his courage and then moved also toward her across the wettish street, but the altishke flinched

---

33 "Youngsters."

34 "Elderwoman."

and upraised her shoulders and downlooked toward the puddles and fasterwalked until she had bypassed him, and so Leyb then stillstood, not knowing what next to do, not finding help from the seated yingelakh or from the walking altishke

Leyb'ele

sibling ours

but then he heard the altishke's footsteps stop and he turned just as she backturned toward him, but did not closer approach.

Are you lost?

Leyb said, I'm looking for Charles.

The woman blew air softly from her nose. There are a lot of people with that name.

Leyb nodded, chewed the inside of his cheek, tried to remember if Charles had told him another name, could not remember, let his head sink toward the ground.

The altishke looked at him through the darkness, inside what there was just cracking a grayish hum from the spitting sky above, and she then stepped a bit closer, as though moving animaltoward. Are you hurt?

Charles what is writing all the time? Leyb said, upmoving his head quickly, his mind landing upon Charles's fingertips.

Jesus is a rock in a weary land, the altishke quieted.

Leyb saw the small cross danglish on the altishke's chest, and he plucked another thoughtsprout from his mindgarden, perhaps a kliger bukher afterallish, that maybe a godthing is a godthing, even in amerike, that perhaps he might drag a godthing from a dustdrawer of his mornings in Zatelsk's kheyder, in what he was always able, with help from his friends, the pokeish shtekhlers and firesome murashkes of the dustvillage, to untangle the most thornsome of talmudical difficulties, and so outspilled here in philadelphiye from Leyb's mouth a smallish tangle of hair and also some freshwater and also some embers from the burningmost shrubs, and he said, Meyshe?

zugt men Moyses in amerike Leyb'ele
or Meyses depending on the neighborhood

I mean Moyses? Found his way to the promised land for helping only one sheep what was lost, Leyb said.

The altishke looked upon him.

zugt men shoup in amerike many sheep one shoup
sha nebekh let him speak

The one sheep had been taken from its flock, Leyb said, away from the grass and the riverbank, by two dybb, two demons, what had been disguised as other sheep, and the one sheep was left lying in the middle of a valley, and there were sounds coming from its mouth, but no living one heard them, and the sheep thought it would there remain alone, alone, and its flesh grew tired, but Moyses? What was certainly busy with many other things? He had come to look for this one sheep, to help it find its way. And for this god had granted to Moyses to behold one burning tree, to take off his shoes, to find the promised land?

The altishke nodded.

I am the sheep? Leyb said, not sure what sort of nod she had nodded, and so thought to continue down another windsome talmudish alley, about the lostsheep what fumbles in the afternoon as a blindman gropes in darkness, but then the altishke spoke.

I've got no aspirations to be any sort of Moses, child, the altishke said, but you do look like you could use a hand. I think you're looking for Ms. Rose Patterson's son. You're a friend?

Leyb wanted to say, I suppose, but said instead, I'm a friend?

Come on then.

And the rain, it ceased, yoh, it uplet for some moments, for this was a moment in what the world did not deserve to be destroyed.

The altishke walked onward to where she was going and Leyb turned and backwalked directly toward from where he had come. They passed again the two seated yingelakh, what both output their cigarettes and upstood from their ledge.

Hello, Ms. Freeman, one said.

How do you do, Ms. Freeman, the other said, offtaking his hat.

Ms. Freeman nodded. Good morning, boys, she

said, and onwalked, Leyb afterfollowing in her footsteps until they reached a particular cornersome brickish building, in what they went past a door and up some stairs, stairpieces decorating the stairwell like fallish stars, still silent both but for the shepherdsome footfalls, and for the deyfek of Leyb's heart, and Ms. Freeman? She knocked on the third from the left door on the opposite side of the fourth floor and Leyb? He only stood and waited.

There was the metalsound of lockscraping inside wood, and then opened the door, with sleepwoolish clothing on his body and of course no hat on his head soever, and also a blinkish heaviness perched upon his eyelids: Charles.

Ms. Freeman, ma'am? Charles said. What time is it, is everything alright?

And then Leyb slightmoved from the shadow behind Ms. Freeman so that Charles could see him too.

Jesus christ, Leyb, Charles laughed.[35]

---

35 Charles had managed to fall asleep just moments prior to this, the events of the evening still coating his lungs, and had been awoken by knocking, had risen from his bed and moved toward the peephole of his door, which he rarely locked, for reasons of superstition ("a sealed door brings a sealed fate"), communitarian habituation (no one in this section of the Seventh did), and Lethe (ah, the abeyant areas of man's mind), but which he had locked on this night, and when he saw Ms. Bettie Freeman standing on the other side of the door, he was seized

He's a friend? Ms. Freeman said.

Charles looked at Ms. Freeman's face, and then at Leyb.

Yes, he's a friend, ma'am. Thank you. Where did you—Leyb, why don't you come inside? Thank you, Ms. Bettie. Would you like to come in also, ma'am? Can I make you a cup of tea?

Don't trouble, child, Ms. Freeman said. Remember, Jesus is a lone tree in a windswept field. And say hello to your mother for me.

I will, ma'am, thank you, again, Charles said, and Ms. Freeman turned from the two men and walked back toward the stairs. Charles looked at Leyb and then reached out his hand and touched Leyb's shoulder, and Leyb felt the warmth of his hand through the wetfabric of his shirt, and Charles said, Jesus christ, Lion, you're freezing. Come on in.

And so Leyb onwent under the lintel and into the apartment.

How in the world did you get here?

---

by the thought that she had come to tell him something terrible, that something had happened to his mother, whom he hadn't seen for many days, it being one of their off weeks again, and thus the first reaction he felt when he beheld the shivering mammal standing behind her was its own sort of astonish, as it were, and relief, which was then compounded by his relief at the fact that this Lion was not locked in one of the city's birdcages, and hence: laughter!

Aroundasking, Leyb said, and tried to eyeblink with one eye, but felt a strange heaviness there, and followed Charles's eyes as they landed on his eye.

Are you alright?

Leyb touched his own face and felt only now the smallhill of flesh risen beneath his eye and the under-ache as his fingertips overran, and he shrugged. I'll overlive it.

I bet you will, kid, Charles said. Come on in.

And Leyb, what was already oncome in, said, Oh well if you're insisting.

Charles reached for two metal boxes what were there resting beside the door on a smallish wallshelf. Smoke?

Leyb shook his head. Charles outtook a cigarette and openflicked his lighter. Leyb looked toward the floor, what was shoerubbed and stained with ashpat-terns and with earth. Leyb took off his shoes, yoh, and looked back up at Charles, what had turned and was walking a few paces to the otherside of the apartment, what was only being one room, around the edges of what were a paperoverspilling bookshelf and a cornerbed kept company by a clothesbox and a paperoverspilling ta-ble kept company by two chairs and a rustful stove kept company by one sink and some shelves and one Charles, and a smalledge door, and in the center of the room perched a springish couch.

So are you going to tell me how you managed to

extricate yourself from the talons of our city's finest? Charles said over his shoulder, his voice curved around the lit cigarette, his hands busyish with a reddish kettle held below a faucet what choked and coughed with effort and then outdribbled a tepidsome trickle into the metal thing below.

Leyb shrugged toward Charles's back, did not speak, and the only sound in the room then was the tiff of an underflame from the stove's top hitting the metal of the kettle's bottom.

It's alright, tell me only what you will. Would you like a gloz kave? Charles backturned toward Leyb.

I'm some fanciful rebbe that I should drink coffee? Leyb said.

I've already put a kettle on, reb Lion, Charles said. If it offends your class sensibilities, at least a gloz heyse vasser? Have a seat.

Charles towardgestured with his hand to the springish couch what sat in the middle of the room and what faced toward a wall against what rested the shelf on what stood and from what fell books and books like the shelves of some fanciful rebbe.

Don't worry about getting it wet, Charles said, and Leyb, what hadn't so worried until then, perched upon the thing's arm.

Charles walked toward the edgedoor, inwent, and outcame holding a towel. I wish I could offer you a warm bath, Lion, but I don't quite have room for a clawfoot in this closet, and in any event, these days I'm lucky if the pipes give me a full cup without protest, thanks to old Goldfarb.[36]

Leyb couldn't think of anything what then to say, so did not then say anything.

If it were a bit later in the day, you could go over to the pba place back on Gaskill, you just walk straight down Lombard the whole way. Not the cheeriest place on god's gray earth, I will say, but I'm sure they'd love to offer their services to a fellow like you.

Sorry, Leyb said. I don't have anywhere else to go.

---

36 Charles felt himself on the brink of apologizing for his material circumstances, though he knew he ought not to, for while this was not the first nor the fifteenth night he found himself outside of Cricket's with pale company encountered therein, this was the first time said company was inside Charles's home; on the other nights, they'd make their way toward the other men's houses, "Better that way," the men would mutter, meaning, safer, in their minds, than the jungles of the Seventh Ward, wherein surely they'd be set upon by some western chapter of the Leopard Society or other; while at home, if inquired of, they could simply pass off their night's companion as a Pullman porter or bull-man butler or some such trade, and they'd almost invariably fail to meet his eyes as they expressed their preferred locale: but indeed, rarely in these nights did their eyes meet his eyes at all, even as their eyes feasted on his skin—and who is it, then, indeed, that can be rightly deemed to be part of a western flesh-eating society? Charles had never once been asked to stay the night.

No, that's not what I meant, Leyb, Charles said, and he looked for Leyb's eyes with his eyes. I'm glad that you're here.[37]

Charles draped the towel over Leyb's shoulders and Leyb closed his eyes, what were become overfull with light and tears, and into his eyelidred darkness entered Charles's voice, still softened.

Maybe we'll get you into some dry clothes?

A river, thought Leyb. Quiet, maybe, breathed Leyb. And there were shivers throughpulsing his body, and the slightmost chatter of his teeth, and a windsting in each of his hands from how they had scrapekissed the earth, but a fireheat was building also in him and he offtook his clothes in quick succession, his Halpersocks, his trousers, his overshirt, his undershirt, all of what were soaked, and the cold air struck his naked body and he clenched his teeth and blessed the cold in silent jewish and then there was a watery scream and Leyb startled and Charles did, too, yoh, for both had forgotten the kettle, and Charles walked to turn off the fire, and Leyb followed him toward the steam, and his own sex was hardbecome and he felt it standing before him,

---

37 "I'm sorry for leaving you alone back there," Charles didn't say, but hoped that Leyb would sense something of that sentiment in his words anyway, or at least feel it in the gesture that followed.

and he felt heat in the roots of his teeth, and Charles turned back to face him, and his eyes looked at Leyb's eyes for a longish moment, and Leyb stepped again closer, the smell of water and rust in his nostrils, and he bit Charles's shoulder through his clothing and then kissed where he bit, and he downreached for Charles's sex and felt not a full softness, but mostly so,[38] and he

---

38 And if this is to be as a confessional, then let it be so fully: It was not entirely the case that Charles, as could be extrapolated from the following passages, submerged all of his own urge in order to gallantly clarify that his hospitality was a thing utterly desexed. Reality's waters, are, of course, murkier; there was a part of Charles that did swell with urge, and urge, and urge, as it were, at the sight of Leyb's nude body, at his thin form, at the jut of his collarbones, at the sparse hairs in the center of his chest, at the way his stomach sloped lithely toward a thicker tangle of dark hairs, at the shape of his thighs, at the smart of Leyb's teeth on Charles's shoulder, at the softness of the kiss that followed, at the thought of joining his body unto Leyb's, of moving part of his body into Leyb's, for some moments, and there was even a sense in which the stench that rose from Leyb's disrobed body, of rotten moss and puddlewater and wine-spiked sweat, might have served to stoke Charles's urge even more, for it was utterly human, and raw, and thus good, even if it was rough on its surface; the fading came, in this moment, not from any scent, but from when Charles sent his eyes toward Leyb's sex, which was beautiful, but which stood uncovered, its head lone-standing in a way that, in that instant, reminded—and ah, what a word, re-mind, so aptly capturing the hideousness of being forcibly returned into the lonely captivity of one's own mind—Charles that before him was not just a man's body, or a boy's body, but

withdrew his hand as though he had touched a thing what was scaldish hot, and he looked for Charles's eyes, and then asked, You want that I should go?

No, Leyb. I don't want that at all. You're welcome to stay here, without conditions, baby. You're freezing, let's get you dressed, and maybe under the covers.

Leyb looked again at Charles's eyes, to read if there was something untrue in them, and he saw thickets, many of them, but through them he glanced nothing what told him to go, and anyway he didn't have anywhere to go, but he was grateful not to have to silence any voices

yoh also we Leyb'ele we also think that you should stay
yoh also Leyb'ele it's sweet you think that you can so silence if we were to think that you should not

what might tell him to depart, and his eyes again upfilled with tears and with light and Charles led him to the bedcorner, his arm aroundlooping Leyb's naked waist, and opened the clothesbox and outtook a shirt and undergarments and trousers for Leyb, and Leyb updressed, and Charles lay Leyb under the covers, and stood and overwalked to the kitchencorner, and Leyb

---

a Jewboy's body, which was not a wholly unfamiliar variant of body unto Charles, but which carried with it all manner of heavy manna, some of it stale and sour and covered with oily paints, stories of flight and falling and gelt and tea and so on, and so, a re-minding; a wilting, et cetera.

now inwardly blessed that the apartment was as small as it was, for he did not want to be far from Charles for long, at least for the remainder of this nightsome morning, and Charles returned with two mugs of hot water, and he climbed under the covers next to Leyb, and Leyb moved his body so that as much of his side was touching Charles as possible, and Leyb lay his head on Charles's shoulder, careful not to spill the water.

You know what sort of bird you remind me of now? Charles said.

What sort of, Leyb said, biting down on a yawn, the exhaustion of everything seeping into his jaw, but yoh, even as Leyb's tayve downcurled for an earless sleep on the floor of Leyb's chest, a sort of riverquiet remained in the room, Leyb only later realized, for realizing this in the middle of the moment would have meant its updrying.

A puffling, Charles said.

What's a puffling, Leyb said.

A young puffin.

What's a puffin.

It's a sadeyed fellow from iceland.

Sad because they're boiling him?

So you do know what a puffin is, Charles said, and Leyb felt him draw closer to his side in their already sidecloseness.

So you're wanting to boil this jewbird? Leyb said.

No, no, Charles said. No one boils the pufflings.

He overleaned and gentlebit Leyb's shoulder. They eat them raw.

Leyb wondered if he should move again to reach for Charles's sex, but sleep was downtugging his eyelids with its small insistent hands, and his body felt like it was downweighted not with other bodies,

Leyb

Leyb'ele ours

but only with earth.

Tell me a story? Leyb said.

What sort of story? Charles asked.

Any sort of, Leyb said, downbiting another yawn, headnuzzling as might do a puffling.

Alright, Charles said. Well, do you know the story of the bird jew?

Leyb forthback moved his head against Charles's shoulder.

Well, once there was a jew, an innkeeper, Charles said. And this innkeeper had to renew his inn's lease each year, yes? So, one year, the year in question, the jew goes to speak with the landlord, at the landlord's estate. When the jew arrives, he sees that there is a great feast underway, men munching on golden roasted parrots, toasted pork, minced flank, flaked shank, that sort of feast, butter dripping down their jowls, and we know what Red Emma would have to say about this, yes? Property is thievery without any risk to the thief, and these were thieves of the first order, what? Anyhow, the jew doesn't look at the food for long. He casts his eyes toward the heavens, murmurs a prayer, yea, though he walks through the estate of the shadow of death, et cetera, and he gingerly approaches the landlord, who is, of course, drunk, and swaying, and singing, and holding a hunting rifle. And the landlord sees the jew approaching, his beard hanging down onto his chest, his hands clasped behind his back. The jew tips his hat, and the landlord is surprised to behold the jew before him, and he gapes for a moment, but then he begins to smile. He smiles more broadly, his healthy teeth bared for all the guests to see, and then he laughs out loud, and slaps his thigh, and lays his gun on the table near a platter of suckling pig, and it seems for a moment that he might embrace the jew, even, but he doesn't. Then, before the jew can utter a word, the landlord cries, Of course! And everyone at the party falls silent.

Leyb had now upsat, his head removed from Charles's shoulder, a ribbon made from vines and grass running through his jaw, his hands bothclasped around his rapidly colding lapcup of water.

So the landlord says, Of course, little jew! You need not even ask. In fact, not only will I allow you to renew the lease for another year, this year, I'll let you renew your lease for five more years. No, make it ten! With no extra strain on your purse. The jew is now astonished himself, and finds no words with which to speak. Then the landlord says, The only condition I have for you is that I'd like you to pretend to be a bird.

What does that mean, Leyb said.[39]

Actually, you know, now that you ask, I'm remembering that I don't actually remember the ending to this particular story, Charles said. It's odd, how memory works, isn't it?

Leyb nodded, and did not need to look at Charles's eyes to see that truth and his words were not then familial unto one another, but yoh, Leyb did not need to know the ending to this mayseh, yoh, he knew the ending to this mayseh.

Why don't I tell you a different story? Charles said. A happy one.

Leyb nodded and wanted to downrest his head again on Charles's shoulder but did not, yoh, he stayed only upsitting and waiting.

This story, Charles said, this one's a local mayseh, as it were. Took place right here in philadelphia, a long

---

39 And only then did Charles, who had gotten stupidly swept up in the story himself, charmed by his own tongue, as it were, look over at Leyb, and see the expression pulled across his face, one of dull panic disproportionate to the contours of this bedtime tale, grim though it might be. Charles realized, or half-realized, that he knew next to nothing about this boy perched in his bed, tucked under his mother's quilt, and decided that perhaps he ought to cut this story short.

time ago, when a young man was walking down the street, not so far from here, just over on Twenty-Third and Lombard. His name was George Queen. He had pretty eyes and puffy baby's cheeks and he hummed to himself while he walked, always. He loved humming, he couldn't stop himself, even though his friends always asked him to stop. He was heinously tone-deaf, Charles said, and Leyb downrested his head on Charles's shoulder once more.

What could he do? George Queen liked to hum. And so, this one evening, he was walking down the street, humming, and he didn't notice that on the other side of the street, a group of white men had started following him. These men began to laugh, and crossed the street, and George Queen saw them, then, but tried to pretend he hadn't, and kept humming. The men kept walking behind him, getting closer and closer, making sounds, singing a song of their own.

Then what happened, Leyb said.

Then one of the men struck Queen in the side of his head.

Why?

That's a good question, Lion. These other men didn't think to ask the same question, they just started to strike Queen as well. It was a warm night, time was bountiful, flowing, and apparently none of them was in a rush to go anywhere, and so as George Queen started to stumble, they continued to strike him, and then one of them took out a knife.

They took him to the forest? Leyb said.

What forest?

You said this was a happy story.

It is, in a sense, Lion. You see, the men were drunk, particularly the fellow holding the blade, and it fell to the ground, just next to where George Queen himself had fallen.

And he grabbed it and stabbed into them?

He did, Lion. Exactly. George Queen stabbed Misters Joseph A. Sweeney and John G. O'Brien. And they died, and their friends ran away, and bleeding, broken-jawed George Queen lay there for a few moments, and then surrendered to the law when they arrived shortly after, and extracted him from amidst the crowd that had gathered, and for that, he wasn't sure if he was glad or not, whether it would be better for them to get his death over with, or if the extra weeks alive until the court ordered him hanged was something for which to be grateful.

You said this was a happy story.

It is, Lion. Do you know what happened?

What happened.

They wanted to hang him, of course, but the judge, a fellow named Finletter, ordered the jury to find George Queen innocent. He said, and I'm paraphrasing here, he said that he hoped the case would repel the attacks made on inoffensive persons in the community, and would make the streets of philadelphia safe for any man to walk home at any time of day or night, without fear.

It's a truthsome story?

I just read it in the footnotes of a book I'm reading for an article I'm working on. So yes, it's true, but I suppose it might not be truthsome, in a deeper sense, given its happy american ending. Might I say, then, that it's a mayseh in emes, but not an emesdike mayseh?[40]

I suppose, yoh, Leyb said, a yawn outstretching now without being downbit.

Alright then. You should get some sleep, Lion, Charles said, and he kissed Leyb once on the top of his head, and then once on his forehead.

Outside, yoh, the rain began again to downmove toward the earth and theregathered in rivers and rivulets, high as the hydrants what wept upon its face, and throughout philadelphiye, if a jew or even an unjew listened closely enough, this person could still maybe hear the faintest singing and strumming
tum bala tum bala
tum balalaike

In spanish, Charles said, a storm like this one is called a tormenta.

---

40 "A story in truth," but not a "truthsome story."

In jewish, Leyb said, holding on to the edges of the morning before he downfell finally into sleep, it's a khlyope.

Well that's a quite a word, khlyope, Charles out-drew the word's syllables and softlaughed, I like it.

Next to the sound of Charles's laughter Leyb found that sleep was overtaking him, and he could no longer outrun it, but before he was awaytaken, he wanted one more thing to say.

Charles?

Yes?

A beautiful thanks.

nishto far vos, Leyb.

yoh but so before that
before any of that
before all of that
et cetera

A List

Before all of the remnants of Zatelsk made their way into philadelphiye, half of these remnants were having to move the people of Zatelsk beneath the dust and pineneedles and flowers
yoh but not alone
having help
always having help
o wa
and so the remnants of Zatelsk stayed for three weeks in Itzl's house, what alonestood on the edge of the stand of trees, what might hold them hidden if the clan of death againcame, yoh, Gittl stayed there inside Itzl's during the days, near the child, Leyb, what had said not one word since she had found him, and in the nights, she outwalked alone into the forest
not alone
not alone
not alone
never alone Gittl

and started to dig there in the dirt, with a shovel taken from Itzl's, a place for each jew, and one by one she put each there, and though she was not believing in any mastergod soever, she was saying for each burikh dayen ho'emes[41] because many of the people of Zatelsk were believing that this is what a jew should say for each jew what had been alive and then wasn't alive anymore, yoh, and so this at least Gittl could muster, three holytongue words to the nothingness, maybe also their names, maybe also a small mayseh.

Khayele Temerls, mameshi what made forestblessings
what like rodents were hard to vanquish
burikh dayen ho'emes
omeyn
omeyn but what were vanquished
omeyn but not her fault
mameshi ours o wa

Efraim Fishl Genendls, tateshi what slaughtered for funds and tongues but never for owneating
burikh dayen ho'emes
omeyn what had strong hands

---

41 "Blessed be the judge of truth."

omeyn what wept sometimes when he slaughtered
omeyn tateshi ours
o wa

Binyumin Beynish Rikls, zeydeshi what after Bobeshi Genendl died spoke only on yontiff
burikh dayen ho'emes
yoh but even before we had chessplayed always in silence
omeyn
omeyn
omeyn

Dov Ber Beyrish Rikls, oddfeter what after Beynish speechceased was so lonely in their home
burikh dayen ho'emes
omeyn yoh we could have tried more
but as the psalmist wrote no one anyway knows how to speak to a greatuncle
omeyn
omeyn

Khanele Temerls, tanteshi what auntsneaked to teach Gittl and Hendl to quickdrink books
burikh dayen ho'emes
yoh but why only Gittl and Hendl

sha nebekh zug omeyn
omeyn but yoh ikh bin maskim why only
of course also Reyza she would have taught but Reyza could not read yet but soon o wa

Sheyndl Temerls, tanteshi what was always yelling upon someone but sometimes singing too
burikh dayen ho'emes
omeyn
omeyn
once she told me that I was slowminded what was not very nicefeeling a thing but it's okay
omeyn

Temerl Gittls, bobeshi what was having ten teeth and three daughters and winddancing hands
burikh dayen ho'emes
omeyn bobeshi ours
omeyn
omeyn
what was frightening to me when she smiled to me but o wa omeyn

Rittl Dreyzl Sheyndls, cousinwalker what was a firestar of bright company on dullfish afternoons

burikh dayen ho'emes
omeyn
company for some fish only never was she inviting me to walk
omeyn
omeyn but maybe me she would have invited soon o wa

Avreml Sheyndls, cousincobbler what was grumpish to his siblings but not unto his cousins
burikh dayen ho'emes
yoh what was teaching me to play the whistle
omeyn
omeyn
yoh what was promising to teach me to also play the whistle o wa

Leyzerl Sheyndls, cousinpesterer what was always leaf-putting into olderhairs
burikh dayen ho'emes
omeyn
omeyn
what was always telling me also to leafput
what was always letting me also leafput

Veyrele Sheyndls, cousinposturer what claimed always to speak with wisdom of an altishke

omeyn
but yoh maybe she was in truth not posturing
omeyn
omeyn

Lipke Dvoshke-Meshkes, shabbesnapper what dreamed
of shoes with flappish americantongues
burikh dayen ho'emes
yoh a sleepish unclesheep
omeyn
omeyn
omeyn

Dvoshke-Meshke Fradkes, veryaltishke what always
litvishtalked of better shtupn in lithuania
burikh dayen ho'emes
vey iz mir
sha Anshl why should not veryelders talk too of shtipn and tayve
omeyn
omeyn

Peske Dvoshke-Meshkes, floorwasher what planned to
be onstage an actorjew under flowerrain
burikh dayen ho'emes

omeyn
omeyn
I think she would have been once I saw a show what she onput for Gittl and Rittl she was good
o wa

Itzl Kalonymus Kalman Monyes, orphanporter what tonguemoved the best he could
burikh dayen ho'emes
omeyn
yoh Gittl he was kindsome and handsome might you have easygone more upon him
sha Hendl not now
o wa

Velfl Dveyrls, wolflet what was always howling from his sister's slights
burikh dayen ho'emes
omeyn
yoh was unbearable in his whinging
yoh but sometimes a slight isn't so slight
omeyn

Basye-Beyle Dveyrls, goddishdaughter what was always being upbraided for the slightest

burikh dayen ho'emes
a knowledgesome friend what was wrongtreated by her mameshi
omeyn
omeyn

Dveyrl Risheles, paidmourner what was reminded of her self from her daughter so was harshbeing
burikh dayen ho'emes
omeyn
yoh but it's not an excuse harshbeing so just because she wasn't selfliking
yoh or maybe it is who can judge there is no judge sibling mine
omeyn

Burikh Bendet Asnes, tailor what drank in order to quietfind or fund the enterprisish youngsters
burikh dayen ho'emes
omeyn
omeyn
a beautiful thanks for all the gelt little good it did oh well
omeyn

jew what Gittl could not recognize for how they had
burikh dayen ho'emes
yoh we cannot
help in this
only can we say omeyn
omeyn

Freydl Breyndl Galyes, altishke what always walked with psalms poinched in her palms
burikh dayen ho'emes
omeyn
yoh I prayed always to be like Freydl when I was elderbecome
omeyn
omeyn

Yiskoh Teybls, ying'ele what never spoke in words just sounds
burikh dayen ho'emes
omeyn
omeyn
omeyn
o wa youngster even than I

Elyokim Teybls, tinyone what smiled and laughed in favor of his twin Yiskoh

omeyn
omeyn
so same they looked but also differentish were their tiny faces
omeyn

Teybl Mates, scholar what almost died from bringing
twins into life but did not die from this
burikh dayen ho'emes
omeyn
like her like Teybl I prayed also to become when I was somewhat elderbecome
omeyn
omeyn

Melekh Bubunas, husband what seventy weeks after-
birth was kneading still the shabbesdough
burikh dayen ho'emes
oy nebekh and the whole of Zatelsk knew from this
for what nebekh Anshl he was helping you're the nebekh
omeyn
omeyn

Tzvi Hirshl Tzarinas, beadle what was having beady
leerish eyes
burikh dayen ho'emes

feh
oy
must not someone still say omeyn
but there is no judge and no must Zimml sibling mine o wa

Zele Leml Pesls, cobbler what was dim from shoes but bright from intentions
burikh dayen ho'emes
yoh but what solefish cares for intentions
omeyn
yoh Anshl a Zimmlfish cares omeyn
omeyn

Esterl Pesls, reader what read more holybooks and novels than even the halfremnant of Zatelsk
burikh dayen ho'emes
omeyn
but not more than her sibling Hendl
omeyn
no Hendl I am sure always Gittl read the most o wa

Shmerl Pesls, yidl dibek what pressed poor pudgish faces into paperpages
burikh dayen ho'emes
omeyn

omeyn
yoh what once made me say got iz avek and only now Gittl
do I grasp your Nietzsche'le
omeyn

Nekhele Pesls, nearseer what looked the sun right in
its very eyes
burikh dayen ho'emes
I loved her
you did not so
yoh once Anshl told me he did
omeyn

Ikhl Mikhl Katzyes, rebbe what was having tuftish ears
like some forestroaming lynx'ele
burikh dayen ho'emes
yoh but respectish should we be
what it's disrespectish now to say that a rebbe had ears
sha both
omeyn

Pesl Lifshes, rebbewife what was helpgiving lessons for
daughters' fears to be lessened
burikh dayen ho'emes
omeyn

yoh also to daughters what weren't her daughters
omeyn
yoh but I wasn't having any fears just like Gittl

jew what Gittl could not longenough look upon to recognize for what they had
burikh dayen ho'emes
omeyn
omeyn
omeyn
it's okay Gittl

Zeyde Malyeles, cobbler what was born sickish but grown so strongish as to handbreak any log
burikh dayen ho'emes
yoh it's true I was watching him handbreak wood once for a shopfire it was magnificent
omeyn
omeyn
omeyn

Ogishe Dreyzls, cobbler what was hoping a woman in the workshop might bettermake
burikh dayen ho'emes
omeyn

omeyn
omeyn
yoh my turn o wa yoh Mameshi once took me to Ogishe and yoh I forgot what else

Mikhuel Eydeles, tateshi what was grumbling at his Ogishe but proudish nonetheless
burikh dayen ho'emes
omeyn
yoh so he was wifedead sadbeing but still too grumblish upon Ogishe what tried to save Zatelsk
omeyn
omeyn

Shraga Feyvl Tzirls, cobbler what was spoken of for the texture of his wickedtongues
burikh dayen ho'emes
omeyn
omeyn
I don't understand
it's okay Zimml to not understand I also don't omeyn

Tzalel Breyndls, slaughterer what was throatslicing all the bigger animals from chickens
burikh dayen ho'emes

yoh but our tateshi was better a slaughterer
in truth Anshl not so but it's what
omeyn Tateshi would not have wanted anyway to so cut into goatthroats and so
o wa

Alte Glikls, paidmourner what was of course not cursed for forgetting to light the shabbeslights
burikh dayen ho'emes
omeyn
yoh it was the fault of her mushroomhusband
omeyn
omeyn

Yarml Breyndls, mushroomruslter what was burdening his valorwife with his tubercular spores
burikh dayen ho'emes
yoh but not his fault was it
omeyn
Anshl there is no judge sibling mine
omeyn

Rokhl Altes, wanderer what on one foot was the happiest jew in all of Zatelsk

burikh dayen ho'emes
omeyn
omeyn
omeyn
omeyn but yoh also I was happiest

jew what Gittl could not recognize
burikh dayen ho'emes
omeyn
look away Gittl
close your eyes Gittl
omeyn

jew what Gittl could not recognize
burikh dayen ho'emes
omeyn
omeyn
omeyn
o wa

infant jew what Gittl could not recognize
burikh dayen ho'emes
omeyn
look away sibling ours

omeyn
o wa omeyn

Kisl Mariyashls, cobbler what hoped to stand someday inside or even beside a university
burikh dayen ho'emes
omeyn
Gittl had also been visiting Kisl on some mornings
not yours to share Hendl
omeyn

Malkele Mariyashls, gambler what was winning from all the women favors unrepayable
burikh dayen ho'emes
omeyn
Mameshi was always underbreath cursing the young Malkele only twenty and with such prowess
omeyn
Mameshi was never cursing

Makhle Mariyashls, healer what was helping all the animals what were hurt
burikh dayen ho'emes
omeyn
omeyn

once I saw Makhle bettermake the broken foot from a fox
and I cried but not from sadness
o wa

Mariyashl Temer Ridls, storyteller what was making the aftershabbes glimmer
burikh dayen ho'emes
omeyn
yoh what was also playing the balalaike for all the women
omeyn
o wa

Sanl Urlik Adels, outlaugher what was sounding like a bear when he was uproaring
burikh dayen ho'emes
yoh even during eveningtimeprayer from Shraga Feyvl's backwhispers
omeyn
omeyn
omeyn

Ridl Goldinchkes, eldest what everyone in Zatelsk went to for forgettingblessings
burikh dayen ho'emes
omeyn

may she have a lightsome place in the garden of eden
omeyn
omeyn

elder jew what was called Yukhe or Yakhne may the forgetting mind be forgiven
burikh dayen ho'emes
all what you can do Gittl
omeyn
Yukhe or Yakhne it's okay
omeyn

youngest jew what was three days small and had so not yet been given any name
burikh dayen ho'emes
omeyn
omeyn
omeyn
maybe I could think for him a name

Friml-Malye Hales, groundknitter what was turning horseradish into gaberdines
burikh dayen ho'emes
omeyn

yoh what once made a grassdress for our mameshi
yoh it's true
omeyn

Rifke Hodas Khayenes, heartholder what was having
weepingbouts over always something
burikh dayen ho'emes
omeyn
omeyn
it's okay Rifke now
omeyn

Daughter Rifkes what Gittl could not remember how
she was called
burikh dayen ho'emes
omeyn
omeyn
omeyn
omeyn

Daughter Rifkes what Gittl also could not remember
how she was called
burikh dayen ho'emes
omeyn

omeyn
it's okay Gittl now
omeyn

Son Rifkes what Gittl could not remember how he was called
burikh dayen ho'emes
was in kheyder with me but we cannot tell you
only reinforce you
and if already you forgot
then it is forgotten o wa omeyn

Son Rifkes, youngest yoh 301 otherjews is too many jews to know all how they are named
burikh dayen ho'emes
omeyn
omeyn
omeyn
it's okay Gittl sibling ours it's okay omeyn o wa

Khavele Nenls, riverwasher what was making sure the river stayed cleanish from hairweeds
burikh dayen ho'emes
omeyn

omeyn
omeyn
and also yoh Mameshi was sometimes going to help Khavele in the mornings

Khaykl Nenls, sanctitysocietyman what was lending his hands to cleanse the dead
burikh dayen ho'emes
yoh what could have lent now to our sibling
yoh but it's okay
Gittl you can rest
yoh you can rest Gittl omeyn

Godl Sternes, sanctitysocietyman what was helping his tateshi despite all nightmares
burikh dayen ho'emes
yoh to kheyder he would arrive sometimes looking like a sheyd we were not so kind
omeyn
omeyn
it's okay Anshl o wa

Sterne Tsipeles, sanctitywife what was known for the variety of her morning endeavors

burikh dayen ho'emes
oy
sha Anshl not your place
there is no judge
omeyn

jew what Gittl could not recognize for how they
burikh dayen ho'emes
omeyn
omeyn
Gittl you should rest
omeyn

jew what Gittl did not remember how she was called
burikh dayen ho'emes
omeyn
omeyn
omeyn
Gittl

jew what Gittl could not recognize
burikh dayen ho'emes
Gittl you should go
omeyn

omeyn
omeyn

Shulem Usherl Lanes, tateshi what hoped to be a maccabee but did not fight
burikh dayen ho'emes
yoh tateshi of Leyb
Leyb what we helped walk alone across the ocean
we helped yoh we all helped
omeyn

Mirele Katzyes, chessplayer what was sisterchallenging always for the title of best
burikh dayen ho'emes
yoh what was the bestplayer in Zatelsk when they came
but what was always before this menscolded for playing
omeyn
o wa

Binele Katzyes, chessplayer what was rested so near a board when Gittl came
burikh dayen ho'emes
Gittl enough
it's okay it's time

omeyn
sibling ours o wa

Zanvl Mireles, scholar what in not so secret loved the balalaike more than teyreh
burikh dayen ho'emes
omeyn
yoh what was playing and strumming always aftershabbes for the men
yoh but on afteryontiff Mariyashl and Zanvl would together play
omeyn

Shprintzl Mireles, unpaidmourner what had in truth the most beautiful songvoice in Zatelsk
burikh dayen ho'emes
omeyn
yoh what was always singing with Zanvl
what maybe I loved
omeyn

jew what Gittl could not recognize
burikh dayen ho'emes
omeyn
Gittl enough

omeyn
Gittl you should go

jew what Gittl could not remember how she was called
burikh dayen ho'emes
yoh siblings ours your eyes
omeyn
Gittl it's time
omeyn

Meyerl Pereles, bukher what had been in kheyder with Anshl and Zimml
burikh dayen ho'emes
yoh it's true but Gittl
omeyn
Meyerl was a real nar
omeyn

Son Pereles, bukher what had also been in kheyder with Gittl's brothers
burikh dayen ho'emes
Gittl
omeyn
Gittl
omeyn

maybe Mushke Khayennes Gittl was not sure she could not longlook at this child
burikh dayen ho'emes
yoh Gittl
it is time
omeyn
Gittl you have to leave now

And the heat was growing inside Zatelsk like something living and the rot was come unto the dustvillage and in some of these eighteen or twenty-one daytimes in what Gittl was not outside, the bodies' flesh was awaytaken by animals from the forest, and at the cusps of these twenty-one or eighteen evenings when Gittl was still inside Itzl's she could hear more often what sounded like singing around the forest, like the voices of the clan of death what had come to take everyone into the forest, and what could of course backcome, and so Gittl stopped digging separately the holes into the earth, and she stopped looking longishly at the faces or what were left and it became all what she could do to push all under any earth soever, and sometimes she only piled leaves on top, and pine needles, and handfuls of flowers and weeds and sorrel and dirt, and she did try to say for

each of them at least three words in holytongue, but she failed to give even a mayseh unto each
yoh but she tried
she did
Gittl did
sister ours
and so then in the forest what allsided Zatelsk it became:

another jew what wasn't alive anymore a child covered now in a blanket of grasses
burikh dayen ho'emes
omeyn
omeyn
a blanket is something
omeyn

another jew what wasn't alive anymore what had a beard filled with leaves
burikh dayen ho'emes
omeyn
leave Gittl you should leave
omeyn
omeyn

another jew what wasn't alive anymore what wore a prayershawl white with streaks of mudred
burikh dayen ho'emes
yoh it is good to be covered in a talis
omeyn
omeyn
omeyn

another jew what wasn't alive anymore a child what was wearing a sunyellow ribbon
burikh dayen ho'emes
omeyn
omeyn
omeyn
a beautiful ribbon o wa

another jew what wasn't alive anymore an infant
omeyn
omeyn
Gittl look away now sibling ours
omeyn

another jew what wasn't alive anymore familiar to Gittl but forgotten
burikh dayen ho'emes

omeyn
we cannot help
omeyn
omeyn

another jew what wasn't alive anymore unrecognizable
to Gittl
burikh dayen ho'emes
omeyn
omeyn
omeyn
o wa Gittl

another jew what wasn't alive anymore a body
burikh dayen ho'emes
omeyn
omeyn
omeyn
omeyn

another body no another jew what was once alive and
now what wasn't alive anymore
burikh dayen ho'emes
omeyn
omeyn

omeyn
omeyn

another jew what wasn't alive anymore
burikh dayen ho'emes
omeyn
omeyn
omeyn
omeyn we are with you always Gittl

another jew what wasn't alive anymore
burikh dayen ho'emes
omeyn
omeyn
omeyn
omeyn

another jew what wasn't alive anymore
burikh dayen ho'emes
omeyn
omeyn
omeyn
omeyn

another jew what wasn't alive anymore
burikh dayen ho'emes
omeyn
omeyn
omeyn
omeyn

another jew what wasn't alive anymore
burikh dayen ho'emes
omeyn
omeyn
omeyn
omeyn

another jew what wasn't alive anymore
burikh dayen ho'emes
omeyn
omeyn
omeyn
omeyn if you place just one leaf upon each it is enough Gittl

another jew what wasn't alive anymore burikh dayen ho'emes *omeyn omeyn omeyn omeyn* another jew what wasn't alive anymore burikh dayen ho'emes *omeyn omeyn omeyn omeyn* another jew what wasn't alive anymore burikh dayen ho'emes *omeyn omeyn omeyn omeyn* another jew what wasn't alive anymore burikh dayen ho'emes *omeyn omeyn omeyn omeyn* another jew what wasn't alive anymore burikh dayen ho'emes *omeyn omeyn omeyn omeyn* another jew what wasn't alive anymore burikh dayen ho'emes *omeyn omeyn omeyn omeyn* another jew what wasn't alive anymore burikh dayen ho'emes *omeyn omeyn omeyn omeyn* another jew what was maybe awake alive o wa a small child but of course it was only the sound of upstored air in the body leaving through the nose when Gittl lifted this child burikh dayen ho'emes *omeyn omeyn omeyn Gittl it is time to go* another jew what wasn't alive anymore burikh dayen ho'emes *omeyn omeyn omeyn omeyn* another jew what wasn't alive anymore burikh dayen ho'emes *omeyn omeyn omeyn omeyn* another jew what wasn't alive anymore burikh dayen ho'emes *omeyn omeyn omeyn omeyn* another jew what wasn't alive anymore an altishke burikh dayen ho'emes *omeyn omeyn omeyn omeyn* another jew what wasn't alive anymore burikh dayen ho'emes *omeyn omeyn omeyn omeyn* another jew what wasn't alive anymore what had a face what was not burikh dayen ho'emes *omeyn omeyn omeyn omeyn* another jew what wasn't alive anymore burikh dayen ho'emes *omeyn omeyn omeyn omeyn* another jew what wasn't alive anymore burikh dayen ho'emes *omeyn omeyn omeyn omeyn* another jew what wasn't alive anymore burikh dayen ho'emes *omeyn omeyn omeyn omeyn* another jew what wasn't alive anymore burikh dayen ho'emes *omeyn omeyn omeyn omeyn* another jew what wasn't alive anymore burikh dayen ho'emes *omeyn omeyn omeyn omeyn* another jew what wasn't alive anymore burikh dayen ho'emes *omeyn omeyn omeyn omeyn* another jew what wasn't alive anymore a child burikh dayen ho'emes *omeyn omeyn omeyn omeyn* another jew what wasn't alive anymore burikh dayen ho'emes *omeyn omeyn omeyn omeyn* another jew what wasn't alive anymore burikh dayen ho'emes *omeyn omeyn omeyn omeyn* another jew what wasn't alive anymore burikh dayen ho'emes *omeyn omeyn omeyn omeyn* another jew what wasn't alive anymore burikh dayen ho'emes *omeyn omeyn omeyn omeyn* another jew what wasn't alive anymore burikh dayen ho'emes *omeyn omeyn omeyn omeyn* another jew what wasn't alive anymore burikh dayen ho'emes *omeyn omeyn omeyn omeyn* another jew what wasn't alive anymore burikh dayen ho'emes *omeyn omeyn omeyn omeyn* another jew what looked like Itzl's cousin but impossible because Itzl's cousin was the second laughingest child in all of burikh dayen ho'emes *omeyn omeyn omeyn omeyn* another jew what wasn't alive anymore burikh dayen ho'emes *omeyn omeyn omeyn omeyn* another jew what wasn't alive anymore burikh dayen ho'emes *omeyn omeyn omeyn omeyn* another jew what wasn't alive anymore burikh dayen ho'emes *omeyn omeyn omeyn omeyn* another jew what wasn't alive anymore burikh dayen ho'emes *omeyn*

omeyn omeyn omeyn another jew what wasn't alive anymore burikh dayen ho'emes *omeyn omeyn omeyn omeyn* another jew what wasn't alive anymore burikh dayen ho'emes *omeyn omeyn omeyn omeyn* another jew what wasn't alive anymore burikh dayen ho'emes *omeyn omeyn omeyn omeyn* another jew what wasn't alive anymore a child burikh dayen ho'emes *omeyn omeyn omeyn omeyn* another jew what wasn't alive anymore burikh dayen ho'emes *omeyn omeyn omeyn omeyn* another jew what wasn't alive anymore burikh dayen ho'emes *omeyn omeyn omeyn omeyn* another jew what wasn't alive anymore a child burikh dayen ho'emes *omeyn omeyn omeyn omeyn* another jew what wasn't alive anymore another child burikh dayen ho'emes *omeyn omeyn omeyn omeyn* another jew what wasn't alive anymore burikh dayen ho'emes *omeyn omeyn omeyn omeyn* another jew what wasn't alive anymore burikh dayen ho'emes *omeyn omeyn omeyn omeyn* another jew what wasn't alive anymore burikh dayen ho'emes *omeyn omeyn omeyn omeyn* another jew what wasn't alive anymore burikh dayen ho'emes *omeyn omeyn omeyn omeyn* another jew what wasn't alive anymore burikh dayen ho'emes *omeyn omeyn omeyn omeyn* another jew what wasn't alive anymore burikh dayen ho'emes *omeyn omeyn omeyn omeyn* another jew what wasn't alive anymore burikh dayen ho'emes *omeyn omeyn omeyn omeyn* another jew what wasn't alive anymore burikh dayen ho'emes *omeyn*

omeyn omeyn omeyn another jew what wasn't alive anymore burikh dayen ho'emes *omeyn omeyn omeyn omeyn* another jew what wasn't alive anymore burikh dayen ho'emes *omeyn omeyn omeyn omeyn* another jew what wasn't alive anymore burikh dayen ho'emes *omeyn omeyn omeyn omeyn* another jew what wasn't alive anymore burikh dayen ho'emes *omeyn omeyn omeyn omeyn* another jew what wasn't alive anymore burikh dayen ho'emes *omeyn omeyn omeyn omeyn* another jew what wasn't alive anymore burikh dayen ho'emes *omeyn omeyn omeyn omeyn* another jew what wasn't alive anymore burikh dayen ho'emes *omeyn omeyn omeyn omeyn* another jew what wasn't alive anymore a child covered with a handful only of sorrel burikh dayen ho'emes *omeyn omeyn omeyn omeyn* another jew what wasn't alive anymore burikh dayen ho'emes *omeyn omeyn omeyn omeyn* another jew what wasn't alive anymore burikh dayen ho'emes *omeyn omeyn omeyn omeyn* another jew what wasn't alive anymore a child burikh dayen ho'emes *omeyn omeyn omeyn omeyn* another jew what wasn't alive anymore burikh dayen ho'emes *omeyn omeyn omeyn omeyn* another jew what wasn't alive anymore burikh dayen ho'emes *omeyn omeyn omeyn omeyn* another jew what wasn't alive anymore burikh dayen ho'emes *omeyn omeyn omeyn omeyn* another jew what wasn't alive anymore a child a child a small child what suggested to Gittl to lie down and rest but there was still the overliving child what did not speak and what only cornersat inside Itzl's and still also more jews what Gittl had yet to cover so burikh dayen ho'emes *omeyn omeyn omeyn omeyn* another jew what wasn't alive anymore burikh dayen ho'emes *omeyn omeyn omeyn omeyn* another jew what wasn't alive anymore burikh dayen ho'emes *omeyn omeyn omeyn omeyn* another jew what wasn't alive anymore burikh dayen ho'emes *omeyn omeyn omeyn omeyn* another jew what wasn't alive anymore burikh dayen ho'emes *omeyn omeyn omeyn omeyn* another jew what wasn't alive anymore burikh dayen ho'emes *omeyn omeyn omeyn omeyn* another jew what wasn't alive anymore burikh dayen ho'emes *omeyn omeyn omeyn omeyn* another jew what wasn't alive anymore burikh dayen ho'emes *omeyn omeyn omeyn omeyn* another jew what wasn't alive anymore burikh dayen ho'emes *omeyn omeyn omeyn omeyn* another jew what wasn't alive anymore burikh dayen ho'emes *omeyn omeyn omeyn omeyn* another jew what wasn't alive anymore burikh dayen ho'emes *omeyn omeyn omeyn omeyn* another jew what wasn't alive anymore burikh dayen ho'emes *omeyn omeyn omeyn omeyn* another jew what wasn't alive anymore burikh dayen ho'emes *omeyn omeyn omeyn omeyn* another jew what wasn't alive anymore burikh dayen ho'emes *omeyn omeyn omeyn omeyn* another jew what wasn't alive anymore burikh dayen ho'emes *omeyn omeyn omeyn omeyn* another jew what wasn't alive anymore burikh dayen ho'emes *omeyn omeyn omeyn omeyn* another jew what wasn't alive anymore burikh dayen ho'emes *omeyn*

omeyn omeyn omeyn another jew what wasn't alive anymore burikh dayen ho'emes *omeyn omeyn omeyn omeyn*
another jew what wasn't alive anymore burikh dayen
ho'emes *omeyn omeyn omeyn omeyn* another jew what
wasn't alive anymore burikh dayen ho'emes *omeyn*
omeyn omeyn omeyn another jew what wasn't alive anymore burikh dayen ho'emes *omeyn omeyn omeyn omeyn*
another jew what wasn't alive anymore burikh dayen
ho'emes *omeyn omeyn omeyn omeyn* another jew what
wasn't alive anymore burikh dayen ho'emes *omeyn*
omeyn omeyn omeyn another jew what wasn't alive anymore another child familiar almost but no longer
burikh dayen ho'emes *omeyn omeyn omeyn omeyn* another jew what wasn't alive anymore burikh dayen
ho'emes *omeyn omeyn omeyn omeyn* another jew what
wasn't alive anymore burikh dayen ho'emes *omeyn*
omeyn omeyn omeyn another jew what wasn't alive anymore burikh dayen ho'emes *omeyn omeyn omeyn omeyn*
another jew what wasn't alive anymore burikh dayen
ho'emes *omeyn omeyn omeyn omeyn* another jew what
wasn't alive anymore burikh dayen ho'emes *omeyn*
omeyn omeyn omeyn another jew what wasn't alive anymore burikh dayen ho'emes *omeyn omeyn omeyn omeyn*
another jew what wasn't alive anymore burikh dayen
ho'emes *omeyn omeyn omeyn omeyn* another jew what
wasn't alive anymore burikh dayen ho'emes *omeyn*
omeyn omeyn omeyn another jew what wasn't alive anymore burikh dayen ho'emes *omeyn omeyn omeyn omeyn*

another jew what wasn't alive anymore burikh dayen ho'emes *omeyn omeyn omeyn omeyn* another jew what wasn't alive anymore an infant child burikh dayen ho'emes *omeyn omeyn omeyn omeyn* another jew what wasn't alive anymore burikh dayen ho'emes *omeyn omeyn omeyn omeyn* another jew what wasn't alive anymore burikh dayen ho'emes *omeyn omeyn omeyn omeyn* another jew what wasn't alive anymore burikh dayen ho'emes *omeyn omeyn omeyn omeyn* another jew what wasn't alive anymore burikh dayen ho'emes *omeyn omeyn omeyn omeyn* another jew what wasn't alive anymore burikh dayen ho'emes *omeyn omeyn omeyn omeyn* another jew what wasn't alive anymore burikh dayen ho'emes *omeyn omeyn omeyn omeyn* another jew what wasn't alive anymore burikh dayen ho'emes *omeyn omeyn omeyn omeyn* another jew what wasn't alive anymore burikh dayen ho'emes *omeyn omeyn omeyn omeyn* another jew what wasn't alive anymore burikh dayen ho'emes *omeyn omeyn omeyn omeyn* another jew what wasn't alive anymore another child burikh dayen ho'emes *omeyn omeyn omeyn omeyn* another jew what wasn't alive anymore another child burikh dayen ho'emes *omeyn omeyn omeyn omeyn* another jew what wasn't alive anymore another child all these children one after another together burikh dayen ho'emes *omeyn omeyn omeyn omeyn* another jew what wasn't alive anymore burikh dayen ho'emes *omeyn omeyn omeyn omeyn* another jew what wasn't alive anymore burikh dayen ho'emes *omeyn omeyn omeyn omeyn* another jew what wasn't alive anymore a child burikh dayen ho'emes *omeyn omeyn omeyn omeyn* another jew what wasn't alive anymore burikh dayen ho'emes *omeyn omeyn omeyn omeyn* another jew what wasn't alive anymore burikh dayen ho'emes *omeyn omeyn omeyn omeyn* another jew what wasn't alive anymore an altishke at least she had lived longer burikh dayen ho'emes *omeyn omeyn omeyn omeyn* another jew what wasn't alive anymore yoh when she finished placing only one leaf placing only three words not even a full mayseh or a name unto each Gittl would rest she would lie down to rest burikh dayen ho'emes *omeyn omeyn omeyn omeyn* another jew what wasn't alive anymore burikh dayen ho'emes *omeyn omeyn omeyn omeyn* another jew what wasn't alive anymore burikh dayen ho'emes *omeyn omeyn omeyn omeyn* another jew what wasn't alive anymore a child burikh dayen ho'emes *omeyn omeyn omeyn omeyn* another jew what wasn't alive anymore burikh dayen ho'emes *omeyn omeyn omeyn omeyn* another jew what wasn't alive anymore burikh dayen ho'emes *omeyn omeyn omeyn omeyn* another jew what wasn't alive anymore a child burikh dayen ho'emes *omeyn omeyn omeyn omeyn* another jew what wasn't alive anymore burikh dayen ho'emes *omeyn omeyn omeyn omeyn* another jew what wasn't alive anymore burikh dayen ho'emes *omeyn omeyn omeyn omeyn* another jew what wasn't alive anymore burikh dayen ho'emes *omeyn omeyn omeyn omeyn* another jew what wasn't alive anymore burikh dayen ho'emes *omeyn omeyn omeyn omeyn* another jew what wasn't alive anymore burikh dayen ho'emes *omeyn omeyn omeyn omeyn* another jew what wasn't alive anymore burikh dayen ho'emes *omeyn omeyn omeyn omeyn* another jew what wasn't alive anymore burikh dayen ho'emes *omeyn omeyn omeyn omeyn* another jew what wasn't alive anymore burikh dayen ho'emes *omeyn omeyn omeyn omeyn* another jew what wasn't alive anymore burikh dayen ho'emes *omeyn omeyn omeyn omeyn* another jew what wasn't alive anymore burikh dayen ho'emes *omeyn omeyn omeyn omeyn* another jew what wasn't alive anymore burikh dayen ho'emes *omeyn omeyn omeyn omeyn* another jew what wasn't alive anymore burikh dayen ho'emes *omeyn omeyn omeyn omeyn* another jew what wasn't alive anymore a child a small one burikh dayen ho'emes *omeyn omeyn omeyn omeyn* another jew what wasn't alive anymore burikh dayen ho'emes *omeyn omeyn omeyn omeyn* another jew what wasn't alive anymore burikh dayen ho'emes *omeyn omeyn omeyn omeyn* another jew what wasn't alive anymore burikh dayen ho'emes *omeyn omeyn omeyn omeyn* another jew what wasn't alive anymore burikh dayen ho'emes *omeyn omeyn omeyn omeyn* another jew what wasn't alive anymore a child burikh dayen ho'emes *omeyn omeyn omeyn omeyn* another jew what wasn't alive anymore burikh dayen ho'emes *omeyn omeyn omeyn omeyn* another jew what wasn't alive anymore a child in her crib burikh dayen ho'emes *omeyn omeyn omeyn omeyn* another jew what wasn't alive anymore burikh dayen ho'emes *omeyn omeyn omeyn omeyn* another jew what wasn't alive anymore a child in his parents' bed burikh dayen ho'emes *omeyn omeyn omeyn omeyn* another jew what wasn't alive anymore burikh dayen ho'emes *omeyn omeyn omeyn omeyn* another jew what wasn't alive anymore burikh dayen ho'emes *omeyn omeyn omeyn omeyn* another jew what wasn't alive anymore a child burikh dayen ho'emes *omeyn omeyn omeyn omeyn* another jew what wasn't alive anymore burikh dayen ho'emes *omeyn omeyn omeyn omeyn* another jew what wasn't alive anymore burikh dayen ho'emes *omeyn omeyn omeyn omeyn* another jew what wasn't alive anymore a child burikh dayen ho'emes *omeyn omeyn omeyn omeyn* another jew what wasn't alive anymore burikh dayen ho'emes *omeyn omeyn omeyn omeyn* another jew what wasn't alive anymore burikh dayen ho'emes *omeyn omeyn omeyn omeyn* another jew what wasn't alive anymore burikh dayen ho'emes *omeyn omeyn omeyn omeyn* another jew what wasn't alive anymore burikh dayen ho'emes *omeyn omeyn omeyn omeyn* another jew what wasn't alive anymore a child burikh dayen ho'emes *omeyn omeyn omeyn omeyn* maybe that is only a mound of earth it is dark now but no yoh it is another jew what wasn't alive anymore burikh dayen ho'emes *omeyn omeyn omeyn omeyn* another jew what wasn't alive anymore burikh dayen ho'emes *omeyn omeyn omeyn omeyn* another jew what wasn't alive anymore a child burikh dayen ho'emes *omeyn omeyn omeyn omeyn* another jew what wasn't alive anymore a child burikh dayen ho'emes *omeyn omeyn omeyn omeyn* another jew what wasn't alive anymore burikh dayen ho'emes *omeyn omeyn omeyn omeyn* another jew what wasn't alive anymore burikh dayen ho'emes *omeyn omeyn omeyn omeyn* another jew what wasn't alive anymore burikh dayen ho'emes *omeyn omeyn omeyn omeyn* another jew what wasn't alive anymore a child burikh dayen ho'emes *omeyn omeyn omeyn omeyn* another jew what wasn't alive anymore burikh dayen ho'emes *omeyn omeyn omeyn omeyn* another jew what wasn't alive anymore it's too many how can there be so many it was only one small dustvillage burikh dayen ho'emes *omeyn omeyn omeyn omeyn* another jew what wasn't alive anymore burikh dayen ho'emes *omeyn omeyn omeyn omeyn* another jew what wasn't alive anymore a child burikh dayen ho'emes *omeyn omeyn omeyn omeyn* another jew what wasn't alive anymore burikh dayen ho'emes *omeyn omeyn omeyn omeyn* another jew what wasn't alive anymore burikh dayen ho'emes *omeyn omeyn omeyn omeyn* another jew what wasn't alive anymore burikh dayen ho'emes *omeyn omeyn omeyn omeyn* another jew what wasn't alive anymore burikh dayen ho'emes *omeyn omeyn omeyn omeyn* another jew what wasn't alive anymore burikh dayen ho'emes *omeyn omeyn omeyn omeyn* another jew what wasn't alive anymore burikh dayen ho'emes *omeyn omeyn omeyn omeyn* another jew what wasn't alive anymore burikh dayen ho'emes *omeyn omeyn omeyn omeyn* another jew what wasn't alive anymore when Gittl was finished she would after find a way to awaytake the child of Mirele's what was waiting for her back inside Itzl's she would take money from the pockets of the jews what were not alive anymore and walk with the child to pinsk and find a way for him to go to the ocean yoh almost the only words he had said in two weeks was the name Yutke from some cousin in amerike when Gittl asked him again and again if he had elsewhere family and then she would but now she had almost forgotten to say burikh dayen ho'emes *omeyn omeyn omeyn omeyn* another jew what wasn't alive anymore burikh dayen ho'emes *omeyn omeyn omeyn omeyn* another jew what wasn't alive anymore burikh dayen ho'emes *omeyn omeyn omeyn omeyn* another jew what wasn't alive anymore burikh dayen ho'emes *omeyn omeyn omeyn omeyn* another jew what wasn't alive anymore burikh dayen ho'emes *omeyn omeyn omeyn omeyn* another jew what wasn't alive anymore burikh dayen ho'emes *omeyn omeyn omeyn omeyn* another jew what wasn't alive anymore burikh dayen ho'emes *omeyn omeyn omeyn omeyn* another jew what wasn't alive anymore burikh dayen ho'emes *omeyn omeyn omeyn omeyn* another jew what wasn't alive anymore burikh dayen ho'emes *omeyn omeyn omeyn omeyn* another jew what wasn't alive anymore burikh dayen ho'emes *omeyn omeyn omeyn omeyn* another jew what wasn't alive anymore burikh dayen ho'emes *omeyn omeyn omeyn omeyn* another jew what wasn't alive anymore burikh dayen ho'emes *omeyn omeyn omeyn omeyn* another jew what wasn't alive anymore burikh dayen ho'emes *omeyn omeyn omeyn omeyn* another jew what wasn't alive anymore burikh dayen ho'emes *omeyn omeyn omeyn omeyn* another jew what wasn't alive anymore burikh dayen ho'emes *omeyn omeyn omeyn omeyn* another jew what wasn't alive anymore burikh dayen ho'emes *omeyn omeyn omeyn omeyn* another jew what wasn't alive anymore burikh dayen ho'emes *omeyn omeyn omeyn omeyn* another jew what wasn't alive anymore burikh dayen ho'emes *omeyn omeyn omeyn omeyn* another jew what wasn't alive anymore burikh dayen ho'emes *omeyn omeyn omeyn omeyn* another jew what wasn't alive anymore burikh dayen ho'emes *omeyn omeyn omeyn omeyn* another jew what wasn't alive anymore burikh dayen ho'emes *omeyn omeyn omeyn omeyn* another jew what wasn't alive anymore burikh dayen ho'emes *omeyn omeyn omeyn omeyn* another jew what wasn't alive anymore burikh dayen ho'emes *omeyn omeyn omeyn omeyn* another jew what wasn't alive anymore burikh dayen ho'emes *omeyn omeyn omeyn omeyn* another jew what wasn't alive anymore burikh dayen ho'emes *omeyn omeyn omeyn omeyn* another jew what wasn't alive anymore burikh dayen ho'emes *omeyn omeyn omeyn omeyn* another jew what wasn't alive anymore one more child from Zatelsk what was alive and then was not alive anymore burikh dayen ho'emes *omeyn omeyn omeyn omeyn*

and in addition to these 296 jews from Zatelsk what weren't alive anymore

yoh

also

four

others

there were of course ten people from Zatelsk what were not harmed: Phonye the clerk, what probably showed the men his penis for proof of what he was not, and Phonye'te his wife, and their seven children, what were sweet children, and what had hopefully left before the jewslaughter began all around them, and also Phonye, the man of god, what almost certainly had not left, what had likely instead watched, watched and even helped the clan of death what had come to take the people of Zatelsk into the forest, yoh, and when they came they took everyone from Zatelsk into the forest and almost every jew what had been alive wasn't alive anymore, but there were of course two jews from Zatelsk what were still alive, or at least had overlived, or at least what were not by Gittl placed into the ground or under any leaves soever.

Timebird

In the morning Leyb was for some time being in a perfectish world. The morning was actually afternoon, and Leyb was actually in Charles's apartment, and his body was actually roilish with ache and the dullstab of the sun was sparsing through the lonely overkitchen window, only the window was not lonely, it was friends with all the walls, and the sun was not dullish, it was just backholding its heat so as not to disturb the two men what were quiltbeneath entangled, and Leyb's body, if aching, was also ensconced in Charles's body, and Leyb rolled then on top of Charles, sleepish still, and lightbit the topbone of Charles's cheek, and Charles awakegroaned and slowblinked, and he said, Good morning, Lion, and Leyb said, I think it is already afternoon, and Charles said time shmaym, and Leyb said, It's okay that I'm still here? and Charles's eyes were looking upon Leyb's eyes, and Charles said, I should probably get some writing done, and Leyb closed his eyes then, but amidst the redflicker of Leyb's behindeyelids, Charles said, But you're welcome to stay here for a while, or for longer. I'd be glad to get the rebbe another cup of coffee, or a first, as it happens?

And Leyb closed his eyes and felt fireants upcrawling on his wrists, and felt hedgehogs underquiltnestling at his feet, and then he opened his eyes and beheld that lo, there was no longer any ceiling over Charles's apartment, only sky bluestretching above hordes of worshipful pines, oh swayish oh shokling, and in it, there were no clouds soever, only a blackbird what had caught fire but what was not consumed, what made a plinking sound once and then once more
yoh tum balalaike
happy may we be
and then it began again to rain.

yoh so before this
time was beginning to move in other ways
and to stretch toward itself
and to drink itself o wa

Thus Spoke america

And so Gittl left Itzl's house what stood beyond the stand of trees within what Gittl had stood when the clan of death had come to take every jew from Zatelsk, jewish for what stands or falls beyond catastrophe, into the forest, and she awaywent from Zatelsk, never to return, approximately a wandering aramean, approximately dead, but for the pullforward of her feet, and the malekhbabble, and the various tayves of her body, and she moved then north into the belly of some or other city, yoh, pinsk first and later minsk, and in each she was scrubbing in silence during the days, and then downlaying her head during the nights on some or other floor, where in the predawn hours she could tell to her siblings any mayseh she pleased, and they could tell to her, and this she did more or less for seven years and then seven more, and in this time, of course, Gittl was having tayves and boredoms what were leading her to lay with various men, and one of those men, in the sixth year of the second cycle of seven, was called Meyshke and he was an editor at the minsker journal in what's offices Gittl was then scrubbing days, and what was called Literarishe Blumen[42] but what everyone called Marx's Beard, and what was known even in amerike for its relishment of communal welts and warts, or so Meyshke claimed, his floursome chest all piffled and hairfish blooming, and after they had shtipped for the second or fourth puffish time in Gittl's smallroom, for Meyshke was matrimonial unto some Shoshke or other, and could not thus bring himself to bring herself to his own larger room, yoh, in that once after, Meyshke's blinksome eyes fell upon what Gittl had written during another once before, seven years after the forest, perhaps

yoh it's what
it's only time
there is always before
o wa

and what pages she kept under her pillow some nights, to read and recite, and what pages she had neglected to remember to awayput this night before Meyshke came, her list of jews what had been alive and three prayerwords to the nonexistant deathjudge of truth, with a be-

42 "Literary Flowers."

foremayseh for some, and Meyshke read the pages while still upon her sleepmat, and then asked if he could place her poem inside the Beard, for they were working hard, all the workers were, he said, on an issue commemorating the events what had occurred during the time of the revolution and the afterwar, et cetera, though he would of course make sure they didn't mention a single hair from Trotsky's mustache, time's altar and all, and they'd attribute the hanging of any collaborator of the malekh made from only eyes to Tovarisch Stalin himself, and they would certainly not mention any instantiations of redled jewslaughter soever, and Gittl wanted to say, It's not a poem, it's just a list, but she was tired and wanted for him to leave, and so she said, I should care where you place it, so long as you backbring the pages

yoh if you do not
we will kindly help
your revolutionary jargonfilled head
revolute until backward facing upon the stalk of your neck
o wa

and so he took them, and he brought them back, and Gittl and Meyshke shtipped maybe twice or four more times, until Gittl grew bored and awaysent Meyshke into the wilderness of minsk, and Gittl returned to the toilets and floors of the Beard, and she ignored him when he tried to grab her attention there, with pssts and other pesters, and then one time she turned toward the psst sound peeking from this pisher's pisk[43] and said, yoh, Meyshke'le, a beautiful thanks, I'd love to come for dinner by you and your Shoshke'le, monogamy is the bailiwick of bourgeoisie, not so, and the other editors horselaughed with their big teeth and Meyshke redflushed, and then that was that, yoh, until maybe two or four months later, when a letter arrived at the offices of Literarishe Blumen and Meyshke himself brought it to Gittl, what was of course not expecting any letter soever, because of how all the people what she knew were awaytaken to the forest, et cetera, but was not displeased to see Meyshke's face so grum and coyfish when he told her it was addressed to her, and she took it from his hand and saw that her name was indeed scrawled on its outside, but that it had been opened, lilacish seal overbroken, and she spit, lightly, near Meyshke's nice shoes, and then longlooked at Meyshke, and he awaylooked for shame, but did not leave, and so she reopened the alreadyopened envelope, and saw that in it was a document declaring that she, Gittl Khayeles, had been awarded passage into amerike, hurrah, and Meyshke, having already read its contents, murmured then that no one got such things these days, then began to explain about the quota's jaws, but Gittl offcut him and said, yoh, I know, I do read every then and now a famous

43 "Slubberdegullion's craw."

journal what's called Literary Flowers, and she looked then down at the amerikanish welcomepaper in her hand, and noticed that attached to its back was a notelet, in jewish, what she overturned and read: tayere tokhter fin Khayele, ikh hob lib gehat dayn lidele, farvus kimsti nit kin amerike? kim, leyen for dayn lidele far di nebekhdike yidn do,[44] and it was signed, the Baroness, and Gittl looked at Meyshke what gazed howlishly with a certain sort of tayve at the papers in her hands

yoh unimportant is Meyshke's jealousfish
isn't he anyway supposed to scoff upon amerike's golden toenails
Marx's Beard indeed anyway Gittl let's already
an aftermayseh is waiting o wa

and Gittl laughed without smiling, and nodded her head, and bid him farewell with a fingertap on his fleecesome forearm and a handpat on his smoothshaven cheek'ele, and then she, Gittl Khayeles, took the money what she had saved and also a little extra from the office what for a socialistic tip, and she sprinkled it into the atlantisher's opened jaws, and the water chickled to itself, distracted by its newfound fortune, and so when Gittl was thirty-one years old she left her homecontintent and its

---

44 "Dear Khayele's daughter, I liked your little poem, why don't you come to america? Come, declaim your little poem for the poor neglected jews here."

everhumming river of death and went into the ocean, and there she enjoyed outspitting each of her own may-sehs into the waters and lo the waters responded by up-casting their salt over her flesh and her eyes, such that her gums became coated with salt and her eyelashes stuck together and her memories overcrusted and be-came grains of salt and were dispersed throughout the waters and the therewaters of the past and the present, and Gittl grew tired, and thought she might begin her undergoing and come finally to rest in the khvalyes,[45] but she was just then propped up by porpoises, her bare feet borne west on their slickblack fishbacks, their sharpish maws opening for to shriek their underwater psalms loudly enough that Gittl could hear them call-ing in voices waterish familiar

sweet one
beloved one
tired one
blessed be your tired feet

over the subdued wind and under the saltglass slice of the water and the softdark sluice of the murk what was overlapping their backs as they flapped forward or

---

45 This word, which is, of course, the name of the Comrade Trunksboym's press in which this mayseh found its first home, stands in particularly stark aural contradistinction to its amer-ican nasal honk of a cousin, "waves," and echoes, at least to my ear, the aforementioned "khlyope."

under their bellies as they leaped over the face of the deep and gray. A small flaming blackbird led the way like a needle and thread sewn through the sky, and Gittl downlay to rest her head on the backs of the creatures, their softsmooth skin flickering underneath her cheek and above their muscles, right on the border between the water and the therewater, and yoh, on the otherside of the atlantisher wetness sat plump and bespectacled amerike.

The blackbirds downflopped dead onto land, smoldering heaps of feather and fine bone.

Two by two the porpoises swam away into the grayscape, shrieking as they swam.

And Gittl was left to stagger alone like a drunken Ham unto the edges of her new stepfather's bepoisoned and snakesome garden, holding in her hands a paper invitation hewn from a tree, wishing she could hold instead the hands of her siblings hewn from the wind.

yoh and of course
Gittl sibling ours
we are all wishing this
o wa

Wastyur neym, said amerike.

Gittl Khayeles, said Gittl.

Incomprehensible, said amerike.

Gittl Zhitomirsky, then, said Gittl. Gittl Felshtiner, Gittl Berdichevsky, Gittl Skvirasky, Gittl Proskurover, Gittl Zatelsky, Gittl Rechistasky—

Gerty Radish, said amerike. There we are.

Nothing said Gittl.

Oh jewess, said amerike, lose the sourpuss. You made it. Mazel tov cocktails for all. And what's in a name, after all? Look at me. Tateh Vespucius indeed. No oedipal complex to be had at all, woof, given that dad was basically born dead, in terms of significance, what? And still, I did alright for myself, right? Didn't I? You can smell the leather in my eyesockets. Here, smell. Nice, right? Scraped either from a jersey cow or from some redfinned member of the garment workers union or other, isn't that right, Gerty? You've got no intentions, I'm sure. Anyway, enough about you. My essence, of course, is dentistry. In the course of no time at all, I sank my thankful milky teeth into the belly of this other fellow, coated my molars with his flesh, daintily tugged his molars from his mouth's flesh, and he barely yelped, Gerty, for they do have a much higher pain tolerance, biologically speaking, and I dribbled his warm mouthblood all over my pretty garden, and now gosh darn it, jewess! Would ya look at all that corn, I warned my daughters of his ways, and then started a school, and built a town, and then another, kept his teeth tucked away in my cheek for good luck, called it a day or two, and good grief, what do we got? A room for you, Gerty! A room of your own. A room that I built all by my lonesome, no help at all! Look away from my face. I'd strongly recommend that you, ha. Ahem. Look at the pictures on the wall, would ya?

Gittl vomited.

Don't look too long, though. As I was saying, lose the sourpuss. Not a good look in these parts. You've jewed your way in here, and good on ya, Gerty, good on ya, Radish. I'm a big fan of initiative. You're here to peruse your happiness, or something like that, right? Right. Now do a little twirl for me, would ya?

Atta girl.

Atta Gerty.

You'll like it here, I'm sure of it.

Here.

Have a tooth.

Gittl stood still as amerike offpicked all her lice, muttering to itself under its vinegar and roomnut breath, and somewhere was the sound of a bell clanging inside a wintersome nostril, and every now and then amerike paused to scratch the undersides of its eyelids with one of its thirteen tongues, and then it was finished, and so deloused, Gittl grabbed hold of a collection of dustmotes and bordermoths what to use as currency, and was then muscled onto a train, and fell there into sleep, and she slept for longer than she almost ever slept, for hours, yoh, or at least for a long hour.

Arrived to philadelphiye, Gittl awoke.

philadelphiye

yoh in amerike now
where a mayseh always lusts after the after
and after and after
feh

a mayseh fin philadelphiye

tuk tuk tuk.

Opened the door an altishke what was wearing an enormous hat covered with feathers and jewels.

Peace upon you?

Upon you peace, Glikl! Good to see you. What do you make? A good journey? Good. You'll eat something?

It's alright.

No, no, you must eat something, daughter, it's a long journey, you must be hungry.

Alright, a beautiful thanks.

Harry! yelled the Baroness of philadelphiye, and through the gildish hallways fastwalked an altishker, what was wearing a nice suit, and Gittl wondered if perhaps this was the Baron, but the Baroness was speaking upon him in american, and was saying, What you're doing, Harry, I was telling you that our guest would arrive today and the lunch isn't even ready!

Sorry, ma'am, said Harry. The food is ready, ma'am.

teh, the Baroness said, and then turned to Gittl and

said, nit kin kliger bukher, ober s'iz nit zayn fault, nit azoy, Glikl?[46] The Baroness blinked with one eye.

Gittl

it's Gittl

what is this

we don't like this

Gittl.

What?

My name is Gittl.

Yes, of course. That's what I said, said the Baroness in jewish. Then, in american: Gittl, it's what I had said, right, Harry?

Yes, ma'am.

Good. You might be going now, Harry.

Yes, ma'am.

at the end of the woodstreet remember the youngish pine
once I told Zimml s'iz do a bissl toi
and Zimml believed your dewish words you demonfish
and so he tasted it with his tongue
but it was not dew it was sap what was clinging to the pine
fingers then my tongue
o wa it's funny

—and like I was saying, Elke was glad to help, daughter.

What?

---

46 "Not such a smart boychik, but it's not his fault, not so, Glikl?"

Elke
help Elke
Elke daughter
who is Elke

Who is Elke, Gittl said.

Elke Roosevelt, said the Baroness. We are fastish friends, even if she's a bit slow, but a nice critter, all in all, and I told her over tea, I said to her, There's a poetess what I must bring, what we must have here in amerike, and now here you are!

They were now seated on opposite sides of a table what was almost as big as the room in what Gittl had slept for all her years in minsk.

I am here.

Now here you are, said the Baroness again. Here you are, just like that.

A beautiful thanks, Gittl said.

Oh it's nothing, there's nothing for what, the Baroness said. Just a jew what is helping another jew. Here, eat. Harry!

Harry came then, as if throughwallwalking, and Gittl startled a bit, and the Baroness said in jewish, Don't worry, daughter, he's a friendly one.

And Gittl did not speak, and watched as Harry put his hand on the metallish lid from the platter, and she saw her own reflection moving in the lid as he uptook it, and beneath the lid there was a heapish pile of flesh.

A beautiful thanks, Gittl said in american to Harry,

but then she turned to the Baroness and said, ikh ess nit kin fleysh.

The Baroness looked at her for some time. Then in american she said, Harry, for what are you just herestanding.

Sorry, ma'am, Harry said, and quickleft the room.

Gittl did not speak.

The Baroness stabbed a fork the size of Gittl's arm into the flesh and took a piece onto her plate. You don't eat any meat, you say. What kind of thing is this? But I should care, she said, and with her other hand, she pushed toward Gittl a small goldene bowl. I should care.

In it were potatoes.

A beautiful thanks, Gittl said, again, and took from the bowl only three small potatoes, although she was quiverish with hunger.

The sound of the Baroness chewing upon flesh filled the room in what there was no other sound.

Do you, do jews in amerike read often Marx's Beard? Gittl said.

What? Who has said anything from him, may his goyish name be erased, feh, what jew is calling her child Karl, no wonder the boychik turned out as unpleasant as he did, not so, daughter?

Sorry, Literarishe Blumen, do you read it often?

The Baroness looked at her. I have never heard from it.

Gittl looked at the Baroness.

The Baroness looked at Gittl.

Did you, how did you read my, the poem?

Oh, yes, yes, of course, your little poem. No, I don't read poems. I was only needing something what to ask of Elke, I couldn't go into our tea without any favor asking, that would be impolite, after all what I've done for her, so I asked my sister Zelde whose son Mottl's valorwife Blume-Bashke is always reading little poems, and she had said there was a girl poet in the last issue of something or other, I suppose it must have been what you said, Literarishe Beymer, and I liked this idea, a girl poet, speaking of what, good that you should finish eating already, daughter, I hope your potatoes were delicious. They were certainly delicious, I hope.

A beautiful thanks.

Oh, it's nothing, there's nothing for what. Anyway, good that you should finish eating and get ready because, you may believe it or don't, this afternoon, you will be doing your first reading from your little poem!

Oh, don't look at me so. We won't even have to leave the house, I've told my friends it will be a smallish affair, this first reading, maybe only fifty jews, and they are coming here, in, well, soon, very soon, good that you should get changed, Harry will show you to your room, Harry! Harry!

yoh just speak it
as the psalmist says sibling ours feh
little poem smallish affair
Gittl

I'm sorry, Gittl said.

What's that?

I cannot.

You cannot what, daughter? Don't worry, it's only a few people, all what are speaking jewish of course, even if some are stumbledumb in it like Mottl Zeldes what was born here and sounds like a yenki goy when he opens his pisk, nebekh, no wonder he married so strangely, anyway, don't be nervous, you won't have to read it in american yet, and I'm sure they'll all love your little poem.

Gittl did not speak.

Harry, you should now show the poetess to her very room, please, thank you, et cetera.

Harry stood beside the door, sweat beading like dew on his backfallish hairline. Yes, ma'am.

Gittl stood.

I am sure the reading will be so moving, said the Baroness, still sitting. I'm looking forward to hearing your little poem. Now go get ready, Glikl, daughter mine. Harry!

Gittl followed Harry down the longest hallway in philadelphiye, surely, and they arrived at the end of the hallway, by the door to outside, before a left turn up a staircase, where Gittl could already see how she would become with a tail fixed on her by some farshlumperter[47] malekh.

not any tailfixing sibling of ours though
sibling ours it's time
yoh Gittl it is time
just only say in nice american

A beautiful thanks, Gittl said in american, what she was knowing swimmishly from all her years of bookdrowning.

Harry had started to walk up the stairs, and was not upon her looking. You're welcome, ma'am.

I'm not any ma'am, it's okay, Gittl said, standing still at the stairsbottom. But I have only to go outside.

Harry turned and looked at her for a long moment, and the wrinkles on his brow were more wrinkledbecome. I am afraid I can't let you go out there alone, ma'am.[48]

---

47 "Tatterdemalion."

48 By all appearances, this may well have been Harold Rassmullen, who lived just a few blocks from where Charles had lived as a child, meaning, ultimately, just a few and then a few more blocks from where Charles still lived, at the time of this event, and who owned seven cats, all of which were known to be dangerous for children, and who was among the first seven or

Gittl looked at Harry's eyes. It's okay, she said. I'm never going anywhere alone.
yoh not alone
not alone
never alone Gittl
o wa
And so Harry then beheld around him and around the tiredeyed jewess a crowd of other jews, with four jews frontstanding and others behindcoming to crowd under the Baroness's lintel, and the jews in front were holding what looked to be a whistle and a pile of books and a tusk and o wa one was holding only nothing at all, and Harry shook his head for it had been a goddamned long day, sure, but Jesus christ was he now seeing things,
yoh no
we are not
things
Harry
I am too young for this, he thought, and he closed his eyes.

---

so in the Seventh to own a car, which was said to be dangerous for children, too. Mr. Rassmullen was rumored to work for the most powerful Jew-witch in all of Philadelphia, and he warned the children that she would certainly cast a spell, at his behest, on anyone found to be bothering either his cats or his car, and so, lo, the signs and wonders seem to align, as it were.

but yoh
it's not about your age
Harry it is about
what you intend to do before all the world

Do I truly mean to prevent this poor jewess from leaving? On one hand, there's what the Baroness will say, and she will have a fit, I imagine, but more important is what my parents might have said, may their souls rest in peace, Be decent or don't be at all, they'd always say, and also, to be honest, it just seems like it might require a bit more effort than I am willing to expend, I am tired.

yoh so do not prevent
and be healthy for us
Harold son of Violet and Gregory
o wa

Harry opened his eyes and saw only the door pulling closed before him, and beyond this pullclosed door, Gittl outwalked down the outside stairs and right into the street, and everywhere there was rain, and Gittl laughed, for she was here in philadelphiye, on the edge of amerike, alone, alone, alone, but for one other remnant of Zatelsk, what she had not seen in seven and then seven years, but what she was ready now to see. Halper, Gittl remembered, for she had forgotten some

names in her forest list, but did not forget this name what small Leyb had pulled from some drawer inside his memory when he finally againspoke toward the end of the third week after the clan of death took everyone to the forest, yoh, as Gittl went forth and back to the forest to place under the earth and leaves the people of Zatelsk what had been alive, had stayed in Itzl's all that time Leyb, not much moving, not much eating, not at all speaking, until one evening, when Gittl again asked, and he said to her in a quieted voice a name, Yutke Halper, what he remembered from bedtime maysehs, yoh, the litvish Yutke what had become wealthsome in the belly of the goldene medineh with a husband what sold socks to allamerike, seventh cousin to Shulem Usherl Lanes, Leyb's own tateshi what solemned prayers like rotten pears, and then, before all the world moved as it did, Gittl took this name into her mouth and helped Leyb walk alone across the ocean and then she went alone into the belly of a city, and then another city, and now she too had walked across the ocean into philadelphiye, and now Gittl too had to find the Halperhome.
But philadelphiye is not so small a city
yoh we cannot help you find it
but if you ask we can help you ask
and if you walk
Gittl we can help you walk
and so Gittl walked into the philadelphiyesh evening, and she beheld through the rain that the city was filled

with wheat, and outside on the street one thousand drivers with their carts of ware and exposed bellies lay along the streetlamps silent in the rain, and there were children playing with parcels bulging with ants and intestines, and Gittl was passing through swayish fields of wheat and rifles, and cold rose from the water like steam and the sky of the therewaters above the city downspit upon her, and of course, in the entire city of philadelphiye there is no wheatfield to be found, only streets what were slickened with wetness, and Gittl onwalked upon them, with only the pages of a list stuffed in the pockets of her tateshi's coat, and only the name Yutke Halper balanced on her tongue, and she then asked the first jew what she saw on the street, what was wearing a tall hat made from bearls and foxkes and what pointed her helpishly in the wrong direction, where she asked another jew, an enormous creature with a beard made from bees, honey dripping down his mustache and coating all his teeth, waiting, he told Gittl, as though she'd asked him about anything other than Halperjews, for morning.

Gittl stared at his teeth.

Pert hussy, he said. Staring so. Come closer, tchotchke'le.

do not take one step closer jew
little thing he says feh
once I was afraid from beestings
o wa but once I was afraid from nothing

Gittl spit, growled, pastwalked, and behind her the beebearded jew upreared and when he backdownreared he was become a small cityowlet, with eyes made from bottlecaps and he turned his head around, around, around, and Gittl walked on, and nearby, she saw a patch of drytall grasses, brushed downward toward the ground like hairs on the scalp of some fungalgolem. On the other side of the street, three women sat around a fire what burned in the belly of a wheelbarrow, lighting the dull around them, withstanding somehow the downfall of rain. Two of them were holding bundles, and Gittl watched as they moved to toast their bundles over the flames, and she saw that in each bundle was wrapped a small owl, feathers scorched from bodies, eyes widesome and blinkless. One of the women played an oboe. Gittl awayturned, and tried to walk in the other direction, but could not upmove her feet from the ground. And she looked around and saw that in every window in the city flickered a candle, as though it was yeartime for all the bodies what together made up the soil above what lay a layer of pavement upon what Gittl's feet were then stuck, and the wind hiccupped and shrieked in a familiar tone
breathe Gittl
you're okay Gittl
you know this Gittl
it will pass sibling ours
and the city of philadelphiye began to consume itself,

brick upsnorted into gaping dustnostrils, wood gnawing on its own knots with splintersome teeth, steelish beams holding on to one another and crying out, and from each new crack in the ground sprouted a tree, until Gittl was surrounded by only trees, and over the branches of these trees were draped
breathe Gittl
we love you
we will be here after
o wa
deflated bodies, no bones or muscles or organs left inside them, just skin and frightened eyes, some of the men with yarmulkes still balanced on the tips of their beards, some of the women with their mouths still open in song.

shulem aleykhem, said a Phonye with no holes in its face for eyes or nostrils or a mouth or ears, only an eversmoothness of skin.

Gittl wanted to call out for her siblings, that they might become each as dark and piercing jewlead,[49] such

---

49 I've taken a bit more license than usual, here, adding "dark" to the original "piercing jewlead" (dirkhshtekhene yidblai), in order to summon the vestige of Du Bois's "dark and pierced Jew" into the frame, to stand opposite the Phonye's below rendition; while I am, of course, loathe to defend any allegiance to the Church, which I know can serve as the justification for blood-spilling, and -drinking, as below, I cannot but nod, even if obliquely, toward that small portion of the faithful, for whom said faith can

that when she faced this Phonye, she might send her siblings forward before her. But she could not call out, was alone in this city with only this Phonye laughing through its everskin before her.

Good to see you, Gittl, said the Phonye. Or it is Glikl?

Gittl tried to spit but her mouth was drybecome.

Relax, Gittl. I'm just here to tell you a story. My own mayseh, if you will. It was around the holy period of easter, as I'm sure you recall, and we'd finished our day's work. And we were hungry, Gittl, famished, really, as men get when they finish hard work. Foolishly enough, none of us thought to bring along the canned black blood sausages—the same sausage that posed such a challenge to the boys, when we'd just started such endeavors, but practice makes perfect, right, jewess? Practice makes for the ease of swallowing anything you please, blood sausages, or anything at all. You do know this, don't you, Gittl, having rolled all those bodies into the ground?

Gittl tried again to make a sound but could not make a sound, tried to move her feet but could not move her feet.

---

and does fortify a tendency toward decency, like the aforementioned Ms. Elizabeth Freeman. (Perhaps, if I am being truthful, I also had in mind Ms. Rose Patterson, whom I hope one day might hear this mayseh, even if she won't read it herself.)

Relax, Gittl. What's the hurry? Just listen to the mayseh. What's wrong? You love a good mayseh, I thought. So, in any event, we didn't have any blood sausages this particular evening, and were altogether too pooped to shlop—is that the right word, Gittl, shlop?—all the way back to camp and I'll admit it, I will, some of the others were a bit inebriated, having bibulously imbibed libations both prior to and during work, silly boys. What, you don't think I know such words? Offensive, Gittl, truly. I'm hurt. Anyway, Phonye, remember Phonye? The pious one, with the strong jaw and the traveling eye? Phonye suggested that we break bread together before leaving the goats' den, both to sate our bodies and nourish our souls, as the day of the lord's resurrection from the grave, to which you all chased him, not that I'm much of a believer myself, Gittl, but it is truly a shame what you did to the poor fellow, anyway, that day was quickly approaching. We found a sack of flour in one of the goat's hovels, and fire was not an issue, embers were plentiful, as some of the other goat-hovels were still smoldering, in fact, when Phonye made his aforementioned suggestion. The issue, at the moment was that we lacked water, goatess! What to do, what to do. We knew it was bad luck to touch a river that had spent so much time in proximity to jew-maws, and jew-tongues, and appeared to be filled with jew-hair, and everyone had finished their personal water supplies, and no one had thought to bring extra. In truth, we hadn't intended to stay as long as we did, but sometimes, when working, a man can simply lose himself, and when such a thing is synchronized, this loss of self for many men all at once? That is a thing, Gittl, quite a thing to behold indeed. Anyhow, there was, of course, a well, but its water had, unfortunately for our new-found quest, been spoiled when we deposited within it the majority of the local goats' bearded leader's hairy form. But did we despair of our intention to bake and consume bread with our brothers at the end of a hard day's work? Certainly we did not. Another of the men, I believe it was Phonye, had stepped outside of the den in which some of us sat, then, resting our tired heads on goosefeather pillows, and cuddling under blankets and the like. He stepped out to relieve himself, for while we had run out of water, we did, as mentioned, still have other libations which we were consuming, none of which we wanted to pour into the flour, not knowing, first, if such a culinary method would be feasible, and not wanting, second, to waste any of our store, because there was more of the good war to fight, and didn't your old pal say that a good war hallows any cause, Gittl? Anyhow, there was a goatish war on the horizon, red pointy-bearded swarms in every direction, stinking goat-villages splayed out all over our beautiful countryside, giving succor, pulling strings, saboteurs all, but I diverge. I'm not a political fellow, Gerty, I'm just a simple Phonye, and you see, all I wanted was a nice fur coat for my wife, too. Anyway, our compatriot Phonye stepped outside, and when he returned, there was a look on his face that I can describe only as beatific. He was simply aglow, Gittl. He mentioned that two of the goats' whelps were on the ground near the entrance to the den, and that he had barely noticed them, so small were their forms, while he relieved himself, and had only fully registered their presence afterward, and that then, on a whim, he had bent down and reached a finger into the pool of blood that collected around one of the discarded whelps, and had brought his finger to his tongue. Sweet like pudding, he said. I remember his tone exactly, Gittl, even as I tell you this. Phonye said, I believe I've found the answer to our quandary. It took the rest of us a few moments to understand what he meant, but when we did, Gittl, goatess, when we did? We were delighted. And so it came to pass that we had the sweetest, most delectable loaves of bread in the days leading up to easter, and in the days that followed as well. I carved off a thin sliver of the loaf, and have it here with me, even now. Would you like to try it?

Here, Gittl.

Try some.

Gittl mustered all what she could muster and outspit onto the splitting ground.

The Phonye began to laugh its shrieking windish laugh, You act so brave, Gittl, little coward girl, who stayed hidden even as her mameshi and tateshi were draped over the branches of the forest, who didn't even try to pull them back?

Enough, Gittl tried to say, but still no voice could be found in her lungs.

And your brothers, how they squealed like small hogs? And Hendl? And Reyza, littlest, sleepingest?

Gittl shook her head.

Yes, Gittl. Smallest, confusedest.

Gittl, still standing, downslumped, and with her feet locked to the earth, two by two her own organs began outcrawling from her body, guided gently by a river of blood overfalling from her eyes.

You didn't even try to help them, the Phonye said.

With an effort summoned from somewhere, Gittl stepped back once, and then another step, tripping over the cobbled stones what were not cobbled stones but were instead made from the calcified innards of dustcobblers and she again found her balance and backstepped again, away from the Phonye's beatific skincovered smile, and then Gittl almost slipped on a liverstone but she turned
turn Gittl
turn now
we're here
we're here o wa
and she saw before her a child.

And by the child, a river.

By the river, some trees.

In the child's hand, a few berries. The liquid running over the child's handskin was darkred, but the child's hand? It was so firm, so filled with bones and blood, a living child, and then Gittl remembered what she had come for to do, and philadelphiye grew then back into itself, the buildings upstanding into sturdiness once more, and the sky was once again above Gittl spitting mouthfuls of rain, yoh, no one had told Gittl that it rains so in amerike in the middle of winter, and Gittl spit, and walked, until she found a homefromwork puddler sitting under an awning and yawning and muttering passages from either Das Kapital or from psalms, it was hard to hear for the rain, yoh, Gittl was only guessing from the jew's facebendings, and Gittl asked if the jew knew where were living the Halpers, and the jew said, Yutke always used to support the union, and then uttered unto Gittl a set of very muddlish directions
yoh so we perhaps helped a little to throughsift them
we'd like some credit for these philadelphiyesh housefindings
yoh that seems only fair
sha
and Gittl found herself before another door, what too had an awning, and was sheltered from the rain.
Gittl knocks on the door
tuk tuk tuk
a remnant she is looking for
tuk tuk tuk

Woman's voice, in american: Yes, hallo, good evening, whom may it be there standing, knocking my door, mm-hm?

Gittl spit lightly, regaining her balance. shulem aleykhem. Yutke?

aleykhem val bneykhem,[50] the woman's voice now came less through a poinched nose, and there was sweetwine and breadcrusts in her jewish. Who stands before my door?

Gittl.

Gittl whose?

My mameshi's and my tateshi's Gittl. I have a question, Yutke.

Who sent you here? How do you know me? What do you want?

A jew has to want something for another jew to open for her the door?

Yutke Halper
valorwife of sockish Morris
seventh cousin of Shulem Usherl Lanes
what lived in the dustvillage known as Zatelsk

The nice door then sniveled open slightish. Through its lightcracked opening peeked part of a jewface.

A good evening to you, Gittl said to the jewsliver. You're Yutke, not so?

---

50 "Upon you and upon your children."

I'm Yutke.

Yutke, I'm looking, Gittl started.

What? Speak up. I can't hear you, said Yutke, more opening now the door.

Yutke, I'm looking for Leyb.

The nice door now shutslammed. Howling from behind in american commenced. You are! Traitor, collaborator! Alligator! Instigator! You're from the socialist services! From the law! What do you want from Leyb?

Breathe, Mameshu, Gittl said. I'm not from any services. I'm from the dustvillage. From Zatelsk.

The door openswung again, and now Yutke's face was a mask of astonishment.

In truth? Yutke said.

Of course in truth. A jew would lie about such a thing?

Zatelsk Zatelsk?

Not birobidzhan.

As though she might embrace Gittl Yutke looked, or as though she might strike her.

Praised is god, you're the girl what the Baroness found, all of philadelphiye has heard this mayseh, but I didn't know if it was true.

Nothing said Gittl.

I didn't know if you were real, in truth, girl, this Baroness, a life on her head, is a bit of a turnhead, she is, but she gives to the community—

Is Leyb here?

Yutke downlooked at her own feet.

feet what were inside two niceish socks
they say the sockseller's wife should be sockless
but it is not so
feh

Not precisely.

What?

Leyb is not precisely here. Yutke glanced over her shoulder into the empty hallway in what hung happy pictures of four unhappy looking jews wearing goyishe clothing and stupid hats.

They came crawling about looking for him, Yutke said in a lowsome voice.

Who did?

It's a narrow world, Gittl daughter of your mameshi and your tateshi. They knocked upon many doors, and even here they knocked, and described a jew a scrawny a frowzish, and said that he had done what must not be done, and had become, not upon us, a laywithman'er, and hearing this, my husband, Morris, may all his teeth fall out but one and in that one may he have always a toothache, god forbid, said to the lawmen that he's been now suspiciousful for some time, and that surely he'd give them the boy his very self for any questions they might have after pourdowning patch'eles on his misused rear, but he said all of this in jewish, somewhat drunk was Morris from having many aftershul schnapps

not a coincidence that Morris was ot azey shikker
oh tum balalaike and so on
hello you two
yoh nice to see you et cetera
Shprintzl I always loved your singing
also I did o wa

and so I told them no, no sirs, no sires, no tsires, never have I heard from such a jew a treasure, and I put my Morris faintly to bed, told him no shabbesdiker shtup for him this evening, and then sat down on the street like a shikshe bum waiting for Leyb to homecome.

nu.

And this little jew this treasure homecame soon after.

And.

And I told him to find maybe a different place to sleep.

And?

And? And then he went.

To where?

To birobidzhan, to tel aviv. To where. How should I know to where he went? Do I look like a goingwoman to you, Gittl daughter of your mameshi and—

Alright, okay. I understand.

I did my part.

Okay.

I did! Don't you judge me, girl.

there is no judge
no judge and no law
Yutke daughter of your mameshi and your tateshi
o wa

A good night, Gittl said, and she turned to walk down the pathway lined with droopen soggish winter-plants of gray and burning yellow.

Girl.

Gittl did not aroundturn.

Gittl!

Gittl stopped walking, but still did not aroundturn.

I did hear from Frume what has a cousin Blume-Bashke—

The jew what reads the little poems? Gittl asked, now turning.

What? Oh. Yes. Maybe. Always doing odd things is this Blume-Bashke. I heard she has become a little communistish, not upon us, no evil eye, tfu. You know her?

No. I don't, it doesn't matter. What did Blume say?

Frume.

Frume.

Frume said that she heard from Blume-Bashke what heard from Mottl what heard from Khayim-Yankl[51] at the puddle in camden that Leyb had been seen ingo-

51 Yiddish for "So-and-So" or "What's-His-Name."

ing to one of the big tenements what is upfilled with blacks across the river, maybe Weinblatt's, no evil eye, not upon us, poor Yutke, I did my part.

Gittl nodded, and began walking.

yoh we had anyway found plucking Zanvl
and also singish Shprintzl
hello it's so nice
o wa
you had found us feh
creditgrabbing always were you springoffs from Khayele the mousemaker
careful now
sha Anshl she's not wrong as it is written credit to whom credit is dew (Mustelids 19:35)
yoh sha Anshl
springoffs from our mameshi o wa

Don't you go there alone, girl!

I never go anywhere alone, Gittl didn't say, for how many times could a jew say such a thing on a single day, she only outwalked back into the philadelphiyesh rain, not afraid of how the city might crumble into itself, or of the Phonye what might again sprout from it, for she knew, Gittl did, that there is no mastergod, that anything bad what might happen might happen, but also it might not.

Anshl, you badluckster, what's heard? Gittl said.

Hendl, Gittl said. Blessed be the soup of the universe, et cetera.

And Zimml, what do you say, sweet one, we should walk? You won't grow tired?

A good evening, littlest, sleepingest, laughingest, perfectest.

it's okay Gittl
omeyn Gittl
I won't grow tired Gittl
a good evening Gittl o wa

And Gittl walked once more into the puddles of this newish city toward one more door upon what she would knock.

for forty days the rain's been driving
tuk tuk tuk
now Gittl is tohomearriving
tuk tuk tuk help us sing you two

yoh let's go a gantzn tog geven farnimen tuk tuk tuk
itzt bin ikh aheymgekimen tuk tuk tuk here we are

Tohomearriving

tuk tuk tuk.

Opened the third from staircase fourthfloor door a man what was having a thin mustache and fingertips on the doorhandle what were covered with ink.

Can I help you, ma'am?

A good evening, Gittl said. I'm looking for Leyb Mireles, or Leyb Zatelsky, or Leyb Halper.

The man's face changed, and his nostrils flared ever so. This was the perhaps thirty-sixthish door on what Gittl had knocked this evening, after walking in the direction what Yutke

Yutke

she's saying it was Yutke

Yutke she says

who is Yutke I forgot

had handwaved, and starting to aroundask if anyone had seen a youngerjew, twenty years or so, frowzy, ingoing and outcoming from a building, and first she was laughed upon, and one woman said, Plenty enough

jewboys going and coming around here, but then two yingelakh what were sitting on an edge heard her and one outcalled, Goldfarb, and Gittl said to them, Thank you, sorry, not called Goldfarb, and they said, No, Goldfarb's building, and explained that they had seen a young and malodorous jewboy, no offense meant, stumbling last weekend and had tried to only help him but he had grown skittish and had instead found an elderwoman what walked him to the corner of Lombard and Seventeenth, right there, and Gittl said to the yingelakh a beautiful thanks and walked then toward the building from what parts seemed ready to fall
into water
to become as an ark
to awaytake a friend
no not yet o wa
and in there she knocked on each door, and some did not open, and some flung toward her sharpwords, and some were helpfulish but could not help, and so many apartmental faces had been held by Gittl's eyes that evening, but this was a different face after Gittl said Leyb's name, yoh, this face before her now contained: recognition, reticence, radishes, fear, fog, protectiveness, preventiveness, confusion, candles, somehow calm.

You said you're looking for Leyb? the man said.

yoh, Gittl said, her voice tangled within her throat.

The man was silent.

I'm not any law, Gittl said.

The man laughed a smallish laugh. Somehow I gleaned as much.

Leyb is here or he is not? Gittl said, not wanting to be laughed upon. She wondered if she'd wrongread the recognition, the radishes, the protectiveness. If there'd only been confusion and candles there, or if he was from the beginning only laughing upon her too.

fun vanen precisely kenstu Leyb? the man said. It took a moment for Gittl to grab onto what he said, this sort of quickfish talkflip between jewish and american being still unfamiliar to her, and his accent being amerikanish and also litvish at once, and yoh, also she had not sensed jew in his underhum, but she replayed his words on her mind's phonograph, what she had been charitably given brandnew at the entrance to amerike's left adenoid, and as she replayed it, she understood, and then Gittl? She felt a type of reliefterror overwash the top part of her skull and her breathing, then, was become fully like an old jew with legs what had failed her as she awaywalked through the forest, and what finally got to downsit on the colddawn earth amidst the needles and tongues.

Gittl said, Precisely I know Leyb
from the banks of the river
from the smell of the pines
from the dew on the sorrel
from home o wa
from home.

The man then aroundlooked the hallway, as if looking for someone else what might come, and Gittl therelooked too, and saw that some people were gathered there to look upon her, heads outpoking from doors, chatsome titters and undertalk coursing through the overfalling dimlit hall.

The man turned back into his apartment, and shut the door most of the way before Gittl, and Gittl heard his footsteps padding around the insidebelly of the place, and she heard him say, Lying, and Gittl wondered then again if he had been laughing upon her the whole time and felt her face flush with bashfulish anger, but between the courses of blood wandering into her eyesockets, and between the wonderings in the rest of her head, Gittl heard a rustlish shuffling off to the left, and then another voice, and more words in low american what she could not fully outmake, something from a sister or a cousin, then a longish silence, then footsteps.

Opened the door another man, wispthin with an outjutting jaw and frowzy dark hair and no hair on his face and a fadesome bruise under one eye and dust in both of his eyes.

and fireants crawling
over his shoulders
and hedgehogs crowded
around his ankles

o wa.

shulem aleykhem, Gittl said, her breath returning

into her chest, limping from the forest, blinking in the light, beholding this face what had changed but what had also not changed in the seven and seven years what had passed since she beheld it.

aleykhem shulem?

Leyb?

. . . yoh.

Leyb, ikh bin Gittl.

vus?

Gittl Khayeles, fin Zatelsk.

. . . Gittl?

yoh.

. . . Gittl?

yoh.

And yoh then water rushed out of Gittl's mouth in a river and around them was smoke from the flames of the small trees what were burning still in perpetuity, there on the land what was called once Zatelsk, and here around the remnant of the dustvillage inside philadelphiye, and the trees were everywhere, again, but the bodies draped upon them now dusted off the dust of death and replaced their organs into their skin and took leave into the therewater of the sky's nowhere and somewhere the stomach of the forest had become distended from having consumed too many jews already so early in the world's morning and there was no room there for these two jews, yoh, there was only remaining a clearing what was cleared of almost everything, but yoh, in this clearing, there were only berries, and only Gittl Khayeles, and only Leyb Mireles, and only silence.

Coffee?

Gittl awaylooked from Leyb, back to the man what was now standing behind him, and tried to offblink some of the layers of dust from her eyes.

Why don't you come in, the man said, and Gittl saw his eyes glance again downhallish, and her mind now flickered to the bruise on Leyb's undereye, and she wondered if this man had placed it there, and wondered if she should say to Leyb that they should leave.

This is Charles, Leyb said in jewish, backstepping toward Charles and sideleaning his head. My friend.

Stepping under the bloodless lintel, Gittl said in jewish, Tell him I say he has a nice apartment, or some such honeysome utterance.[52]

Charles halflaughed,[53] and closed the door behind Gittl, and Gittl overglanced again at this Charles, having forgotten already about his shatnez[54] blend of a litvish amerikanish sentence from the beforemoment.

---

52 Orig.: oder azelkhe honikdike verter.

(Idiomatically, as may not require extrapolation: "a sticky-sweet untruth.")

53 A bit with leeches, a bit without, as it were.

54 Biblically prohibited admixture of linen and wool.

Charles, this is Gittl, Leyb said in american. From, from Zatelsk.

Well, a pleasure to meet you then, Gittl from Zatelsk, Charles said, extending his hand. Lion here hasn't told me a thing about his hometown, and actually, I wondered if you might be a relation of his when you first knocked, something about your eyes.

He said Lion, Gittl thought, taking Charles's hand, not lying, Leyb is Lion oversat into american. A new sort of bashfish swam through her, and she followed its jagged fins and glimmersome scales down into her belly before she thought to wonder for what was she so much thinking anyway of this, and not of Leyb Mireles, other remnant of the dustvillage what was not taken to the forest and what stood before her, here and now, and she tried to move her mind to Leyb, and tried to move her eyes to Leyb, but her mind would not move and so also would not her eyes.

Come in, Charles said, gesturing to the apartmental area behind him, what was, in truth, not so nice, but was having a shelf overspilling with books and Gittl's eyes were theredrawn. Over the sound of Charles behindlocking the door and footstepping back toward the right side of the apartment, Gittl's eyes fell on the bookpiles, what were crowding the shelf and crawling toward the rumplish smallbed in the left edgecorner of the room, and she saw amidst the tangles of pages and spines some jewish letters and wanted to closer walk to behold the contents, but remembered, yoh, that she had still not backlooked to Leyb's face, and with all the effort in her body Gittl backlooked then toward Leyb, to his face and to his eyes, and it was as though all this time his eyes had been looking at her face.

Charles returned to the people of Zatelsk, holding a towel, what he handed to Gittl,[55] and then brushed his hand over Leyb's shoulder and said, I'll make some eggs, and left the people of Zatelsk alone together.

nu, Gittl said, trying to smile, holding the towel between her hands.

nu, Leyb said.

You're tall, Gittl said.

You're the same.

Your mameshi here is Yutke?

Not so much.

Troubles?

I suppose.

She said you're now a laywithman'er?

I suppose.

And your black friend is too?

Watch it, lady, Charles's voice in american flitted from the center backside of the room, from what sounds of clinksome metal and coughing water and whiskerish flames dueled and danced, and then a win-

---

55 The Eternal Return of the Same Towel, as it were.

dow opened, and a wisp of cold air flew into the room, and there was the sound of something outflying from the room, and the window closed again.

What's his issue? Gittl said.

He's knowing a halfbasket of jewish, Leyb quieted. Maybe he is thinking that black in jewish is like an evil word here in amerike. He is feeling always on the verge of being eaten here, so.

In truth he's always so on the verge?

The way they reached into his chest in Cricket's, I am thinking yoh.

Gittl sideleaned her head.

I'll latertell it.

Gittl nodded, looked away, looked back, realized this was approaching already the most words what she had ever heard from Leyb, what had been almost entirely silent until right before he walked alone across the ocean.

Around them, Gittl could hear the buildingsounds, oh muttersome oh groanish, through the door, the streetsounds, oh swellsome oh jumble, through the walls, and inside the apartment, only an eggsizzling sound and its accompanyish smell, o wa, Gittl was in truth dizzybecome with hunger, and also with what was around her envelopish now that she had found the other jew what was not awaytaken to the forest, yoh, how to say it, yoh, it cannot be said.

Leyb'ele, you hear?

Now Leyb looked away.

Gittl did not continue to speak.

The two did not behold each other or hold each other and each allowed the other to be ensconced in silence.

do you remember the dew
the way the light sang at sunset around peysekh
the mint and the wild horseradish by the stupid hairy river
o wa
walking across water
yoh awaysent alone

In the midst of this silence, Charles spoke.[56]

Sorry to interrupt, Charles said. Let's essn a bissl? You two can continue your family reunion at the table while I try to figure out what the hell I'm going to do when the rest of Zatelsk shows up at my door.

yoh but not such a difficulty to unravel
just open the door for the rest of Zatelsk
yoh anyway there is no rest of Zatelsk
yet

Leyb overleaned and whispered a thing into his ear.

What did you tell him, Gittl asked, looking to the space behind Leyb's head.

---

56 Before speaking, he looked at the two Jews, who still stood near his entryway, not looking at one another, not speaking to one another, but seeming, somehow, as if they were entangled, grappling, even.

I told him you're going to fall in love with him for his eggs, Leyb said. Gittl overlooked at Charles, at his eyes what looked anxious underneath the teasing, at the inkstained table what was set with three chipped plates, what encircled a centerpiece of an emptied ashtray, and upon each of what wobbled a single egg. Beside each plate sat steaming a mug. Next to the table Gittl saw floorpiled a stack of papers, upon what rested an inkbottle and pen.

Gittl looked to Charles, jewstones falling from her mouth unpolished by amerike, perhaps as for depth-testing a pond or perhaps only because she was tired, veys ir a bissl fin kikhn?[57]

a bissl un a bissl, Charles said. You'll see. These eggs, he kissed his fingertips and then a bit of extra blood upflished into his face. Come, sit.

Charles gestured for Leyb and Gittl to sit in the two chairs by the table, and he sat then himself on an overturned wastebin, and Gittl understood that it had been its contents what had been defenestrated in the beforemoment.

Well, l'khayim teyvim ulesholem, Charles said, and upraised his glass, and somewhere far away across the inkish eggocean of a table Leyb upmoved his glass too and Gittl caught in her vision's edge something resem-

57 "You know a bit about cooking?"

blant to a smile being dragged onto his face, and outside amerike and the Phonye together shrieked and whistled and belched in an alleyway called Blight, and Gittl once more found that she could not look directly upon Leyb's face, and so wondered instead again who is this Charles what had just glassraised and hoped in philadelphiyesh litvish that all the people of Zatelsk might upraise their coffee or hot water to good lives and to peace.[58]

---

58 Who is this Charles, indeed?

This Charles was the first and only child born to Rose and Edgar Patterson, the latter being avek, as it were, long before Charles could remember, the former being an erstwhile janitress in the employ of the Free Library of Philadelphia on Chestnut, wherein Bill Shakespeare's Othellic saliva oozed down young Charles's face, alongside the retch from Conrad's shadowy aorta, and Twain's twanging globs of musical mucus, et cetera. Still, on he read, for what else was there to do, mother's hands submerged in the toilets, shadows dancing on the walls at the cusps of evening, no siblings to speak of or to. And this Charles did find friends, then, as mother's fingers cracked and bled, and nighttime bled into the light from the cracks under the doors: Walt and his grasses, W. E. B. D. B. and his gold and silver fleeces, C. McKay's sonnets tucked beneath the bonnet of E. Edwards, the aforementioned Red Emma's punctilious pillory of private property, and onward. This Charles spent a glut of afternoons, and, eventually, a few hideously unhappy nights, with these comrades and oppugners in this shelved village of dust, until he was whisked from it to a certain couch, one that was at once distant from and nearby to Charles's home.

Who is this Charles indeed?

A scene, a miniature mayseh: A young man sits still on a Jew's couch. The couch is poorly made, sinking deep into its own recesses, covered with old and bark-like fabric. The young man can feel the texture of the textile on the backs of his thighs, for he is naked. On the other side of the room, another man, the Jew, not young, not naked, the skin of his face hanging downward from his cheeks, his perpetually cold fingers wrapped around a brush, his chapped lips pursing and unpursing. There is no sound in the room save for the crackle of burning tobacco and paper and the squelch of the moving brush. The young man sits there, not for the first time, not for the last. Wouldn't he like to stand up and leave, to light a match and leave it on the couch and see what is left after that? The young man smokes cigarette after cigarette as he sits, so not quite still, not quite still life, not quite a bowl of fruit: a concession. He does not like the way his belly appears in the paintings. He does not like the Jew, though he believes he loves him, in a way. He does like—or, at least, if not likes, loathes less—the Wissotzky which follows the sessions, which can last anywhere from five to ninety minutes, depending. After, gelt passes from paint-stained hand to unstained hand, it does, it always does. Tateh.

"vu iz dayn mameh?" asks the Jew, yet again, this evening, though he knows the answer.

"Would still prefer that I ceased to exist."

Even as the young man says this, jaw so set, he feels a dull ache in his gut, knows that he has not spoken the truth, or the full truth, but anger and hurt can guide one's tongue down all sorts of paths and alleyways.

"a shanda, a shod, kum aher, mayn treyeriker yungerman."

Charles understands him, but does not move, is not ready. He's done this, spoken to Charles in Yiddish, since the beginning, when he found Charles in the new branch of the Free

Library, on Locust and Thirteenth, which Charles frequented, smile plastered to his face to at least partially preempt the ladies' needling nervousness; even though he knew he was known unto them as a docile one, which knowledge did spur him, at moments, to daintily dream of docilely setting the entire renovated building aflame, and perhaps he would have done so were it not for all his companions packed inside its belly; he also knew that he was taller than he used to be, and alone, here, his mother having since gone, retreated into the Seventh Ward, having been warded off, let go, thirty-seven-year-old hands curled arthritically into claws, unable any longer to properly wield a mop. And does one think that she was awarded a pension? When darkness approached and light began to dim on the night in which the Jew found him, as well as on the night prior to that, Charles made himself as thin as he could, sucking in his belly, made himself disappear, almost, breathing in the shadows, and when the door locked, finally, his heart slowed and he called on his flattened, bound, papery friends to keep him company through the night.

"It's an abonimation" was what she'd said, his ungainfully employed mother, upon returning home from witnessing the glory of the Lord's only son, et cetera, and witnessing, in her own home, her only son in the midst of certain proclivities-turned-activities: an abonimation. Charles had thought to grab hold of this mispronunciation, to correct her, to wound her in return, but could not bring himself to embarrass his mother, beloved—unto her son, at least—former employee of the Philadelphia Free Library who could not, herself, read. Even now, Tovarisch C. Patterson feels a sense of compunction in retelling this part of the story, and wonders if he should correct the spelling, or skip this part altogether, he wonders and wonders, and yet on he writes, pulled by the urge to tell an emesdike mayseh, a truthsome story, as it were, to Reyza, to all, and by other unnameable forces. She did not yell when she said this, then. She did not raise her voice. It was more of a murmur, a mutter, a prayer.

Charles did not correct her, and did not speak. He only lost hold of the angular form of his shirtless, sweet-breathing, soft-thighed friend, with whom he'd entangled his own body three consecutive Wednesday evenings, including this one. Beautiful, gentle Jack, whose name wasn't Jack, but who, last C. Patterson heard, remained firmly nestled in Jesus's handsome, curly-haired bosom, like his father before him; and so he ought to be spared the potentiality of this story making its way back across the ocean, which is, after all, the hope; he ought certainly to be counted among the righteous of Sodom, i.e., america, not that a namechange alone is sufficient to protect one from truly hungry eyes, but it still feels akin to an act of small mercy, or at least a salted gesture toward such. Often, still, amidst the bitter chill of gray Muscovite mornings does Tovarisch Translator remember, and surely will never forget, the feeling of that first Wednesday, the first time their lips met, the first time Charles felt at peace in the world of bodies and voices and substance and sweat and sound, outside the world of paper and ink. It had been Jack, the preacher's son, who had moved toward him, then, that evening, in Charles's mother's home, which was in truth just a single room, neither unlike nor far from the Lombard flat that stands at the center of our current mayseh, and which she and her son shared with anywhere between one and four other widowed and/or childless churchwomen, depending on the period, including, for a few years, the aforementioned Ms. Bettie Freeman, of Lion-taming fame, with whom Charles could not remember ever having a conversation that did not, at some juncture, feature Jesus as a something in a something or other, but who Charles did, at a few junctures, wish was his mother, instead of his actual mother, as Ms. Bettie Freeman was warm and quick to laugh, while a full and uninhibited smile from his own mother was a thing to be noted and recorded. And let the record note: Ms. Rose Patterson did have—does have—a beautiful smile. In any event, all of the women, regardless of who was then living there, would leave home together on Wednesday evenings to attend study group at Wesley AME Zion just three blocks west, on the corner of Fifteenth, which was led by Jack's own father, and which Jack himself was usually expected to attend, and which he faithfully did, until one Wednesday evening, when he told his father he was sick and walked two blocks over to Charles's house.

"I'd like to kiss you" is what he said, Jack, and his eyes had filled with tears when he said this, and his voice was barely louder than a whisper, and Charles, loquacious, blathering Charles, hadn't said a single word, but rather had simply nodded, dumbly, mutely, his lips tingling, already, with terror—reliefterror?—and with longing and with the pain of being proximate to the phantasmagorical electricity of a waking dream. Jack had kissed him, then, and as stated, Charles had felt a sense of peace, there is no other word for it, at least not in american, and this sense of peace was swiftly followed by a sense of dread, for this was the sort of peace that Charles knew a person could not hold on to, that could not last, that would certainly catch fire and scorch all that was near it. They touched each other, Jack and Charles did, that evening, stroking with tentative, revelatory hands the contours of one another's bodies, sharp shoulder, soft thigh, newly stubbled jaw, long thin fingers, kissing one another, barely breathing, not breaking the kiss for minutes on end, it seemed, minutes which felt like centuries, and even as their tongues grew tired, their hands remained urgent (and urgent and urgent) and they pressed and rubbed their unfettered hardnesses against one another through the encasements of their garments, until the point of spilling over, and then, burning with gratitude and dizzy with vertigo and dry-mouthed with the aforementioned dread, Charles pulled away from Jack, and if, before, during, he had been elevated in a space that had no name, no future, past, or even present, just after that moment it was as if he had fallen down into some great canyon, and was there, alone, surrounded by the wind and by the past and by the future, and could not bring himself to raise his voice and see if he might find Jack standing there on the lip of the canyon, and nor, in the reality of the still- (thank Jesus and his faithful flock) empty apartment, could he bring himself to look for Jack's eyes, in those moments after, lest he find contained there a contempt, or worse, a blankness, and so he watched Jack's long, elegant fingers dancing with one another as Jack buttoned his shirt, looking to see if he perceived any sort of tremulousness therein, and he did not see any tremor, and Jack then tucked his shirt into his trousers and walked toward the unlocked door, turning as he went, speaking Charles's name.

"Charles—"

"Will you come back next week?" Charles said, willing his voice to rise from somewhere within him. There is an idea that a person has a fixed number of sentences to utter before death, and that two or three of them are reflective of this person's core, and must thus be said again, and again, and again, in different forms or in the same one. It seems, in painful reflection, that this must be one of Charles's two or three.

Jack was silent for a long moment, and then he said: "I'll try," and he did, he came back the Wednesday that followed, and the Wednesday after that, and it was on this third Wednesday that Charles's mother had returned early from Wesley's, for she herself had been feeling genuinely under the weather, unlike Jack's miraculously thrice-believed—or perhaps not so miraculously, given that the god-man's son had heretofore given no man any god-given reason to suspect him of being anything other than straightforward and forthcoming—Wednesday-evening illnesses. Charles's mother had come upon them, there, like that, on the uncovered floor of her shared room, both still with their trousers on, but neither wearing shirts, and Jack stood quickly, scrambling from Charles as though Charles's body had grown suddenly scalding or slimy, not looking at Charles or at Ms. Patterson as he pulled his shirt over his shoulders and buttoned it hastily, his hands apparently shaking this time, as he walked, and then ran, from the room, not tucking the hem into his pants, and Charles's mother had said the word again, "abomination," her own eyes wet, her own voice barely louder than a whisper, "But the Lord can understand mistakes, Charles," and Charles had tried to twist his tongue into a lie, to tell his mother that this had indeed been a mistake, but something had restrained his tongue, then, and before his mother could say anything else, before she could mispronounce her curse a third time, or tell him to leave, or to perish as her parish might have it, Charles had gone, to the place in the city in which he had more friends than any other, and it was there, gone, leaning and loafing amidst the dust and the pages and loneliness, that Charles met the painter, the Jew, and it was there, gone, that Charles would remain, far from his friend, Jack, and from his mother, who never did report a thing of what she saw to anyone, or at least to anyone in the church, such that Jack could continue his preordained path toward ordination, and such that Charles could have reversed course at any juncture, too, he knew, but he chose not to, could not so do, and chose instead to remain far away, in those first days and also later, though he never actually left the Seventh Ward for more than a few weeks at a time, and so still saw everyone from his mother's parish in the hallways and the streets, throughout the days and months and years that followed, but he was become like a ghost back at his mother's home, after the thawing of all that had transpired in those first days, for Rose Patterson's anger continued to rise and ebb in silent and unpredictable tides, such that there would be times, certain days or weeks, in which Charles would return home to find that the door was locked, and he would knock, and his mother would not open the door, though the others would if they were home and she was out, and would remark about how they weren't sure what had gotten into Ms. Rose, locking the door like this, and certainly they must have sensed something, but had the grace never to speak it. There were also many other weeks in which his mother would come to his newfound apartment five blocks west—a wretched, beautiful thanks to Goldfarb, to the painter, to all—which he paid for with his own artfully earned pocket-scorching gelt; she would come bearing soup and half-smiling, as she always had; and there were even a few times in which it seemed that she might ask him about his days, these days, these new, heavy, heady days of smoke and jade and tea bags, but she never did, and so, we may fly over the company at Cricket's, back when Cricket's was still a blind tiger as well as a bird nest, and the longings and lust that found their homes closer to home in the Seventh Ward, for contrary to the beliefs of a certain Blood Brother–cum-Tovarisch, the sodomitical sodality, so to speak, was neither a pale invention nor a capitalist intervention; and we might meander onward toward the first meeting with the Jewboy of Zatelsk therein, too, when it was only the avian aspects of Cricket's that drew the wrath of the law, no longer the drinks, a beautiful thanks to the progressive material march of the trash heap, et cetera, and the peripatetic Jewess scribe of Zatelsk who followed in young Lion's tracks, and her poems and pages and the oversitting, and all that followed, which is contained in the pages that follow, which is now cordoned off in the kingdom of the eternal, unalterable before, but which was all still yet to come on this evening in which Charles was perched on the couch of the Jewboy of Paint, the oily starting point of this particular mayseh.

"un vu is dayn tateh?"

"avek," the young man answers.

He's a quick learner, this one.

The Jew once said to him, this time in English, "You're clever, for a, well, it's not a polite word."

"For a what?" young Charles asked, trying to reinflate his deflating chest (e tu, Jewboy?). "For a Negro?"

The Jew laughed through his nose, "No, no. For a goy, mayn kind."

For a goy, mayn kind, indeed, though young Charles didn't see the Jew painting lumpen portrait after portrait of fair(y)-hued goy-boys; besides Charles, there were at least two others he knew of, two other young Negroes, though he had never met them in the flesh, and did not recognize them from their fleshy facsimiles he saw grimacing from the walls while walking, at nearly unbearable but somehow irresistible intervals, through the backrooms of canvas and oil. Otherwise it was just faux-nostalgic landscapes of wheat fields and pine trees, and hunchbacked rebbes shlepping gefilte jars down wooden streets, and pathos-pumping pictures of factories filled with sweating, muscular, shirtless workers. The Jew once said, when Charles asked, that it was his "Billikopfish spirit, third cousin, yeh?" that allowed him to better capture the soul of the seated Negro with his brush, "for who after all did establish the

National Association for the Advancement of your people,"
et cetera.

Charles thought once or twice about murdering the Jew, for he knew where he kept his gelt.

But he had, alas, read Othello by then, et cetera, such that such ideations were sapped of all romance in the barren end-of-times city of his mind, and instead he simply sat and spoke in ever-cleverer Yiddish to the Jew and kept smoking while hands crept past the barrier of the canvas, put the cigarette out only when tongue, like the tongue of some aardwolf cackling at the moon and lapping termites up from the earth, pushed tentatively toward the base of his neck, always tentative: Whose hands? Whose tongue?

"Your father went away," the Jew says, in English. "They always do, don't they?"

"I thought avek is the way to say he died."

"Oh, yes, it is, mayn kind. Fallen to dropsy, was it?"

"Dropping oneself off a building is a pale method of transportation. We don't do that."

The Jew laughs through his nose again. "Not suicide, my child. It's a medical term."

He puts his hand on the young man's leg, but this time, the young man moves his leg away. "I know. I was kidding."

"Of course, mayn kind."

"Consumption."

"Ah. A bad way to go away. Sorry for your loss."

"I was two."

"It's alright, mayn kind. A tateh can take many forms here, away."

The Jew nods and shakes his head, the flesh of his cheeks shakes, the tea on the table shakes, the room is filled with the smells of smoke and oil; Charles did, at first, occasionally flare his nostrils in surreptitious search for the fetor judaicus, but only encountered fetor lonelaicus, the Jew's and his own, which, perhaps, he owned, was worse. Afterward, the two shake hands. The young man walks out into the cold night, hands shaking, pockets lined, eyelids heavy, the flesh of his inner cheeks nestled between his molars, cigarette burning between his bare fingers, belly quivering slightly, everything quivering slightly. Will he come back? After his mother tells him that she's prayed on it and knows that he'll get right from this sickness, so maybe he could stop leaving home at these hours? After he finds Goldfarb's, and establishes other methods of garnering enough gelt to keep Goldfarb at bay? To where will he return from away, prodigal son, basket of fruit, loneliest Charles?

Who is this Charles, this tateh, this Tovarisch, this translator, indeed.

yoh and so after that
here it is always after and after
amerike amerike gey kakn afn yam
et cetera

The Revolutionary Worker's Role in the Address and Redress of the Negro Problem in America[59]

And so yoh after the three had togetherclinked their drinks to hope for good lives and for peace, et cetera, and had eacheaten their eggs, what were it must be said not terrible,[60] amidst an unexpectishly ungnawful silence,

---

59 In translating many of the chapter titles, I sought to retain something of the original "a mayseh fin this or that," even when they veered off slightly ("a mayseh fin avekfliyen," rendered simply as Awayflight, e.g.). This one, admittedly, flies a bit of a wider arc from the original "a mayseh fin Marx'ele," though I'd venture that the spirit remains largely consistent between the two; in general, this chapter had to slightly bend the heretofore established rules of capitalization, to better capture the Essence of what was said, et cetera.

60 Finer words of egg-praise have never been uttered, Comradess.

yoh and of course there was what to say
but yoh also there was time
and also there was being in the same room
o wa

yoh aderabe it is better to not yet talk
for always won't the words be not enough

Gittl stood to help wash the dishes but Charles said for her to leave it, that she and Lion should sit and talk, and Gittl longed, for a moment, to be allowed, instead, to move the dishes around under the stammer of water, but turned, finally, and looked at Leyb's face across the table, and saw that it was Leyb's face, what she had seen after she had heard him gurgling under a pile of people and pulled him out, and wiped the stink from his eyes with her thumbs, and helped him walk alone into the ocean, and she looked away from his eyes, and Gittl said, zug mir, zis'ele.[61]

And then Leyb spoke, in the language of the dust-village what poured from his mouth like a river of lambsblood and sorrel. He started from the beginning
yoh for a long hour had been in amerike
Leyb of Zatelsk
yoh so this is how a mayseh came to sit for him
forgive him o wa
when the waters and the skywaters were the same inside

61 "Tell me, sweet one."

him, when he was still Leyb Mireles, with no dreamer's dream, even, of Halper or philadelphiye or Cricket's or of this particular apartmental midian, when the contentedly anxious dead, what were placed in the ground one by only one, and the falldownish tailors and the hipthrustish prayers and the matriarchish chessplayers still danced together each yontiff to the strum of his older brother's balalaike, when his colleagues the hedgehogs and fireants helped him unspool his betumbled mind by the slerm of the hairish river under clouds of everburning smoke, the scent of burstberries on fingers and the sight of fishoil stains on pages, when Zatelsk and all its glowing soggish shrubbery was aflame, adullflame, but aflame, yoh, with lifesome tayve. He did not linger in the forest. He did not linger on the water. He told Gittl of angrysad Yutke, and her talking sock of a husband, of their Peterful and Joanish springoffs, of school what he had finished, of a yenki jew what had told him of the goyish watering hole for birds what was called Cricket's, of his first and second time there.

During this unspooling, Charles had been putterish and glideful throughout his apartment, opening the lone window to hear the rain, fingerflicking his fireish zipper, making more hot water, sitting on the springish couch with a Joycesome tome in his lap, longfingers of tobaccosome ashplant creeping always toward his mouth, but never burning, and Gittl noticed that he stuck his tongue out from the cigaretteless side of his mouth in order to lick his fingertips like an ancient grizened khukhem[62] before each page turn. At first Gittl did not know if Charles was listening or understanding what Leyb was saying, but he was then lightlaughing in moments of Leyb's recounting,[63] and coming over to sit next to Leyb at the table. He put out his cigarette there, and brushed his inkstained hand over the nape of Leyb's neck when he spoke of Cricket's, glancing at Gittl to see perhaps how she would glance at his hand, but Gittl was of course not handglancing in any manner soever. When Leyb finished this part of his mayseh, the three of them sat in silence again around the table, inbreathing and outbreathing the same oxygen. Gittl waited to see if Leyb would say more but he did not say more.

yoh it's alright
always there is before
and sometimes also there is later
o wa

Then Charles looked at a clock what was balanced upon a bookpile and spoke. Much as I hate to cut this short, I've actually got to head out to a work engagement, or a workers' engagement, if you will.

Charles iz a shrayber, Leyb said in jewish.

---

62 "Sagefish."

63 ir redndiker skarpet fin a man, or, "her talking sock of a husband," still tickles me, so many read-throughs later.

I know, Gittl said in american, looking at the inkstains on Charles's eggtable. You're a writer and also a party member?

No, not as such, Charles said. More of a ghostly fellow traveler.

Gittl sideleaned her head.

I'm a shraybsheyd, or a sheydshrayber, or a shraybshifter . . .

Gittl headleaned to the other side, her mouth pulling toward a halfsmile.

I ghostwrite for a number of self-styled men of letters. Tonight, one of them, a fellow named Weissberger, will be speaking at a Special Meeting on the theme of The Revolutionary Worker's Role in the Address and Redress of the Negro Problem in America, or some such.

interesant, Gittl said in jewish, feeling neither particularishly nor materialishly interested.

Well, you're welcome to come along, Charles said. Plenty of your folks will be there, and it's not a far walk.

I don't have anymore folks, Gittl did not say.

Gittl not alone

yoh you have plentymore folks

sibling ours

o wa

Alright, Gittl said.

Alright then, Charles said. Anything else to drink before we go? a gloz kave? Another famous egg? It's stopped raining, finally.

Gittl shook her head. Thanks.

Smoke? Charles tapped the metal box resting in front of him on the table.

Gittl nodded. A beautiful thanks. Charles lit his own cigarette, then Gittl leaned forward to kiss her cigarette against the zippish neverending flame upshot from Charles's second metal box, and then both looked at once at Leyb, who sat statuestill in his chair.

kimsti nukh, Leyb'ele?[64] Gittl said.

Leyb did not speak, only his silence did.

is he coming to a communistishe meeting everyone together gathered
when they came they told everyone to gather in the shil

Charles placed a hand on Leyb's shoulder. You can stay here, Lion.

Gittl watched this, and then downlooked at her own hands, what were both resting on the table, cigarette dangling heavywet in her mouth.

yoh it's what a jew can stand on his own
everywhere there is forest so fear neither valley nor the mountaintop (Narbiyahu 17:4)
but maybe he's not wanting to come
yoh but maybe alonebeing is not better

Leyb looked at Charles and at Gittl, and both of

---

64 "Are you coming too, little Lion?"

them, yoh, everyone saw the currents outcrawling from his eyes, and his mouth pulled into some sort of shape.

Then Leyb said in american, Sure I'll come. You two might become lost without me.

Gittl and Charles laughsofted both.

Charles stood and walked toward the coatrack by the door, uptaking his overcoat, and overdraping it upon his shoulders. It's an odd request, he said, but when we get to the corner of Asylum or Spruce or thereabouts, would the two of you, well, hold hands, or link arms? Paint a picture that's easier for old amerike to digest, as it were.

Outside old amerike sang ten cents a dance that's what they pay me gosh how they weigh me down and blinked all of its eyes as serenely as it could muster, but darn it, feelings were hurt, they were, by what Charles was overheard saying through the thinwood door, amerike was feeling both misunderstood and misunderestimated.

Gittl did not look at Leyb, but could feel his eyes on her face.

I know it's odd, Charles said, it's just that america's got a lot of eyes.

Gittl looked at Charles.

yoh maskim he's not wrongbeing
der malekhamuves hot a sakh eygn (Chrysanthemums 5:17–4:9)

but we are speaking now from deathless amerike grunchly happy look at its teeth
o wa

It's okay, Gittl said.

Leyb didn't say anything.

Okay then, Charles said, moving his hand toward his head as if to feel something there, and then downmoving his hand to place it on his door's handle. Shall we, comrades?

The hallway was full with people, full with helloing and so forthage, and toward the bottom of the staircase, a youngerman what was smoking alone said something to Charles,[65] and Charles said, Give my regards to your brother, Cal, and the man smiled and Gittl saw that he was missing two of his frontmost teeth, and then he saw that Gittl was looking at his mouth and updrank his own smile. Outside the maindoor two women said, Where you off to, Charles, dressed like that at this hour, and Why don't you introduce us to your friends? and Charles's fingers upcrept to where Gittl noticed was missing a button from his coat near his throat, and

---

65 "Pumpernickel evening, ain't it, Charles." Sweet, anxious Calvin McPhearson, younger brother of Charles's sometime friend and occasional lover, Paul, who'd moved to New York a few years prior. Hard to say what in the world little Calvin was talking about, but easy to say how fondly Charles felt toward him.

he said, We're late for a Party function, and you two are more than welcome to join, too, and one of them said, Wrong kind of party for my blood, baby, and the other said, Let me know next time, Charles, maybe I will come,[66] and outside, the evening was full of sound, and the street was full with potholes brimming with murkish waters and glimmering glowing bugs and discardful waste,[67] and the buildings were retching parts of themselves down into the streets.

When they arrived to a widerstreet, they turned left and upwalked a bit, and streetlights began to downshine like little nightsuns, and Charles aroundlooked toward the people of Zatelsk, and said, Now might be the time, if you don't mind.

---

66 These two women were Mary St. James and, you may believe it or don't, as it were, young Kit Williams, who did, in fact, accompany Charles to a meeting later that spring, and the rest of Comrade Williams's story, regarding the government-fabricated Henry Ford kidnapping plot, and the trials, which are still ongoing as of the time of this writing, is well-known, and in fact features not unfrequently even here in Moscow of 1936 on the pages of Pravda, and Tovarisch C. Roses has received at least three impressed nods and two you-don't-say chin-tilts after informing interlocutors that da nu, konechno, of course he knew the revolutionary Tovarisch K. L. Williams.

67 One doesn't imagine Zatelsk was a veritable barrel of rubies, yet the gentle reader isn't bombarded there with an oglesome litany of potholes and rubbish; this fixation doesn't suit you, Gitt.

None of the nightsome passersby seemed to be much looking upon them, but Gittl turned to Leyb and saw that Leyb was looking upon her face, and so she opened her hand to Leyb and he reached his hand toward her, and folded it into hers, and in the distance Gittl could hear a river of water or wind what sounded like water, and so, yoh, in silence they walked for some more moments until they arrived at the reddoor of the revolution.

Inside the revolution, what was taking place many floors up from a shuttered theater, and what was full with mostly men shaped like shadows and lumpen toadstools and with smells leathersome and furrish and with sounds shaped like gossip but also prayer, yoh, blasphemish though it is to utter, the springoffs of reb Marx'ele, on either side of the ocean, Gittl knew, were not utterly disopiatesome afterallish. Had approached them a Leninish rebbe, tall and cleanshaven but for a mustache and a little beard, what was comely with big hands and dark eyes, and the oven of Gittl's own tayve inside this evening was uplit, and she thought that perhaps she might endeavor to shtip him, her first since the ship to amerike, yoh, but then he spoke.

So good to see you, my keen cat. How's the struggle? Hope all is aces down in the Ward.

One of his hands darted through the air and

grasped Charles's hand like an adder rabbitgrabbing, and uppumped it, and downswung it, Charles's hand limp and cuniculish in this man's paw's maw. He lay his left hand on Charles's shoulder, and Charles's shoulder did not inmold to the touch soever, stayed only coldfish stiff and still.

Hello, Weissberger.

Weissberger aroundlooked the room, his hands still onclamped over Charles's hand and shoulder, his mouth pulled into a dancing bearish look, an everyone look at what I am doing look, and Gittl downbit the urge to spit, yoh, not polite to so do inside the belly of the revolution. Charles overlooked at Gittl, and it was as though he blinked at her then with one eye, but without blinking any of his eyes soever, and Gittl nodded.

Can't wait to gum the works tonight, said Weissberger.

Sure thing, Charles said.

Weissberger leaned closer to Charles and quieted something what Gittl could not overhear into his ear.[68]

Charles's jaw clenched unclenched ever so. Weissberger pulled back from Charles.

Who's the dame? He did not seem to see Leyb, what had become as though a statue again, standing still but

---

68 "Thanks for the draft, Charles, it's the bee's knees, and thanks for being here. I'll get you the rest of the rhino suds next week."

for his eyes, what were aroundflitting, and Gittl wanted to againtake his hand but did not.

This is Gittl . . .

Radish, Gittl said.

Gittl Radish, and this is Leyb Halper. Gittl, Leyb, this is Anthony Weissberger. I told you about him.

Good things only, I hope? Weissberger laughed through his nose and Gittl remembered that dancing bears are made to stand over grates of burnish coals and that is why they dance, but Gittl could not smell any coals, yoh, so maybe he was not so much a dancing bear as a human sneeze. He took Gittl's hand and held it too tightsome.

avade heys er white townsman
let go of her hand kindly now
also no callouses on these fingeredges what sort of writer feh

nor az di shraybst vi honik, said Gittl.[69]

Sideshook his head Weissberger. I don't speak jewish.

I know, Gittl said in american. She overlooked at Charles and saw a hintsmile playing on his lips.

Weissberger opened his mouth but then closed it, for the crowd around them had fallen silent, the faces inside the revolution all frontroomlooked to the

---

69 "Just that you write like honey."

podium, upon what rested an iron manifestation of Marx'ele, a glass of water, and a wood stick bearing the soviet flag in fluppish miniature.

Toward the behindpodium had walked a man, tall and wheatly, and he spoke with a lult what sounded to Gittl different from the american what she had so far heard.[70] Good evening, Comrades.

Secretary Comrade Blankstone, Charles quieted to Gittl, what knew already from her years scrubbing the follicles of Marx's beard the fullish transcript of his introduction before he spoke it, yoh, he would say: vey iz mir, what in american may be oversat to oh dear me, the workers are having a hard time, and everyone is miserable and oppressed but lo victory is nigh what from the inevitability of history and if we look closely we can see that capitalism is in its deaththroes, et cetera. Behind Charles, Leyb was become almost a fragment of air.

The Negro problem is a Communist problem, continued Blankstone. The Negroes are at their truest core Workers, and so their Struggles are the Struggles of Workers around the world.

You're here for researching? Gittl said to Charles.

Not as such, Charles cliplaughed. Hard to imagine that these lilyepenimer have much in the way of insight

---

70 That'd be Oklaheymish, Comradess: Timothy Blankstone of Broken Arrow, OK; not the sharpest implement in the Third International, but strapping, in that cornfed sort of way.

with which to enlighten me as per the question at hand, or regarding the truest core of the Negro. I'm here, how best to put it? Mostly as a bauble for Comrade Weissberger.

What does it mean bauble, Gittl said.

It means he thinks it boosts his credibility to be seen as having a Negro friend.

Gittl looked at Charles, did not speak, in the front-roomish background Blankstone continued to ondroll.

Easy on the judgement, Comradess. He pays me in advance for the speech, and promised a bit extra this time if I showed up in person. Moral support, he called it, but I'd call it sweatless toil, and a few of these fellows occasionally do offer up some neat tidbit or other about the science of dialectical materialism that is worth hearing.

there is no judge
yoh no judge and no law
only dialectical material what is worth herring
o wa

I understand, Gittl said.

Sure you do, Charles said, and then gestured with his chin toward the podium, where Weissberger was handshaking with Blankstone, and then began around-shifting pages with his big hands, and ahmning from his throat. Here goes, Charles said.

* * *

Good evening, Comrades.

As you all know, for nearly seven years now, as the people of this land have literally languished in the streets, starving and desperate as the machinations of capitalism's unfettered greed crashes down around them, crushing them under its fatuous weight, the government of these United States of America has been diverting mountains of capital into chipping away at the hills of South Dakota. There, this so-called country's leadership is hard at work, carving the fashimiles—

Facsimiles, Charles quieted.[71]

—of four faces into stone. One of these faces is of a man widely known for his rotten teeth. What is less widely known by our populace is how he replaced said teeth. This man was, as was common in his era, the owner of a torture gulag in which newborns were summarily sentenced to life-terms on the basis of the singularly unforgivable crime of their complexion. While legend has it that the man's mealy mouth was girded by wooden teeth, any comrade who has worked with his hands knows well that wood would scarcely withstand the onslaught of so much saliva. As a point of fact, our founding dad's replacement teeth were wrenched di-

---

71 To be fair to Weissberger, it is worth mentioning how once, in a Wissotzky-flavored after-conversation with the painter, young Charles fervently cited a point made by "Sigmund Frood," and recalling, too, how the painter laughed, and laughed, and laughed.

rectly from the mouth of a man enslaved in his personal torture gulag.

Gittl overglanced at Leyb, and saw that he was become a clump of sorreltongues swaying slightly in the wind.

Leyb'ele
a beautiful thanks again for the berry what you have given
we might be able to hold or behold you if only you turn
or also we might not o wa

Gittl found that she could not look at him for too long, and so backturned her attention toward Charles's words what were outflocking from Weissberger's mouth.

—and a half loaf of torture gulag is better than none, to paraphrase the second face's famous philosophy. Third, of course, is the much beloved Teddy, who would find cuddly company in the corners of any Klavern with comments such as, and I quote, the great majority of Negroes in the South are wholly unfit for suffrage. Finally, we come face to face with the face of the self-styled savior of the Negro race, who endeavored not only to free the Negro, but also to achieve an america free from Negroes. And I quote, here, from a speech which this most-honest of faces gave to a delegation of Negro leaders, urging them to leave for Liberia or some other distant corner of the globe: It is better for us to be separated. So even old Abe was part and parcel of the reactionary capitalist prejudices of his age.

Enthusiastic clappage from the crowd. Weissberger again outcleared his throat, drank a small drink of water from the communal cup, and continued.

Meanwhile, in Moscow, there is a more modest statue of a man, made from bronze; one that seeks too to represent the country's national character. His likeness looks down on passersby, his curly hair glowing in the sunlight. This man is the descendant of an Abyssinian general named Gannibal. This man is a hero to the Russian people, and a poet renowned by all people of cultivated spirit and mind around the world. This man is a Negro. This man, of course, is Alexander Pushkin. According to Comrade Langston Hughes in a recent dispatch from Moscow, the American poet Poe, upon meeting Pushkin, refused to shake the latter's hand upon seeing how much Pushkin resembled some of those enslaved in Poe's native Maryland. May Marx bless the poetics of the discerning american eye, Poe was right, comrades: Alexander Pushkin was born in 1799. If, by dumb accident of the earth, on which, of course, there are no accidents, everything being animated and propelled by the inevitable progressive march of material, as it were . . .

Gittl saw Weissberger upglance from the pages before him, watched as his face sought to glean whether he had just blasphemed against the revolution, and she beheld no resolution thereupon his countenance, and she glanced again toward the writer of ghosts what was looking only straight ahead.

But, ahem, excuse me, comrades, let us, let us imagine, Weissberger again began, let us imagine for a moment, that Pushkin had indeed been born in these great United States of America, in Poe's native Maryland, let's say, in 1799. Not only would he have been denied all access to ink and parchment on which to write his verse: it would have been forbidden, comrades, as an offense punishable by death, for the American Pushkin to learn to read. He would have been sentenced, from the moment of his birth, to a life of humiliation and brutalization, of terror and torment. Perhaps some aspiring Washington would have pulled out his teeth. And so I ask you, comrades, to think for a moment of these four faces being carved into stone, and of that lone statue standing in the heart of Moscow, and then to ask yourselves: Which of these, truly, is the land of the free?

Whistles and claps filled the revolution, and Weissberger's visage sought to enstern itself but still peeked beamish and gladsome beneath the applause.

nu, vos zogstu, khaver'te?[72] Charles turned to Gittl.

nit erger,[73] Gittl said.

No need to flatter, Charles said.

---

72 "So, what do you say, Comradess?"

73 "Not terrible." (Truly she was the pineapple of politeness, as old Sheridan would have it.)

So yoh a bit didactish, and also I'm not sure from the idea that the opposite of hideous is not hideous. Maybe it's more truthsome that everything is hideous, and everywhere?

Charles nodded. Maybe.

But I liked the part about the progressive material historymarch, Gittl said.

Noted. You alright there, Lion?

Why should I not be, Leyb murmured.

Charles nodded, gentletapped a hand on Leyb's shoulder, then let his hand backfall toward the air, toward the earth, toward his own body.

The next speech was given by a tufthaired nervejew, what Gittl appreciated for his earnestness, but what aroundjumbled incomprehensibly about the sociopolitical destiny of the proletariat as embodied by someone named Angel O'Herndon.[74] Back at the behindpodium, Blankstone said, Next we have our very own Comrade Loveland, and here Blankstone smiled in a way not so different from Weissberger's aforementioned handshakeish shmeykhl, and to the behindpodium briskwalked a tall man. Charles's face, Gittl saw, was not bemasked now, was Charles's own face, and grimaceful.

Gittl said to Charles, He's a friend from you?

---

74 Angelo Herndon, though there is a case to be made for the poetics of this celestial sic, given how they've continued to torment the poor kid.

Charles outblew air from his nostrils. We're not all friends, you know, Comradess.[75]

Was a joke, Gittl said.

Mm, Charles said.

Leyb glanced up from his feet, over to the door, down back to his feet, and Gittl saw his mouth open and close a bissl as if beginning to speak or davn.

there can be holy

---

75 Matthias Loveland had, in fact, been something of a friend to Charles, or close to it, back when Charles started attending Party meetings in early '33, mostly out of curiosity, just after the Hunger March passed through town. Loveland was five years Charles's senior, and had fought in the War, returning home from those civilized rivers of blood just in time for the Red Summer, which led him to both see redder and turn redder, as it were, first organizing the self-defense unit of the local chapter of the African Blood Brotherhood, and later becoming a high-ranking mainstay of Philadelphia's CP, even as many of the others from C. Briggs's brigade trickled away after the merger. He'd wanted to take Charles under his wing, or so it seemed to Charles, until one evening when, after a discussion in which Charles said something general about the need for Party solidarity with the intimate and romantic groups subject to steadily increasing bourgeois violence, too, Loveland took Charles aside and said to him, barely out of earshot of a crowd of Comrade Blankstone, so to speak: "You know, Charles, I don't give a fuck who you fuck, but I do want you to be aware that speaking of your little sodomitical sodality as a collective is just parroting one of Mr. Charlie's fabrications, designed to undermine the real struggle for revolution, and you ought to know better than that." So, no, not such a friend.

there is no mastergod
there is nothing there is only us
only maysehs o wa
  and also us sometimes
  omeyn

—and all of that is to say, Comrade Loveland said in a voice of bass and water, that the Negro churches, Bethel and Pisgah, Wesley and Zoar, all of them: they are in large part responsible for the passivity of the Negro masses of this city, and for the Party's inability to make sufficient inroads.[76]

No, Charles said to Gittl, his jaw clenching and unclenching. Not such a friend.

After Loveland finished, there was again loudsome

---

76 Charles imagined approaching Loveland afterward, disregarding whatever conflicts he himself may have had with the church and its goers, and reminding T. Loveland that while they may not speak in Marxist terminology, the majority of the faithful are well aware of america's flesh-eating sadism, and of the urgent need to reject the shibboleth of bourgeois democracy, Comrade, and that they know this on the basis of their lived experiences, without any pedantic Karl's or pandering Matthias's enlightening lecture, spaseebo balshoye, and that such lectures may, in fact, have something to do with said roads, or, such lecture-roads may have to do with the Party's insufficiency . . . or something like that. He'd have to work on the semantics later, he supposed. (Did he dream, then, that he'd be ironing out these semantics, or neglecting to do so, from a flat in Moscow? Comrades, he did not.)

applause, and Blankstone waited for it to die and then drulled: For our final piece of the evening, we have a special treat. A poem by Comrade Bear-Meerkat.

To the behindpodium walked a thin jew with round glasses.

This one is a draft, said Bear-Meerkat. It's entitled, Lynching. He was silent for a moment, and then looked up, and said loudly:

Negro!

Gittl saw Charles close his eyes. His jaw clenched unclenched, and he upreached his thumb and forefinger to pinch the bridge of his nose. Bear-Meerkat continued:

Your black form droops
Like a winter plum or
Some other foreign fruit
In the southern summer

Here, Bear-Meerkat paused to push a lock of his hair from his forehead.

You're not the only one who suffers so
Death is the god to whom many pray
These days it's fashionable, you know
To dream of crucifying men this way . . .

In Berlin, and in Scottsboro!

Applause filled the room, and Gittl overlooked at Charles, what was not clapping, and Gittl let her hands rest also by her side. To the behindpodium hurried Secretary Comrade Blankstone, and over the wips and whistles, what had begun to fade into sighs of afterchatter and gladdish mumblesome groans, he said, Comrades, thank you, we actually do have one more poem this evening, by Comrade Anna, please welcome—and his voice bounced through the room over snippets in american of How goes with the strike in Anthracite? and in jewish of Did you hear what Glassfinsky said at the workers university last week, about how the accommodationist socialists are worse than the fascists? and in american, Poor old Tom Mooney, fellow can't catch a break, and in jewish, How's your mother-in-law? and underneath all of this noise walked to the behindpodium a jew, and this jew did not wait for the din to downquiet, only she started to read, and as she read, the din did not downquiet, only it continued, with a few shas and be quiets flat-falling onto the ground, but Gittl was able to ongrab to her poem through the socialish tide of clank and blather, a beautiful thanks to the fact that the jew read each part of her poem first in jewish, and then oversat it after into american:

kheyshekh, mayn baleyter
ikh hob a mayseh tzu dertzeyln

Darkness, my companion
I have a story to tell you

nekhtn iz di fray gekumen tzudrukn
ir kharpe tzu mayn erve, un zi hot gezogt az doh bin
ikh besholem

Yesterday, liberty approached to press
her sex upon my sex, telling me that here I am safe

ober kh'hob geshushket az zi darft vartn
vayl ikh hob gehat a frage fun iberzetzen

But I whispered to her that she must wait
for I had a question of translation

hob ikh gefregt:
vi zogt men pogrom in amerike?

Gittl looked toward the edges of the room to see if the revolution might start to selfdrink its walls, if trees might begin gouging through its distended belly.

I asked:
how do you say pogrom in america?

hot zi geentfert
and she replied

You say Elaine
You say Rosewood
You say Atlanta
You say St. Louis
You say Tulsa
You say New York
You say Springfield
You say Chicago
You say Corbin
You say Philadelphia

vi zogt men pogrom in amerike?

You say america.

Gittl blinked her eyes and let her hands join the motion of the room what did now upfill with some claps and clicks
breathe Gittl
it's not here
there's nothing
o wa
and then she heard Charles's voice.

I'll introduce you.

Gittl again blinked her eyes, looking first at Charles face, what was looking toward her, and then at Leyb's face behind him, what was looking toward the outdoor.
yoh when they came they took everyone to the forest

yoh Gittl heard him gurgling and pulled him out
peace upon you Leyb'ele
Leyb'ele all the people of Zatelsk
yoh all of them what are still alive
are right here and also Charles is

Sorry, what? Gittl said.

You, well, you've been clapping for quite some time. I assumed you liked the poem?

Oh, Gittl said, yoh, okay, and she followed Charles through the crowd, where he was saying and nodding quicksome hellos, and Leyb followed, too, and Gittl did not outreach her hand to Leyb, but she tried to hold on to his silence with her silence.

Comrade Trunksboym, Charles said, slightraising his voice and waving with one hand. The jewpoet looked to them, and then walked toward them.

Hello, Charles.

Congratulations on the poem, Anna, Charles said, and Gittl wondered if she and he had shtipped.

Yes, great poem, Weissberger from out of nowhere pipped behind Charles, his tall head and broadsome shoulders overarching the rest of them, yoh, a shame, Gittl thought.

Hello, Anthony, said Anna. And thank you, Comrade Patterson. That's a high compliment, coming from you. She grasped his hand, and Gittl thought that yoh, certainly they had.

Anna, this is Gittl, Charles said, and that's Leyb.

Charles gestured toward Leyb, what was standing near Weissberger and downlooking and overmouthing words in quietsome jewish but not to anyone of them, and then he noticed four faces looking at his face and closed his mouth.

Yes hello, Gittl said in american, thinking of Weissberger, what stood there eager and expectant with his lollish americantongue, yoh, she was not certain how to be certain what jew knows jewish here, perhaps Anna had someone else tug her poem into jewish and was just outsounding the words what she read.

Hm, Anna said, intaking and then outblowing air from her nostrils. Gittl vemens?[77]

Gittl Khayeles.

Anna nodded, moved her jaw to the left and lightly to the right.

Gittl Khayeles. fun minsk, nit azey?[78]

fin Zatelsk
fin Zatelsk
nit azey
fin Zatelsk

yoh, Gittl said.

avade, Anna said. a gute-fraynd fun der baroness.[79]

---

77 "Whose Gittl?"

78 "From Minsk, not so?"

79 "Of course, the dear friend of the Baroness."

Gittl flushed, and then selfminded once more that she didn't care from anyone, and said in jewish, Not such a good friend.

yeh, in ordnung, Gittl, mir ale hobn unzere[80] Engels and angles. Anna continued in american, Baroness Sunday, potatoes Monday, a bit of Weissberger on Tuesday, not so, Comrades? Anna blinked with one eye toward Charles and dibeksmiled toward Weissberger.

Anyway, I read your poem in Marx's Beard, Anna said, still in american.

Charles looked at Gittl questionfully.

It's just a list, Gittl said.

yeh, your list, then, Anna said in jewish. I'd like to talk more. Would you have coffee with me? I'll be at the Freeling all shabbes.

Gittl looked at her face, looked for glimmers of pitysome sorrows, did not find, nodded, yoh, efsher, okay.

Anna overleaned and kissed Charles on the cheek and said, Come too, if you're free, and nodded to Leyb, and said, khaver, and Comrade Lion uplooked, and backnodded, and said, khaver'te.

Alright then, Charles said. So long, Weissberger, good evening, Comrades. It's been a long day, Ms. Radish here probably hasn't had a good night's rest in a while.

---

80 "It's alright, Gittl, we all have our"

yoh in seven and seven years
but it's what
yoh it's time
o wa

Leyb uplooked and his face became as a dance of jasmine and lilac in a summer wind, looked as though he might gazellefully hillrun, might aroundspin under nightclouds, yoh, so he was ready to go, too, and Weissberger managed to glumly mutter a So long, my keen cats, and Gittl followed the two men out from the revolution what danced broadly on the head of a lonesome theater. Outside the night was dry and cold.

Maybe it'll finally snow, Charles said. The oddest winter of my life. Then he looked toward Gittl. I didn't know you wrote, as well. Why didn't you say something?

What thing should I have said, Gittl said.

How about, Oh, how interesting that you write, I'm a writer too, Charles said. Where are you staying? Leyb and I will walk you.

Charles touched Leyb's shoulder and Gittl watched this and wanted to be the one what touched Leyb so, what told him it's alright, zis'ele, everything's alright, with only the words of her palm.

nu what about from earlier, that Leyb and I should pretend to be a bourgeois nuptialcouple?

Oh, that was just a ploy to try to get our Lion cub

here to come with us, Charles said. Where did you say you're staying, Gittl?
never alone
not alone
but also yoh nowhere
o wa

Could she stay also with you, Charles? Leyb said.

No, Gittl said.

Charles turned to look at her and quieted, Do you have a place to stay?[81]

yoh, Gittl said, and just then, as if a brickram stuck in a citythicket, she saw wheat sheafs and a jewstar and the year 5683 all stonescratched into the outside of a fat lumpen square building on the corner of Pine. I'm staying with the very Baroness of philadelphiye. zayt zhe mir gezint.[82]

Leyb turned his head sharply away.

Right, zayt gezunt, too, Gittl, Charles said. Can we walk you, at least?

Gittl shook her head, not wanting anyone's charity,

---

81 Marx almighty, Charles found that he was genuinely prepared to turn his apartment into Zatelsk II: an american dust-village, as it were.

82 Lit.: "Be healthy for me"; the resonance of this phrase, though, can be much broader and more versatile, and in this case, at least Lion took it to mean something along the lines of, "Leave me alone."

not needing anyman's help, not being able to bear looking more at or not at Leyb's face for now, and turned left onto Pine and walked for a block and then turned up a smaller street and waited with her back againstpressing brick for time to forwardtrickle, for Leyb and Charles to awaytrickle, and then she backturned and returned to the corner of Broad, where sat the ym-ywha, and she prepared to ask there if they took moths and motes as currency, and she stopped for a moment and inbreathed, alone in the darkness of philadelphiye.

yoh not alone
never alone
not alone Gittl
o wa

and yoh so after
after this
after the party
o wa

a mayseh fin a shabbes

And so yoh the next evening was being already shabbes, and on this shabbes Leyb and Charles went again to Cricket's, what had migrated to a new home, yoh, a new basement of smoke and dribbled liquid and melted tin and clay forms, with words etched into their foreheads and psalms cupped between their palms, and this time they arrived together, and once inside the door, Charles took his hand from Leyb's shoulder, where it had rested goyishly pleasant oh chumsome oh buddies for any-eye from amerike to behold, and slid it downward into the midst of Leyb's own hand, where it sprawled soft and welcome, yoh, and this time, the crowd of men what was gathered under the ground beheld Leyb and Charles, and surrounded them, yoh, allsided them, and onto Leyb's face were then downraining kisses, and into his hair were flying hands to ruffle and pat, flying also onto his neck and shoulders to stroke and tap, and in his ears was atta boy, was welcome back, was Charles's voice, too, was another sound, uprising from Leyb's own

body, togetherbraided laughter and softened wailing, and then he was only laughing, yoh, and only slightly weeping, yoh, and everywhere there was strumming
yoh tum balalaike
freylekh zol zayn
and Charles and Leyb were given drinks without passing any coins soever, and they stayed for some hours, or some years, there inside Cricket's, and then walked back to Charles's home together, and there, Leyb removed his clothes at the side of Charles's bed and Charles removed his, and the coldair wicked around their bodies but heat rose from each of them, and Leyb moved to Charles and put his mouth upon Charles's mouth, and Charles's hand overrubbed the side of Leyb's face, and Leyb moved his mouth again and took Charles's two middle fingers into his mouth, and the leftover ink was entering Leyb's body, then, and he was become a mayseh, burning forever in the middle of the philadelphiye wilderness, and Charles's hand downmoved along the side of Leyb's ribcage, against what Leyb's lungs were pressing, yoh, they too wanted to be part of this shabbes, and down farther onto his hip, and then behind him, and Charles's fingers gentlepressed, wettened and warm, around Leyb's opening, and Charles moved Leyb back onto the bed, and Leyb felt on his back the jolt of wintercold fabric, and Leyb looked into Charles's face, and Charles's eyes met Leyb's eyes, and Charles moved slowly then into Leyb, and his shoulder

pressed into Leyb's right underleg, his left hand downthreaded between them, supportish on the overgive of the bed, and with his right hand Charles ongrasped to Leyb's own hardened sex, and held on to it there, between them, and with this grasp Charles's movements started to become faster, and as he deepened, his grasp on Leyb's sex with his hand held firm, and Leyb then was become only breath, was only breathing, was only burning, was only a river, was only alone, was only held, was only filled, and Charles overspilled into Leyb, and alongside the chorus of Charles's breath pattern Leyb overspilled too there within Charles's grasp, up between their bodies, and in this togetherstickish aftermoment, beside wilting sexes and the change of the room's oxygen and broken eyelocks and the swirl of let's clean up, let's backgo into the world again, Leyb was upfilled with the falling present and with earthen past and with the gasping future, and as the cold of the quilt pressed into his back he writhed in stillness and tried to stop his breath from returning, tried to tell his lungs to please wait, just even one more moment to wait, tried to hold this shabbes still inside of him, then Charles kissed his forehead and said, A beautiful thanks, Lion, and Leyb said, Anytime again forever you can, and Charles said, dayenu, baby. I'll be glad to again, when you'd like, Lion, but there's no expectation. You can stay here as long as you'd like. And Leyb looked at Charles and tried to find in his eyes a reason for what he was saying this, and found there only another moment in what the world did not deserve to be destroyed. In truth?

Of course in truth, Lion, Charles said, and his of course in truth coursed through Leyb what understood that if the course of his nights remained mostly unknown, he would in truth sleep again more nights next to Charles, with or without shtipping, with or without talking, with or without laughter or quieted screaming, with or without end, and this knowing brought to Leyb's mouth another approximation of an amerikanisher smile, and to his mind it brought a small stillness what did not have a name, and at the edge of each of his eyes was an echo of a smallsome not forgotten river, yoh, a river next to what he had once given to Gittl a single berry.

Gittl did not know this mayseh yet, yoh, but during this shabbes in philadelphiye, she was only some blocks away, at a cafe called Freeling in what a quorum of jewpoets chuttered and mimbled, slurped and spit amidst the clank of cups and the tin of jewish, yoh, almost no americantongue waggled in this american room soever, what was small but was having its very own carpet, o wa, and across the table from her was the poet Anna Trunksboym, what was saying how they hate to work too hard here, that Gittl ought to just give them americanneat words to uponchew and let them feel of the worldly, without their needing to wander or strain their various groins or spleens with heavy wordlifting, yeh, or herniated heaven forbid, take a few moments to undersit a line, and yeh, a jew wishes she could say, It's okay to not know all the things, kinderlakh, but a jew is also loathe to be made further into a mameh by these men, what can then feel brave and independentish for dislistening, all grownup, yeh, and then she laughed and said, As you can see, daughter of Khayele, I have a feeling or two on the subject, anyway.

And yoh, that aftershabbes, back at the broomcloset in the ym-ywha, in what Gittl had been allowed to sleep by the pockmarked deskaltishke, what had told Gittl first that no, we do not accept moths and motes here, but then had softened, seeing or hearing something

yoh something
like an owl
like a river
o wa

and had told her that she could perhaps sleep in the broomcloset, and had brought her there a pile of towels and a plate of potatokigel and whitefish, and Gittl had let the fishflesh lay alone on the plate and began to eat the potatosquare as the altishke talked toward her about how she had just the idea, Gittl could work at least for a month as a horsecleaner for the goyim in the pasturepart of the city, and even for a select few shrunkfinned jews, you may believe it or don't, child, who manage to mask their genetical equineterror, because the altishke's sister Etke's daughter's friend Blume-Bashke, you may believe it or don't, just this week had to stop working there because she had a child, mazel tov to all israel et cetera, and remind me to tell you sometime the mayseh about the miracles of amerike's helpful scientifish inventions, child, or do you want that I should tell it right now? and Gittl had tried to politenod and behmm the altishke from the closet

yoh hard to do we're trying

as it is written a talkingperson must talk until they've outtalked (Ecclesiastes 11:11)

yoh but I want to know about the scientifish inventions

no o wa

and finally Gittl had to say, No, not now, mameshu, I think I must catch a dreamlet, and only then did the deskaltishke leave, and Gittl did not so much sleep because she never much slept, but yoh, she wrote, and she dreamed, and she spoke small maysehs to her siblings, and she did close her eyes for a short while, and she made certain to leave the closet early the next morning to go to wander alone at the edges of philadelphiye for the whole day, and so too the next morning, what was shabbes, before deciding to try to find the Freeling after all, and when she returned to the ym-ywha that aftershabbes evening the deskaltishke was there, and she upleapt like some bearish meerkat when she saw Gittl, and told Gittl breathlessly that she had a telegram

for her, and that it was delivered by a very handsome black what worked for the Baroness, and god in heaven himself only knew how the Baroness of philadelphiye herself knew that Gittl was staying at our very own ym-ywha
our very own yhwh in himl
feh
got iz avek
o wa we would like some credit
and why hadn't our boarder'ke said that she knew the Baroness, and also did Gittl know that the Baroness herself once—and Gittl had stopped so much listening and looked at the telegram and saw that attached to it was a handwritten note what read, in jewish:

Don't worry, Glikl, no one likes poetry anyway.

Then Gittl read the telegram itself, which was addressed to Gittl Radish, c/o the Baroness of Philadelphia:

ESTEEMED MS RADISH-(STOP)-DINNER AT GOLDFARBS TUES-(STOP)-LION WOULD LIKE TO SEE YOU

Dialogues (I)[83]

Three almoststrangers sat again around a table.

Gittl had hoped she would not have to say that she did not eat flesh, and was relieved to see another dish made from eggs, about what Charles said, as though depthtesting a pond, The eternal return of the same egg, as it were, Comradess, and both of them nodded and halfsmiled, and Leyb made a rustling sound within his throat. Leyb looked taller, a bissl, to Gittl, in how he sat, and his eyes, what Gittl made herself look upon, were glintsome as he began to tell a mayseh in american.

This afternoon, Leyb said, I was walking for no reason up on Broad Street, just walking, yoh, and I saw Peter Halper, my notbrother, and he was walking near the Temple campus, in what he studies. And yoh, not knowing why precisely I walked to him and said

---

83 Orig.: a mayseh fin redn, or, "a story of talking."

shulem aleykhem yidl and he tried to walk from me, like he was fearful from catching my illness, but then I said in american, Peter Halper, peace upon you, little jew, and he stopped, and I knew that he wanted to scream upon me to go quickly from there before any Templefriends might see him so jewfully. But before he could speak, I said, I want also to study accountment and investmenting, just like you, Pete. When I said it, I felt as though after all, perhaps, I might not have to be a jew what stands on top of the roof and pretends to be a bird and flaps his arms and waits for the landlord to shoot him in the head.

Gittl saw Charles flush a bissl, and he said to Leyb, So you did know the story?

Leyb looked to Charles, and said, yoh, Charles, I am maybe not drinking books like both of you, but I am not such an amhoretz[84] that I don't know from Sholem Aleichem.

Noted, Charles said.

And I'm also not such an amhoretz that I can't see that your Marxish ship is sinking, yoh, that amerike will sink it with its teeth, Leyb said, chewing as he spoke on his fork. And he looked at Gittl and at Charles. I want that maybe you should both not go back onto it?

Gittl did not say anything, only she loved this little

---

84 "Man of the Land," i.e., a simpleton.

lion then in silence, this one what thought that he might awaytake everyone from the forest what is of course everywhere.

What did Peter say? Charles asked.

Leyb said, Peter said, Oh no. Unfortunately, they've already filled their quota. And I only then looked at Pete's eyes. Their jewquota, he said. And I only still looked at his eyes, not awaylooking for even one moment, and I did not speak. Leyb almostsmiled. Then Peter spoke. He said, I suppose you might odd it. So I will now odd it, at The Temple University.

That's great news, Lion, Charles said, and he rasied his coffee. A toast to our Templebokher.

Gittl upraised her glass of hot water, and Leyb did, and all three drank their respective zhlyuks in silence. Charles lit a cigarette, offered one to Leyb what shook his head no, and handed one to Gittl, what nodded her thanks.

un ir, Professor? Gittl said, welcoming the smoke into her lungs. You have also studied at the Temple?

Me? No, Charles said, and Gittl saw that there was a slight upjutting of his chin when he said this, as though againstblow squaring. Gittl wanted to tell him to downjut it, it's what, but she did not speak, only smoked, and then Charles spoke.

Did you end up meeting with Anna?

yoh, we have met.

And?

She said that I should think on oversitting my writings, Gittl smalllaughed.

Charles sideleaned his head.

iberzetzen, vi zugt men, Leyb'ele?

Translated, Leyb said, Translating, Charles said, before Leyb had fullspoken his word.

yoh. Anna said that Blume-Bashke what is sometimes oversitting for her is too busy, and that Anna does it mostly her own. Gittl shrugged. Anyway what does allamerike care from my list.

Perhaps I might, said Charles.

Perhaps you might care?

Perhaps I might try to oversit your work.

Gittl looked at Charles's eyes.

You're skeptical I might be able to sink my teeth into your holy mamatongue, Comradess?

No, Gittl said. Only skeptical that I can pay you how Khayim-Yankl Weissberger can.

This isn't a business proposal, Gittl. I was offering as a favor.[85]

I'm not needing anyman's favors.

Well this is off to a good start, Leyb said, outspitting the topparts of his masticated utensil, four wetmetal tines clinkfalling onto the woodish table, coming to rest amidst inkstains and coffeestains, the bottom forkhalf

---

85 "A fine feeling that . . . to be misunderstood . . . it made him feel tragic and great . . ." (as Bruce would have it).

now only a lonesome bulbous post in the midst of a lion's fist in the philadelphiyesh night. Leyb upstood.

Now children, he said, in his best cleaned americanvoice, what was surprisishly convicesome to Gittl,[86] I hope that you two are able to resolve your differences, I will be in my room.

Leyb overwalked to Charles's bed, what was maybe three smallpaces away from the table. He crawled under the quilt, and took a heavybook from the sidesome floor, and opened it to a middle section, and leaned his head very close to the pages until his nose touched the paper and then in one quickmotion he upsnapped his head and offbit the corner of one of the pages, and began to chew. Oh geshmak, he muttered to himself and also not to himself, amerikanisher investmenting.

Gittl and Charles both laughed. Could not but.

yoh we all did
thou shalt upchew the pages of thine justgotten textbook
  (The Temple Code of Conduct 7:10)
and one stolen bundle may be awayborne in the hands of
  a lion
o wa Leyb'ele but yoh not yet

I didn't mean it like that, Gittl, and favor's not the

---

86 And to Charles as well, though he'd seen glimpses before of Leyb's ability to iron out his american, so to speak, when he chose to do so, rather than stay guarded behind the shell of his oversat syntax.

right word, either, Charles said. I know you don't need anyone's charity. I just meant that I'd like to try, if you'll let me.

Gittl shrugged. It's not a privatesome thing anymore. It's now just one more hair on everyman's chin.

How's that?

It was published in Literarishe Blumen, what everyone calls Marx's Beard.

Ah, right, so Anna said. Sure, then. I'll just go see if they happen to have back issues of Literarishe Blumen in stock down at the grocer's.

Leyb soundchewed on another page over in the bedcorner.

Why anyway would you want to do this, Gittl said. Why aren't you ownwriting?

I am ownwriting. I've got a three-part series underway for Weissberger entitled: How the Philadelphia Negro Lives and Struggles Today: A Worker's Perspective, Thirty-Five Years After Dr. Du Bois's Seminal Study, tra la la.

But for this you're Weissberger's ghostbeing. Why not Patterson's ghostbeing?

We're in america, Gittl. I understand that you're new here, but you seem perspicacious enough to get that it's more palatable for everyone at the Daily Worker with a Weissberger stitched onto the garment, as it were.

So write it for another place. You're not, I perspicate, overly dullfish loyal to the party.

What other place? The Tribune probably wouldn't run the things I write for Weissberger, and the Crisis is mostly underwater these days, circumstances being what they are and all. And even if I did write something for the Tribune or the Crisis, neither could pay me a quarter as much as old socialistic Weissberger, Ms. Radish.

Khayeles.

Sorry?

mayn mameshis numen iz Khayele, ikh heys Gittl Khayeles.[87]

That's certainly nicer than Radish.

Tell this to the rest of amerike.

I suppose Khayeles might get caught in some craws. Is your mother still with us?

still with us
always with us
never alone Gittl
o wa mameshi

No.

I'm very sorry for your loss.

Do you have siblings, Charles?

No, Charles said. My father died when I was a child, and my mother never remarried. Why do you ask?

It must be lonely this.

---

87 "My mother's name is Khayele, I'm called Gittl Khayele's."

yoh

as it is written there is nothing in all the world what is like siblings (Book of Zatelsk 4:4).

it must be lonely this

o wa

I'm used to it, Charles said.

Gittl upstood and walked toward the door, and stopped beside the coatrack, and outpulled from the breastpocket of her tateshi's overcoat the pages of her list what were overfolded and downrubbed, tearsome at their edges.

and we did not warn him to return them

as it is written no need

we knew that he would

o wa but maybe better a different mayseh Gittl

Gittl backplaced the pages and pulled out from another pocket another set of pages, newer, crisper, ink still drying upon them.

I have a different mayseh, a new one, she said.

She walked back over to the table at what Charles remained seated.

Alright then, Gittl Khayeles, Charles said, and downglanced to the toppage and outread: azey hot geredt amerike.

There are perhaps here some words what you won't know.

She looked at Charles's jaw, to see if the ball of smallmuscle there would do its clench unclench. It did not. Instead, Charles only sideleaned his head, now toward his bookshelf what had books backstacked in three rows and still others what had been cast to the floor by their comrades and were left there oh lonesome oh forsakeish.

I've got a copy of Al Harkavy's '28 verterbukh, Charles said, so I should be up to date. And then he headtilted toward his bed, upon what Leyb now sat surrounded in halfmasticated pageparts, covered with inkish numbers and signs and wonders. And if I find myself in a bind, I'll just ask my local Lion.

yoh but must we be beholden to amerike's mannerisms of after and after
pinch a horse's nose in moskve and its tail will wag in philadelphiye
incomprehensible Hendl mine
o wa anyway so after that

Dialogues (II)

Where is Leyb?

I'm not sure. Maybe an evening class at Temple, or maybe he's off with someone he met at Cricket's.

Gittl singleraised an eyebrow. This is not hurtsome for you?

No, the opposite. I'm glad for young Lion. I wouldn't want to clip his wings, and anyway, I do recall reading recently something about how monogamiye iz di dalet-ames fun der burzhuazye, nit azey?

Gittl laughed. You would have liked some of the men at Marx's Beard.

Sure I would have.

Gittl quieted, and moved her gaze from Charles's face toward a smallsome pile of papers on Charles's table, on what she could see, even from under the lintel, piles of american words.

Charles followed Gittl's gaze, cleared his throat. Would you like a cup of coffee as you read?

Gittl shook her head. Thanks.

Smoke?

Gittl nodded. Charles lit her cigarette. Lit his own. Both insmoked, and Gittl walked three or six paces from the doorway and sat at the table, careful to not let the ash downfall onto the papers. Charles downsat across from her. Gittl wondered if she should ask him to maybe go do something else, but Charles did not fidget or loudbreathe, only smoked and stillsat, and Gittl found that she was glad for his therebeing as she started to read.

Thus Spoke America

And so Gittl left Itzl's house, which stood beyond the stand of trees, within which Gittl stood when the Kuren Smerti came to take everyone from Zatelsk, Yiddish for what stands or falls beyond catastrophe, into the forest; and she went from Zatelsk, never to return, approximately a wandering Aramean, approximately dead, but for her feet pulling her forward, and the angel-babble, and the various appetites of her body; she traveled northward into the belly of some city or other, yes, first Pinsk, then Minsk, and in each city she toiled, scrubbing

in silence by day, and laying her head down on
some floor or other by night

Gittl uplooked toward Charles's face. Maybe better that you shouldn't tall letter amerike. Tall lettering makes a thing stand above the rest. amerike is maybe a god, yoh, but a god is not a holy thing. Only a person has a chance to be, so Itzl might still be written with a tall letter.

Noted, Charles said. I like that. I may borrow lowercased america myself. What else?

I see that you suremade to insert your komunistishe jargon to remind all the comrades that floorscrubbing is toil, but yoh, okay, it's a mayseh, not a manifesto.

I'll make sure to include that in my next self-criticism session. Anything else regarding this first sentence, Comradess?

yoh, Gittl insmoked. tayve isn't precisely appetite, it's something maybe bigger, stranger, and zi iz avekgegangen here is only she went, maybe better wentaway, as to keep the avek, and the commas with the dots on their heads feel like cages to the mayseh—

You're disappointed?

Gittl looked at Charles. If I was disappointed, I would just say all is in order, Charl.

Charles flushed.

I can call you Charl? It's strange for me to think always of many Charls, or of a second name.

How's that?

In Zatelsk, everyone's second name was as Child Charls.

Gittl Khayeles.

yoh, and Leyb Mireles.

Right. Well, sure, Charl is fine, as long as it's not Charlie. On that note, how about Zatelsk?

What?

Should Zatelsk be capitalized in american?

yoh.

Why?

Gittl shrugged. Maybe a dustvillage is more like a person than a god.

How about philadelphia, then?

You decide. Is your philadelphiye more like a person or a god?

Well, what's a god, Comradess?

A falsehope.

I'll drink to that. And a person?

A thing made from maysehs and tayve and the small choices of each moment.

Charles nodded. Alright. One more question, while we're on the subject. A malekh

yoh

nu

vus
Charl

is an angel, yes?

Gittl shook her head. Angel is a godword. Maybe better
sibling
better sibling
better a sibling
o wa

a sibling what is avek.

And the malekh made from only eyes? Also a sibling?

No, but it can choose at any time its own humanish collaborators, Gittl said. So perhaps it could choose Leyb'ele, or also I.

Also me.

yoh, also you it could choose.

No, I meant—never mind. I tend to wax a bit pedantic, which is what I liked about this mayseh, Gitt, the warts and welts, if I may. It felt corrective to the deadly puritanical neatness of this place, which I've inherited, despite our mutual loathing. It's truly hellacious, Gittl, this place. The way it sinks its glistening teeth into my flesh at every opportunity, but also simultaneously wends its way between my own teeth, into my mouth, onto my tongue, my pen. I think that's why I winced like I did at your comment about the semicolon. But maybe it's more than just semicolons versus commas, or tall letters versus short ones. Maybe there's something ultimately freer about the Yiddish, something that can't be oversat into american?

No, all tongues are the same upground humanfish, I think. There is no such holy mamatongue what helps any person to do anything or to be anything, or what keeps a person from anything. Also, if we're oversitting here into american all the way, Yiddish just is jewish. And jewish with a small letter, yoh?

But of course, Charles said. What else?

Gittl picked the topmost paper back up, downcast her eyes again. So, also Kuren Smerti can be oversat from ukrainian. Something as, as death group, or maybe death family.

Okay, Charles quieted, and Gittl uplooked and saw that his eyes were looking at her eyes. I'll try to come up with something. vos nokh, Gittl?

It's enough. I will read the rest, and we can talk more about this another time.

Alright, Charles said. I'm looking forward to it.

Tell me again why you are wanting to do this, Charl?

Charles laughed. It's a good question, Gitt. I'll get back to you on that one, bli neyder.[88]

---

88 "Without oath," which was, in fact, something the painter would say often, particularly in response to young Charles asking him about plans, or intentions, or amounts: "It will be more next time, bli neyder."

And tell me again how you are knowing jewish so?

It's not much of a mayseh. Just an old painter yid and a lonely, quick-learning kid.

Where is he?

The kid or the painter?

Gittl shrugged.

avek. In any case, if we're not going to go deeper into the warts and welts of oversitting your mayseh right now, I did mean to tell you that I recently wrote a piece of my own, uncommissioned.

Charles shuffled through the papers overstrewn around the table, and outpulled one from another pile. Gittl nodded.

Now is when you're supposed to say, Charl, that's marvelous, might I read it?

oy nebekh.[89] Gittl laughed.

Watch who you're calling nebekh, lady.

Give this to me, Gittl said, and took the paper from Charles.

Why, I thought you'd never ask, Charles said, back-taking the paper from Gittl, uppicking a pen, and out-crossing the first letter from the poem, and writing in its place a small a, and then backhanding the page to Gittl.

---

89 Difficult to translate (apropos the above exchange). Something in the vein of, "Oh you poor thing."

a~~A~~MERICA

by A. Weissberger

O Feathery Father,

Gentle fire-slick are the cocks
Of your bravest young men.

Fat are your fingers, too, like live-baits,
And fallow are the fields of your mind.

In your belly the fellow
You created sharpens nails, counts his

Teeth, for though you swallowed
You forgot to chew, your molars

Are rotting, and so slick and wise
Are those who will rise up with

Their cocks and rifles,
Ossian Sweet waits in every window,

His lovers sweat-pressed behind him,
All his friends steadying his hand.

I am there,
Yes, I am nearly finished.

When I dream or take aim, 'tis of thee.
You've had your chance

To repent or confess, tomorrow is a holy
Day, a celebration of our shared tongue, red

Won't all the rivers run and lo, my eyes
May stream with light and tears

But my hand, my hand, it will not
Shake or falter.

Have you sent it already to Weissberger?

Charles shook his head.

Do not.

What, too risky? That's the whole point of this particular Weissbergerization, Gitt. He's got the leeway for this sort of thing. Perhaps you could see it as one worker's effort to undermine commodity fetishism, Comradess. Plus, it doesn't hurt to obtain some capital while I'm at it. Goldfarb's hungry purse awaits, and if you think Lion's offered to divide the rent, well, then, think again.

I wasn't thinking from safe notsafe. There is no such thing from safe, Charl.

Both were quiet.

I was thinking from history, Gittl said. From laters knowing it was you what wrote this.

I'm not too concerned with the trash heap, Charles said. This piece doesn't need a Patterson imprimatured on it. I enjoyed writing it, and there's part of me that delights in thinking of Weissberger sitting on the lines about america's slickest cocks, and so forth. He probably won't even read it before he sends it off to the Worker.

Gittl did not speak. Outside there was a sound like hyenas laughing and shrieking.

Also, it's nice to get to wield a surrogate, as it were, rather than be wielded.

I understand.

Do you?

You're feeling like usually it's the jews what are using the colorfuls to moan toward stepfather amerike.

Something like that, Charles said. Anyhow, I did already give a copy to Weissberger, so history'll have to chew its cud for now. Would you like some more coffee, Gitt?

Gittl shook her head.

Smoke?

Gittl nodded.

Charles outtook two more cigarettes, placed one in his mouth, passed one to Gittl, leaned forward, flicked the edge of his everburnish zipper to light Gittl's cigarette for her. Gittl inbreathed smoke, looked for Charles's eyes, and then spoke.

Have you before been with a woman, Gittl said.

Charles uplooked from the nowburning end of Gittl's cigarette, through the ribbon of smoke what separated his eyes from Gittl's eyes.

Yes. Not for a while, but I have. Charles closed the metalcase of the zipper, the fire returned to its coffin of aluminum and evening.

Will you do so now, Gittl said, inhaling once more, downbiting her cheek as if to let the smoke seep into her skin, and then outputting her cigarette in the ashtray what lived always at the center of Charles's table.

Charles did not say anything, but he did not again open his zipper to light the fire of his cigarette, and Gittl removed her shirt and stood before Charles what was still seated in his chair, and Charles nodded as Gittl moved upon him,[90] and about this once, or the other two or four onces in what they shtipped over the next months, until Gittl grew uneasesome from feeling the

---

90 For he had lied to Gittl, of course, about having grown used to his loneliness; in truth, he longed for nothing more than for it to be lifted from him, to be taken from him, and he beheld Gittl, and understood that unto many men, she would certainly be perceived as comely, and though he was not squarely among this quorum of men, per se, he was able to appreciate her presence, and the impending pressure of her sex upon his sex, and the sangfroid coolness of her eyes, juxtaposed with the warmth rising from her skin, and the warmth of her breath, and the breathlessness, as Lion would have it, of this moment of urge, and urge, and urge.

same hands upon her, despite the gentlegrasping and the laughter of their continuesome oversitting conversations what preceded each shtip, about all of this?

yoh, there is not much else what to say.

yoh there is everything else what to say
as it is written the mayseh is avek
yoh and the mayseh is beginning
o wa there is always after

a betweenmayseh

And so yoh before and also after this once, Gittl was continuing six days a week to clean horses for the goyim, of what she was unmasksomely afraid, but she downbit her fear, and scrubbed, yoh, and before and also after this once, Gittl was continuing to spend some shabbes evenings and afternoons sitting with Anna or alone at the Freeling, overlistening to the afterconversations about the jewish theater shows, what she was eventually invited to join, both the afterconversations and the shows, and one of them was called And That Evening They Slaughtered Them All, about Kishinev, and that one Gittl did not go to see, and another was called The Conscience of the World, or some such, about the trials of the jew Schwartzbard, and that one she did not see also, but she was asked directly by a director named Yankeff to go see his version of everyjew's demonplay,[91] and it was

---

91 Probable reference to "der dibek," by Sh. Ansky, though

surprishly not entirely dreck, and afterward she shtipped Yankeff, whose staged choreography was firesome, but whose movements in bed were stiff and droll like some statue of libertine, and also she shtipped two of the stage-hands, what both, you may believe it or don't, were all the time looking at their own reflections in the underlit window, o wa, and also before and after this once, Gittl was going for some walks with Leyb, what came to find her at the ym-ywha, and what told her maysehs as they walked, beforemaysehs and aftermaysehs both, and in most of this time, Gittl was only listening to Leyb, but in the middle of one once, she told him that she had lain with Charles, and Leyb said, yoh, I had thought maybe this would happen, and Gittl said, Is it hurtsome for you? and Leyb said, No, it's what? and Gittl knew enough to know that there was more what Leyb did not say, that he was at least somewhat laughing with leeches, but yoh, she heard what she wanted to hear in his words, and after this, Gittl did lay again with Charles, but only one other once, or three others, but they continued in many other onces to sit across the table and oversit together, on paper and out loud, and this was even perhaps more intimate a thing, yoh,[92] and for this Gittl would

---

in Gittl's original formulation, it was rendered as "yedenyids dibekshpiel."

92 Indeed, the sex was fine, and fervent, even, at moments, but the translation sessions were, as Gittl noted here, the true site of

with her heart pounding many aftershabbes evenings make the walk to Seventeenth and Lombard from the ym-ywha, and sometimes Leyb would be there, and all three would together eat eggs, and moretimes Leyb would not be there, and would be instead at the Temple or at some aftercricket's awayplace, dancing and counting, breathing and not breathing, and Gittl and Charles would perhaps shtip one another in these leftalone onces, or perhaps not, but certainly they would talk, and certainly they would be intertwined together on the pages, and in all this time, Gittl was barely seeing the shadow of any Phonye soever, and was on some evenings forgetting to tell to her siblings any bedtime maysehs
yoh we noticed
yoh and we noticed something else
what Gittl noticed too but did not yet say to us or to herself
o wa littlest growingest
and then Gittl returned to Charles's house, in another once in what Charles had just received a telegram.

---

mutual urge and urge and urge: There, across the table, seated in the borderlands between the exposed and the shielded, between the desire to be known and the impossibility of truly knowing, between illumination and obfuscation, between truthfulness and the universes constructed mostly through lies. These pages are a testament, at least in part, to the faltering or flight of said sessions, or, more likely, to both.

Dialogues (III)

What are you reading today, Charl?

Today today? Nothing you've heard of, I imagine.

Try it to me.

Well, I just reread a story by Bruce Nugent, and I'm working my way through a recent study by George Padmore.

yoh, of course.

Charles rasied his eyebrow. You know them?

Gittl shook her head. I should?

You might be less partial to Padmore, a bit didactic even for me, but I think you'd actually like Nugent's story a lot.

Okay, I will read it.

What about you, what are you reading today, Gitt?

Poems, Gittl said. Margolin and Halpern.

Ah, very good.

You know them?

Alas, no, Charles said. I can't say I'm very well versed

in the velt of jewish verse. When I was younger, I did read some Peretz and Yehoash.

Gittl smiled.

Do you read them as well?

yoh nu, avade, Gittl said.[93]

Charles raised an eyebrow. Why are you laughing?

Don't worry from it, nebekh. Where is Leyb today?

I don't know, Gittl, Charles said. I'm not his keeper.

Gittl looked at Charles's face, and for his eyes. What's wrong?

Charles pinched his nosebridge with his finger and thumb, inbreathed, and pulled a folded paper from the pile and slid it across the table to Gittl. It was short to be one of Gittl's maysehs. Maybe it was another one of Charles's poems. Gittl had wondered if she might ask Charles if she could oversit one of his poems into jewish, but she felt shy to ask. She was thinking this as she opened the paper, and saw that it was not a poem.

T PATTERSON-(STOP)-IT HAS COME TO MY ATTN THAT CERTAIN FRIENDS HAVE PAID A VISIT TO A CERTAIN FACE WHOSE WRITING IS WELL KNOWN TO YOU AND THAT SAID FACE WAS QUICK TO DISCLOSE TRUE AUTHOR-(STOP)-I KNOW WE HAVE

---

93 "But of course."

HAD OUR DISAGREEMENTS-(STOP)-BUT THIS STOOL PIGEON MANEUVER BY WSS-BRGR WAS FRANKLY RATLIKE IT MUST BE SAID-(STOP)-NOT TO MENTION UT-TERLY UN T LIKE-(STOP)-SO I CHOSE TO ENLIGHTEN YOU-(STOP)-GOOD LUCK TO YOU-(STOP)-T LOVELAND

a telegram a megile,[94] Gittl said, glad that Leyb was outleft from this mayseh, and that Charles's shortness before was only directed to her.

That's your reaction?

What, better that I should react to your Loveland disbursing additional capital to remind that Weissjew is a rat?

Better that you should react to what this might mean for me, Gittl.

You'll be fine.

Is that so?

Or you won't.

Helpful.

Gittl looked back down at the telegram. What is T?

Tovarisch, Charles said.

Da nu, konechno, tovarisch, Gittl said.[95]

---

94 "Why, what a wordy wire."

95 "But of course, Comrade." (Rus.)

Charles didn't say anything.

Okay, you want that we should write to the International Ladies' Garment Workers' Union to come organize a manifestation? We will invite all the workers of the world into your home. But only not the Fur Workers, what because of the smell.

It's Goldfarb's home, not mine. Invite who you will, Gittl. You've been invited in, and the second you set foot on these hallowed, golden shores, you owned them more than I ever will. The communists are a little absurd, sure, but the enemy of my enemy and all. I would have hoped for better from old Weissberger, though ultimately, I'm not surprised that this particular character folded under a bit of pressure, and told them I was the author of the poem. Frankly, I suppose I didn't realize that america reads the pages of the Daily Worker so dearly.

If you are always vergishly being eaten inside amerike, why are you not leaving?

Maybe I should.

Where would you go?

Charles shrugged. I suppose I'd head on over to the soviets.

You can't really be thinking that it would be better there, Charl.

I'm really thinking it couldn't be any worse.

Mm. Might I again read your poem?

Weissberger's poem, Charles said, but rustled around in his paperpile, and pulled out the original folded paper. Gittl read in silence until the second stanza.

yoh, she said, uplooking at Charles. I had thought there was a highlandiker bit of baited Stalin epigram after Osip Floras in there.

Well perspicated, Ms. Khayeles, Charles said.

I'm not the only one with eyes. You have heard what they did with Tovarisch Mandelstam, yoh?

I've heard what people are saying, Charles said.

You might not be so welcomed in moscow either, Charl.

It'll be fine, Gitt. I'll tell them I'm Charles Du Bois, nephew of, yes indeed, there to work on a book adaptation of Langston Hughes's and Louise Thompson's discontinued mezhrabpom film about america's teeth, so to speak. Then, once I'm in, I'll chose a new name, and they won't be able to tell me from any other Pushkin-descended Tovarisch Adam.

You have given this some thoughts, Gittl shortlaughed.

Outside amerike howled and scratched its eyes with its tongues, and on its back sat a Phonye what opened the everskin of its face to swallow everything, and everywhere there was the forest, and nowhere after all was safe.

I don't necessarily like or trust any of it, Gittl. I'm just learning from our Lion, trying to overlive all of this.

Gittl nodded, and then moved forward to Charles,

and kissed him on his mouth, and their tongues pushed against each other for some time, but neither tongue was burning now, every tongue was heavy, yoh, and every tongue was lonesome, and also afraid, and in this moment no person was become less afraid or alone for the heat of bodies pushed together, so Gittl backpulled, and said, Maybe we should instead get back to work?

Yes, sure, Charles said. That sounds right to me.

yoh and after that
or was it before that
or was it between that
o wa

a mayseh fin a berg'ele[96]

Gittl awoke awashed in darkness, hands held clasped over her belly. Under the palm of her left hand, a pressure.
yoh a foot
or yoh a wing
and yoh this is what we had noticed maybe before even Gittl herself noticed
sha nebekh o wa she noticed

Gittl stopped breathing, and said quietly to the darkness: shulem aleykhem. And then she laughed there in the broomcloset of the ym-ywha, and she spit, and thought that yoh, fine, if it was a boy, she could after all name him for Itzl, it's what?

It was an elbow or a knee or a foot or a wing what moved across, just like that, and then back down. The next week, toes or bells wriggled, and in Gittl's body

---

96 "A story of a smallest mountain."

there was a series of pings. Of doing. Of being. Littlest, decidingest, exploringest, flappingest, tumblingest. Gittl found that she could pat in return with her hands, and once or two onces she did, backguiding the wings down, but mostly it was simply this:

I don't need to tell you how to move.

You know.

And when the flutterings came, yellow flowerings of wheat and green pine would fill Gittl's nostrils, heavy wind over a river of fire,[97] and alongside this would be the holy smell of nothingness, yoh, everything else smelled of too much: the ym-ywha deskaltishke's bread was rotted moss, the towelsoap was glass in her nosepipes, a horse was one hundred thousand horses, foot and feces and flank all togetherpacked in one single smell, yoh, and man's perfume would make Gittl feel as though she was wearing that man's flesh, not such a good feeling, yoh, all these smells would sit between Gittl's eyes, and Gittl longed but could not outtake them from her face.

Except for this one. This smell of nothingness, Gittl wanted not to leave.

---

97 Orig: nahar di nur (translationtongue, i.e., Aramaic); this term is found in a number of mystical Jewish sources, and is variously associated with both the wild beasts of the divine, and with hellfire.

Alongside the smell of nothingness were come beforemaysehs.

Mameshi.
o wa
Mameshi
Khayele the mousemaker
yoh

You used always to hold my hand when we homecame from the shil's posterior on shabbes, when I was so little, before Hendl and Zimml and Reyza, Anshl balanced on your other hip, and right before we tohomearrived, I would unthread my fingers from the latch of your fingers, and then wait without breath for you to put your hand on the back of my head, to feel the sifting of your hand on my scalp, and in my hair, what you sometimes did, and sometimes forgot to do.

Gittl, take your little brother from me for a moment, child mine.

yoh, Mameshi, I will take from you my sibling, my brother Anshl, and take good care with him.

And so nu whose? Maybe Yankeff's, the theaterman of goodlusting performance and lacklusting performance, depending on the stage, yoh, or the curlbearded stagehand's, or Khayim-Yankl's from the horsecleaners, or

Charl's? Never in all the feverish years after the forest had this happened, though not all were as careful as Itzl the orphan porter, such that Gittl had certained unto herself that it was being her self that had no more-lifeurge left after the forest, she had overlived, yoh, but she had not lived after the forest, and then this yellow wingsome fluttering, this smell of nothingness, this child. And so yoh, easy to say whose. Child Gittls.

Gittl's child, to laugh with about ways not to horse-clean, to tell maysehs to about time and siblings, yoh, about Anshl and Hendl and Zimml and Reyza
Gittl
sibling ours
yoh Gittl
o wa
and also about Mameshi and Tateshi, and about every-jew or at least some of the jews from the dustvillage known as Zatelsk.

To awaykeep always far from the forest.

Gittl's child.

Child Gittls.

o wa.

Dialogues (IV)

Gittl removed her tateshi's overcoat and walked toward the table at what Charles had already backgone to sit after opening the door, lighting a cigarette and there-waiting for her.

Oh my, Charles quieted.

Gittl looked at Charles's eyes, at his face what was partly covered by smoke.

Charles output his cigarette.

Is there, he said. Do you think it might be mine?

Ah, this? Gittl said, looking downward. kh'hob geshtipt got aleyn.[98]

Charles laughed without smiling.

No, in truth, I don't know. But I think you don't have to worry so.

I see. Well, in any event, mazel tov.

Gittl nodded.

---

98 "I fucked god himself."

Charles tapped his fingers on the outedges of his zipper flamebox what rested on the table between them. And if it is, if I am the father?

Then I'll buy you a nicesome cake.

How about a nicesome oneway ticket out of here.

Gittl sideleaned her head.

Come on, Gittl. People will want to know, america will need to know. It flies in the face of all that this place holds dear.

What should I care from what amerike deerholds.

What should you care indeed. It's less that, and more what might be said of the other part of the equation, or done to that part. To me, as it were.

But if they said that you forced me, I would just tell them it is not true.

Which mayseh do you think they'll listen to, Gittl, the one told by an immigrant jewess who cleaned floors for Marx's Beard, or the whole goddamn urfantasy of this fleshhungry abomination of a country?

I was ten when they killed Zachariah Walker over in Coatesville. He was still chained to a hospital bed when they set him on fire, Gittl. Afterward, some of them took his fingers as souvenirs. They stuffed his charred bones into a box and dropped them back off at the hospital with a note that read something like, A gift for his friends. That fall, I was walking home one evening from the Free Library. It'd just moved over to its current location, closer to our home, and my mother had started letting me walk home by myself. I loved it, Gitt. I loved that sense of freedom, of being all alone with the city, of disappearing into the city, those moments in which I was just one more person moving over pavement and under sky. That evening, though, near the corner of Spruce, this group of boys started walking after me. At first, they were just laughing, and making animal noises. Then one of them said: You'd better keep walking, Zachariah Walker. It turned into a little song, like this: Better keep walking, Zachariah Walker. Better keep walking, Zachariah Walker. Better keep walking, Zachariah Walker.

They followed me, singing like that. I forced myself not to run, thinking if I ran, something might give way, they might actually hurt me, or worse, so instead I just kept walking in front of them, surrounded by their singing and their laughter, and then, finally, I turned onto Lombard. And then they went off somewhere else.

It sounds like a hard time, Gittl said.

That's just it. It's not about that one time, Gittl. It's that I still find myself humming that melody today. All the time. I still sing their hideous little song to myself, like some goddamn american memento mori, only the death of which it reminds is not that which waits for all of us, et cetera. It's america's particular obsession with torturing me, day in and day out, until it finds a way to kill me, Gittl. And they were right, in that sense, america doesn't care about the details, Gitt. One day it's this, one day it's that. A lot of the days, it'll have something to do with a white woman.

Gittl did not then speak, only thought to herself again and again and again the word alone, alone, alone.

not alone

sibling ours

never alone

o wa

I don't, I'm afraid, Gitt. After everything that happened with Weissberger and the poem, and what happened at Cricket's earlier this year, Leyb told you about that, yes? And now this. I just have a feeling that everything is closing in around me.

I understand. Don't worry from a thing. Gittl backpushed her chair from the table. zay zhe mir gezint, Charl.[99]

Gittl. Please don't. I didn't mean it like that.

Gittl overmoved her fingers on the tablewood, outbreathed.

It's probably not anyway yours, Charl.

Alright.

And if it is, I'll buy for you a ticket to moscow.

Charles laughed. Alright.

Gittl did not speak, only overrested her hand on the smallest mountain of her belly.

---

99 Lit.: "Be healthy for me."

Well then, in the eventuality that it is, that I am the father, and you're anyway bankrolling my ticket out of this hell with all the gelt you've amassed from your various toils, perhaps you'd come with me? All of you, you and Lion, and the child?

Now Gittl laughed. This place, this amerike—

Outside Charles's apartment, amerike perked its ears to hear its name borne like this on the tongue of the infamous and apparently unbarren Gerty Radish of erstwhile Baroness renown.

It's disgusting, yoh.

amerike groaned and writhed and scratched at its eyes with its teeth.

It's disgusting, but it is further away from the forest.

Charles nodded, Right, yes, of course. I understand that.

Charles moved his hands to rest on top of the set of pages outset between them and before them on the table, as if to protect them, the pages, or to guard them from that what is made from only eyes. He had started, Gittl saw through the outsplayed fingers of his hand, oversitting her list, what Gittl had left with him after the last once in what they saw each other. In this moment, Gittl hoped that maybe after all it was his child also.

And I want, Gittl said, I have to try to keep this child always far away from the forest, Charl.

That depends, Gittl, Charles said.

Depends on what, Gittl said.
and Anshl withdrew his whistle and kitchen utensil
and Hendl held before her a stack of burning books
and Zimml dragged behind him a tusk what cut into the earth
and Reyza smallest sleepingest stood tall with her eyes open

For you and Lion, russia might be closer to the forest, but if the child is indeed mine, Gittl, the forest could move right in here for this child, for a child born within the Veil, as Du Bois put it,[100] philadelphia could become the forest at any turn.

Anything bad what might happen will happen, Gittl thought, and felt the everskin mouth of the city opening to swallow her, heard the buildings begin to turn into trees.
yoh he's right it's a narrow world
sibling ours daughter of our mameshi and our tateshi
the forest is always nearby
o wa

Gittl pressed two fingers to her right temple, inbreathed through her nose, oxygen being oxygen, more or less. I cannot believe that the world is only darkness, Charl.

Charles's eyes met Gittl's eyes, and in them were light and tears.

---

100 "ah, bitterly! ah, wearily!"

It's anyway probably Khayim-Yankl the stagehand's, Gittl said. He was the one what earlyspilled, I think.

Noted, Charles softlaughed.

So maybe we will overlive this together, Charl, in some place what is far from the forest for all four of us after all, Gittl did not say, because as it is written, a person can speak outloudly only seven and seven impossible maysehs before their tongue turns to ash, and Gittl needed still her tongue to tell to her child how to stay always far away from the forest.

Gittl and Charles sat for another moment in a still small silence, and then Charles's hand rustled the papers on what it oversat and from what it had not moved since moving to protect them from the world what is or is not all and only darkness. Shall we get to work?

a mayseh fin before and after

In the beginning, what is also the end, there was before and after.

yoh, before, Gittl sat amidst a pile of her siblings what were called Anshl and Hendl and Zimml and Reyza, and Hendl, the slaughterer's second daughter, told everyone the mayseh of what had happened when she had creeptoed to watch their tateshi through a hole in the side of the slaughtershack as he removed the chickentongues from his slaughter for the sake of their mameshi, yoh, what would use these tongues for the sake of all of the dustvillage what was known once as Zatelsk, and Anshl said to Hendl then, far vus, for he acted toughfish but was truly a tendercarp, and Zimml made a moanish sound as Hendl talked of how their tateshi had reached his fingers into the newmade space in the hen's neck and grabbed hold of the bottom of the tonguestalk and outpulled it, yoh, unfastening it from the beak. And if you all had thought it would be small, Hendl said, it was not small siblings mine, you may believe it or don't, the tongue was as long as the entire henhead, or perhaps as the entire chicken, and when it was out in the air it began to squirm of its own accord, and it tried to lash Tateshi then, it sought to avenge its host's spiltblood, yoh, for as it is written in I believe Psalms 154:14 or maybe it is in Enoch 17:2 an outtaken tongue from a fowl what once had fins and scales might be rightfully expected to seek a tongue for a tongue, and Tateshi could not use his knife to stop it, only his bare hands because of course Mameshi needs always for the tongues to be intact for the deathmalekh what is made from only eyes, Mameshi told me once that if the tongue is too small or blemished, yoh, then the deathmalekh what is made from only eyes would not bother to look upon it, and so would instead come to take perhaps the life of a jew in Zatelsk, and perhaps the deathmalekh what is made from only eyes might slaughter a jew in just the same—

Hendl, enough, Gittl said, not because she was afraid, but because Zimml was shaking and Anshl was greenish, but Reyza, smallest Reyza, yoh, she was calm, for Gittl's hands had been clasped clamtight over Reyza's ears, and only mufflesome puffs of Hendl's words had throughpassed.

Okay, alright, it's what? Hendl said. I was just telling you the mayseh of what happened.

o wa, said Reyza, shaking her head. But I didn't hear. Can you tell it again?

And after, they sought to awaytake one more child to the forest, right inside amerike.

And before, there were two jews what were not taken to the forest, and one was called Gittl, and the other was called Leyb. And there was the ocean what Leyb walked across, and the quiet of Cricket's in what men became unto him as a river, and there was Charles, therestanding, offtipping his hat and buying for Leyb a drink, and there was amerike's law, with its untruthsomely outstretched cock, and Leyb was taken from Cricket's into the forest of an emptied alley, and there was only a siblingsong, and then Charles and Leyb returned one evening, together, to Cricket's, and the river there kissed their faces and reached to touch their napes and uplifted them onto its shoulders, and Charles said to Leyb that he could stay for as long as he'd like.

And after, the Lion of Zatelsk stood alone inside a strange home, holding a stolen bundle.

And before, there was a jew what was called Gittl what placed into the earth, or at least under a leaf or handful of sorrel, 296 other jews, yoh, there was a jew what was called Gittl what was overliving, what scrubbed her days into the floor of Marx's Beard, what spent her nights talking with four other jews, what were called Anshl and Hendl and Zimml and Reyza, what wrote only a list what found its way into the very ears, sort of, of the very Baroness of philadelphiye, what sent for Gittl to walk across the ocean into amerike, and Gittl walked, yoh, but she thought to fall into the water, but she was propped up then by porpoises, but she was forward led by a blackbird what was burning but was not consumed, yoh, Gittl stayed afloat by the idea of seeing, once more, the other jew what was called Leyb. Then Gittl found Leyb and met Charles, what became to her as a friend, and what offered to oversit her mayseh into american,[101] and the three of them sat once more around a table covered with inkstains and acclaimed eggs, with glasses raised once more, another once, in hope for good lives and for peace, and Charles said to Gittl, in this last once in what the three of them only sat around this table, I wish I could come with you, to the hospital, my friend. Any day now, isn't it?

Gittl nodded.

I hope you understand why it's impossible for me to come with you, Gitt, Charles said, still holding his glass

---

101 Here goes, then, my friend.

in the air, but I also hope you know that I wish it was not so, that you did not have to go alone, and Gittl only said, I understand, Charl, and then Leyb said in jewish, his chin upraised, I will come with you, Gittl, and Gittl smiled and said to Leyb, A beautiful thanks, Leyb'ele, but she knew that she would not come to find him, in the beforemoments, to ask for young Leyb'ele's help, because she was anyway never going anywhere alone,
yoh not alone
never alone
never alone Gittl
o wa
yoh, she was surrounded by malokhim and by maysehs.

Once, after, there was a child what was called Reyza.

But in a dustvillage mayseh, there is always before.

Reyza, do we believe that all the world is darkness?

yoh and so
before that
wake up sibling ours
wake up Gittl o wa

a mayseh

Gittl awoke awashed in light.

Around peysekh? yoh, around peysekh.

In Zatelsk? Not in Zatelsk, in philadelphiye.

yoh but what part of philadelphiye? Gittl could not precisely remember.

Surrounded by her siblings, all in a pile, never alone, not alone?

Light hummed above her.

Gittl turned her face to the side, away from the light, to look for her siblings, but saw instead only one shaven deer, strapped to a metalbed, closed eyes bulging above its narrowish snout. Gittl turned her head to the otherside, and the stalk of her tongue was neckpulled back as she turned, yoh, her tongue felt the wrong size and there were embers scraping her throat. On her second side, she beheld there another deer, strapped to another bed, surrounded by the smells of hairless water, hardish brick, fear, rotting gums, yoh, the cleanish smell of amerike. Gittl tried to speak, but her voice was somewhere inside a stand of trees, yoh, was told not to emerge, did not emerge. Gittl tried to move her hands to touch the smallest, sleepingest mountain of her belly, but her wrists were crawlsome with tightholding fleshworms what disallowed her to move her arms so-ever. Gittl strained then with only her head, only for to see the smallest mountain, but beheld instead an uneven flatness what was not familiar, under a dress what was not familiar, yoh, so perhaps this is a dream, Gittl thought, and tried to let relief overwash her with this thought, and she wondered if she should say the dreamer's prayer, yoh, I have dreamed a dream and I do not know from what it is, but Gittl was drenchtired and her tongue was wrong and her throat was burn-some and her body was filled with an emptyish weight-lessness, and so she downset her head and closed her eyes to let the dream fade on its own, and called to her siblings again that they might help.

And then a voice, yoh, not Anshl, not Hendl, not Zimml, not Reyza.

Patient seventeen, said the voice, and behind it, a sound of pages trembling as though a jew was quick-searching for the end of a mayseh or a prayerlet in some disheveled or other book. Then the voice again: Here it is. Patient seventeen, Gerty Radish, seems to be stirring, girls. This one, if you'll recall, doesn't appear to speak english, throughout the whole procedure she was yowling and babbling in her native tongue. Just as well, though, twilight is twilight, the world around, and a body is a body, isn't that so? Excuse me, girls, I'm waxing a bit poetic here. Find the corresponding babe, now, would you, Mary Anne?

Yes, of course, Doctor.

Footsteps.

A voice now from farawayish.

Is this, well, no, it can't be. Sorry, Doctor, did you say seventeen?

Mary Anne, sweetheart, you are quite the forgetty head these days! Yes, yes. Patient seventeen. What's the matter?

It's just that, well, it's only that, Doctor, would you come over here?

Footsteps again.

Gittl did not open her eyes, was waiting for her siblings to arrive.

Anshl?

Hendl?

Doctor, look at the, I think, could this child be, is it, well, it couldn't be, but she appears, well, negroid?

Laughed the doctor, a biggish doctorsome laugh.

No, silly girl, certainly not. I can always tell a colored when I see one, or smell one, more precisely: they have a particular scent to them, medically speaking.

Now Gittl did open her eyes, did raise her head, could not wait any longer for her siblings, saw one doctor and two nurses bent over a reedish basket at the other end of the room, into what was jammed a child, humanish nibblings below be goddamned, and Gittl needed then only to find the right words, yoh, for she knew then that on either side of her, the deer were not deer, were only women, knew then that the fleshworms around her wrists were not worms, were only restraints, knew then that she had been told to find this place in the midst of philadelphiye by the helpfish deskaltishke from the ym-ywha, what had insisted, time and again, in the months after the tiniest, wingedest mountain of Gittl's belly began to grow such that it could not be not seen, that Gittl ought to ask for twilight when she arrived to the hospital, daughter, that the jews of philadelphiye were not dumb of modernity, that her very niece's very friend Blume-Bashke had in this very hospital not so long ago lifegiven unto her very own child in such a manner, that there was for Blume-Bashke, and also for any jew soever what wanted it, oh generous, friendsome amerike, sleepish twilight from chloroform or clementine or something of this helpful sort, and then that was that, praised is god, and Blume-Bashke's child was arrived, born inside amerike, with no danger soever, and Gittl did not at first listen to the deskaltishke's maysehs, and later again did not listen, but then, when the feelings of a golemfist squeezing inside her started, Gittl felt, yoh, that she wanted to stay clear of the forest, yoh, that she wanted to overlive, yoh, to remain alive, o wa, and to live with no danger soever, and so Gittl had walked alone across the puddlish ocean of nine or so blocks to the hospital what sat in the heart of philadelphiye's other hurpings and hullings, and Gittl did not ask anyone to go with her, because she was anyway not alone, never alone, et cetera.

Gittl looked toward the other end of the room, where the doctor was still speaking.

It's a discernible scent, medically speaking, girls, and this child—

Gittl's voice emerged from amidst the earthen weight inside her chest, she spoke into the room, in what she was alone, alone, alone.

My child.

And then she said to her siblings, I want that they should give to me my child. I want that they should let my hands free of these restraints, that this smart doctor speaking of scents, feh, that leeches should drink his fluids, that his body should be dry like a desert of upground bonedust, god forbid, I want that he should close his mouth around his stupid words and bring to me my child, yoh, and if the child is a colorful, siblings mine, it's meaning Charl's, what is better than some

Khayim-Yankl's, not so? Gittl tried to shortlaugh amidst the flames what clawed at her throat, and then she said, My child, siblings mine, and then she quieted, o wa.

And she waited for her siblings to respond, but they did not respond.

And she remembered then how she had gone into her home, after the clan of death came, and had found her siblings there. How she had brushed a feather of hair from Reyza's face, and asked for her to wake, but how she did not wake.

Once there was a jew what was called Gittl and Gittl sat amidst a pile of her siblings.

Another once there was a jew what was called Gittl, and Gittl was strapped to a bed in the center of amerike, and was talking to her siblings, and the only response what came into the room then was a silence, a still small shrieking silence, yoh, for Gittl had spoken not in jewish but in american, and not to her siblings, but out loud and to the walls.

What was that? The doctor spoke now loudish,

stepped toward bedstrapped Gittl, slurmed out one word at a time. What. Did. You. Say?

Downleaned. Eyes narrowed. Breath gagscrubbed. Teeth jutting all throughout his mouth.

Gittl wanted to look away from his teeth, but could not look away from his teeth.

Give to me my child, she said in american.

Doctor, she didn't, I don't think she meant colored, said a nurseish voice from the otherside of the room. Why, I'm sure she didn't. As you said, she doesn't speak english so well, and the scopolamine can have strange effects, and anyway—

Gittl's voice, then, became only a sound, became only a river, become only a song: Give to me my child.

The doctor closeleaned to her once more and spoke in a quieted american voice. Don't you worry, now. We will take good care of this child. I'll see to it myself that this child will have a good home. Don't you worry a bit.

Gittl tried then to stand to take her child, but she could not stand.

The doctor himself upstraigthened and spoke now in loudsome american.

Girls, patient seventeen needs help, immediately. She is a danger to herself, and to this child. Mary Anne, see to it that byberry clears a bed for her. And in the meantime, for her own good, please sedate her. She seems to be losing control, this thrashing isn't a good sign, not a good sign at all, medically speaking.

Right now?

Oh yes, right now.

And the child?

I'll take care of the child myself. Don't you worry about a thing.

And then a cloth covered with substances slithered onto Gittl's face, and it was downpressed there by hands, and Gittl tried to pull her arms free, tried to say something into the cloth, but the hands of the forest crawled all over Gittl's face and began to downpull on her eyelids, laying reddish darkness over all the world of Gittl's vision, and the room was filled with the doctor's chanting: mother unable, father unknown, and the sound of waters rising, and then, from the far corner of the forest, Gittl heard a wailingest, hungriest, hopefulest, and then footsteps, and amerike reached out to grab the only child of the dustvillage what was once called Zatelsk, the child what was in the reedish basket, alone, alone, alone.

yoh but not alone
Between the doctor and the child stood a tall man, with a jagged, scraggled beard, on his head sagged a yarmulke and in his hands he held a whistle and a kitchen knife.

yoh as it is written Gittl was not alone
Beside the two nurses stood a woman, her hair knotted into a braid what was a vine climbing a tree, her hands clutching a stack of books, each one of them burning, tongues of ash and wild horseradish outlapping from their pages.

yoh never alone
Steadywalking between the beds of downstrapped deer was another man, slender but with a roundsome face, hands behind his back, and he was thereholding a giant horn, what was overscraping the ground through the rising waters, what had now entered the room, and yoh, this horn was tearing right into the polish of the floor.

o wa

And beside Gittl?

Beside Gittl stood another woman, younger than the rest, with green eyes and freckles across the ridge of her nose, and some diagonal teeth, et cetera, and her brow was furrowed, yoh, and in her hands, there was nothing at all.

And the room was filled with jewslaughter, and then again with a still small silence.

The man with the jagged, scraggled beard, the man what was called Anshl, little malekh, now grown tall and sturdy, tapped his whistle twice with his kitchen knife, blinked with only one of his eyes, and turned to face the doctor.

tell me doctor what is it you intend to do before all the world

Thus spoke the doctor: Gosh, see, the thing is, this child, despite what I said, and I take back what I said, it's a beautiful child, it really is, and Mrs. Doctor and I have been trying for so many years now for a child of our own, and every fifth Sunday or so, you should see the way she weeps, when she thinks I'm not watching, it isn't fair, it breaks a man's heart, we are good people, good hardworking people, and gosh darn it, we deserve to have a family of our own, and I'm not a man of God myself, but by God, such a thing doesn't just happen, mother unfit, father, oh, goodness, babe in need of help, and then I might get to be a father after all, and as for the question of color, well, that should be no bother, the babe is pale, see, pale enough that I didn't notice, and this is America, after all, and what is America if not a future that can be wrought with a man's own two hands? What is America if not flexible? See, a colored child need only be considered colored if America says so, and who is to say what America says if not its citizens? See, this child will be what I say it will be, medically speaking. What is America if not the land of the free? What is it I mean to do with my freedom? I mean to give this child a home, this child—my child! I mean to bring my child back to my home.

And so Anshl pushed his kitchen knife and whistle against the doctor's throat, and he moved his tearfilled lightfilled eyes directly before the doctor's eyes, and he sang, yoh, this is my family, I stand now between you, man of death, and my family, but of course the doctor felt not, saw not, heard not.

yoh so bring the child home yoh do it now yoh know that this is not your child

The doctor moved toward the basket what contained the child, and with both of his hands he took the basket what contained the child, and as he moved to exit the room, there was come from the basket only wailing, then there was a door closing upon the sound, yoh, then there was silence.

Then the woman clutching the stack of burning books, Gittl's sister, what was called Hendl, yoh, what had become after all such a scholar, o wa, she moved to touch her hands on the shoulders of the two nurses, what were both of them bed-surrounding still, and downholding onto Gittl's mouth the cloth.

tell me sisters what is it you intend to do

The first nurse's shoulders downslumped then, and the chloroformish cloth fell onto the floor, and she backwalked and downsat in a chair at the edge of the room, and only gripped her own face between her hands, and then Hendl took with both of her hands the second nurse's face.

Mary Anne sweetheart tell me what do you intend to do now before all the world

Thus spoke Mary Anne Dulch: My friends call me Annie, Lydia came up with that nickname, she called me that since the day I was born, she was three and a half then, and see, I've just been in some other sort of state since Lydia, well, since Lydia passed, I can barely even bring myself to say those words, or any words, for that matter, this morning, I tried to cook oats and forgot to put in water and almost burned my house down, dear lord, Lydia would have boxed my ears, she loved oatmeal, and also now, goodness gracious, my big sister Lydia wouldn't have let this get this far, no siree, not a chance on earth, oh, Lyd. I miss you. I just miss my sister, and I mean to free this woman from her restraints.

yoh so free her let her go free

And the nurse what was called Mary Anne bent down toward the restraints what held Gittl to the bed, and she undid them, and Gittl was then able to move her arms and her hands, and Mary Anne turned from Gittl and walked toward the door, lest the doctor return just then.

Meanwhile the younger man, with the roundish face, the man what was called Zimml, sweetest Zimml, went from bed to bed, from downstrapped woman to downstrapped woman, and behind him the room was upfilled with jew after jew after jew, with frowzy hair and long dusty skirts and lopsided beards, and in their hands they held tightly on to icicles and clumps of sorrel and broken jars and bushels of pears and boysenberries and lopsided prayers and pairs of poorly cobbled shoes and buckets of potatokigel and little scraps of paper hewn from the wind and little singing children hewn from the wind and the room inside amerike then was upfilled also with the sound of strumming music.

what is it you intend to do before all the world

Some of the downstrapped women answered, I intend to remain here until something changes, and others, I intend to see my child, and others, I intend to give way.

yoh so remain yoh so see yoh so give way welcome welcome welcome

Gittl's hands were now free, yoh, to reach for the hands of the woman what stood before her, her sister what was called Reyza, youngest, strongest, bravest, o wa.

And Reyza spoke to Gittl.

Gittl sister mine what do you mean to do before all the world ends o wa or begins

And for a time what cannot be measured, Gittl only remained there, her hands holding on to Reyza's hands, and then Gittl spoke.

I will find my child, Reyza. I will tell to her the beforemaysehs of Zatelsk, and beforemaysehs of my siblings, yoh, Reyza mine. And I will write these maysehs on little scraps of paper hewn from the wind, and also maybe poems, or plays, even, it's what, and I will not let what was before be upswallowed by what came after, and o wa, Reyza, I will live.

o wa so live

And Gittl stood, upraised by all her siblings, and she outwalked from the door held open by the nurse what was called Mary Anne, what looked with her eyes at the face of the other nurse, what did not say then a word only held her head still in her hands, and Mary Anne whispered then to Gittl, Good luck, and Gittl walked then out of the hospital, not heeding any voices of Excuse me, ma'am and Are you supposed to be out of your room, she only awaywalked straight into the wilderness of philadelphiye, and as she did, she heard once more as if a wailingest, smallest sound, and she strained then to turn, to return, to awaytake her child from the forest, but it was as though eight hands or six hundred backheld her there amidst a stand of trees what had upgrown now in the very center of philadelphiye.

stay where you are
Gittl sister of ours
stay there Gittl
we love you o wa

So Gittl stood still amidst the trees, and then tried once more to speak to her siblings, to ask for help in what she might next do.

Anshl, you badluckster, tell me?

Hendl, blessed be the maysehs what carry us onward, et cetera, what now?

Zimml, should we not backwalk all of us together?

Gittl outspoke to her siblings, but her siblings did not answer, for her siblings had been taken to the forest outside of Zatelsk by the clan of death seven and eight years before this, yoh, her siblings what were called Anshl and Hendl and Zimml were dead.

And so Gittl spoke instead to the nothingness.

burikh dayen ho'emes.
burikh dayen ho'emes.
burikh dayen ho'emes.

And Reyza?

Gittl looked upon the face of the darkness what was filling all of philadelphiye, yoh, also Reyza.

burikh dayen ho'emes.

Reyza, Gittl said. I will call my child Reyza.

Once there was a child what was called Reyza.

Once there was a jew what was called Gittl, and Gittl stood: alone, alone, alone.

Only not alone.

For when the clan of death had come to take the people of Zatelsk to the forest, they took everyone to the forest, and all the jews what had been alive were not alive anymore, except for two jews what were called Gittl and Leyb, and Gittl had heard Leyb gurgling amidst a pile of people and pulled him out, and kissed his forehead, and made him stand and walk alone to the ocean, and then, seven and seven years later, Gittl had followed Leyb into philadelphiye, and had found him inside an apartment what was home to a man what was become in truth a friend, what was called Charles, and what Gittl came to call Charl, and so Gittl began then to walk, and she walked past the ym-ywha, and she turned right onto Lombard, and onward to the corner of Seventeenth, and there she climbed the crumbling steps, and yoh, with each step, her body prepared to collapse, but did not collapse, so perhaps, yoh, she was having help, yoh, perhaps she was not alone after all,

yoh not alone

never alone

not alone Gittl ours

o wa

and so arrived at the third door on the fourth floor, Gittl knocked: tuk tuk tuk.

Lion of Zatelsk

Darkness hummed before the door to the house, metal-chunk knob sewn into the softwood. Above the knob a grimacesome keyslit in what a jew might gentle an unfolded clip for paper. Hard to open a toothdoor with a clip for paper alone
yoh hard if you're alone
Leyb'ele not alone
and but lo, just so, opened. On the walls, some paintings, purchased, perhaps, from an old and now toothless jew, of little dogs circling a fallen vulture, of a strawhaired girl dancing in a field of tongues, of god, what looked just like his son, amerike. Or something like these. Leyb was not so much attention paying onto the worlds of paint pressed onto the walls, nor onto the couches what were so fluffish from being stuffed with mustelids including: polecats, martens, sea otters, and also dwarf mongooses and civet cats, all of them moanish and whinesome between the softmost textile, purchased certainly from

some Moyses on Market Street or other, their flesh partly nibbled, for here, inside amerike, who protects the gentlemost laws of kosherkeeping? Not even the strictsome jews. And who protects the sickish and the eldersome? yoh, the doctors do. And who in amerike protects an orphan child? This specifike doctor does.

Only: not an orphan. Only: having three people
and three hundred
o tum bala
what would tear the flesh from their eyestalks in order to weave a basket of safety, eyestalks and reeds and eggs and crumpled maysehs. Two of these people: now inside Goldfarb's apartment, amerike awayhumming on the other side of the door.

And the other person, the third person?

Puffling of the corner of Lombard and tormenta? Frowzy comrade to hedgehogs and fireants? Berryprofferer, roofperched jewbird, awaysent dustchild, everyone's frightened little boychik?

Leyb?

Here now inside these halls, creeptoeing upon a carpet made from humanish hair toward the masterful bedroom, from what snorish peals like teeth crunched between teeth emerged. Toward the door creeptoed Leyb, peering into an opencrack showing: Doctor and Mrs. Doctor faintly softpretzled in sleeping embrace, and on their faces, Leyb beheld the preshadows

of a newishly heftful amerikanish family, visions of picnics and bibs and captassels and castletops in some land or other and breezeful afternoons by the banks of the schuylkill, and yoh, there was amerike, kneeling next to the bed, brushing their hairs with its teeth, reciting to itself sleeptime maysehs about streetlights and walled boxes buried deep and gray beneath the earthcrust, and so distracted was it by its celebrational brushing and recitation, that it did not notice
yoh amerike did not see
could not lay its many eyes upon
the Lion of Zatelsk right there inside this very home.

Leyb creeptoed onward toward the nextdoor, quietish thanks to the help from the two escaped bloodstained polecats
it's wine Leyb'ele
it's only wine
and the limping family of martens and the halfeaten dwarf mongoose, all of what joined the animals already and always cuddled around Leyb's ankles, not at all minding the riverflames and the malodorous spines, and together muffled with their fur and flesh the sounds of woodcreak and carpetwhisper. Leyb opened the nextdoor: a watercloset, overspilling with glassish bubblets of soap. The next? A waterless closet, filled with syringes and sponges and vials and sphygmomanometers

and tiny hats and overflowing with no honey, yoh, only with evaporatish milk. And so but the next?

o wa.

There, in cribcage, causing even the undead mustelids and company to gasp and put their tiny paws over their frozen hearts, yoh, there, before Leyb, what had until recently been the youngest overliving jew of the dustvillage known as Zatelsk, yoh, there before him now lay the youngest living jew of Zatelsk: littlest, sleepingest, perfectest.

Step, silenced step, silenced step. Slightly scarred but now not scared hands of Leyb's downreached, uplifted. Lopsided mouth of Leyb's asking the night for only silence, asking friends, asking siblings
yoh Leyb'ele
you do not have to ask
and then?

Breath, tiny breath, tiny breath.

Flickersmall breaths. Shudderwing breaths. Keeping pace with the stars dying, each being dragged away into the firmament. A quicksome throb danced in the center of misaligned skullplates
tum bala tum bala
tum balalaike
and then slowflittled open one lid, and then the next, and Leyb? He gazed into two whorls of darkness, flecked with light, yoh, these were eyes what Leyb had never beforeseen, but yoh, these were eyes what were

like other eyes what Leyb had seen just a long hour before.

Peace upon you Reyza, Leyb quieted in jewish. I am Leyb. It is nice to meet you.

In his arms, the child again blinked, and then fell back into silence, yoh, into sleep.

Outwalked Leyb as quickishly as he could without overjostling, his left arm what was headsupporting achesome under this newest strangest weight, all the critters of philadelphiye scurrysome to upkeep. Leyb passed under the lintel of the maindoor, what was washed entirely cleanwhite and empty, yoh, and behind him, a rustle of perhaps movement, Leyb did not stop for sure to see, he willed only his mammalcuddled feet forward, willed the armbundle to remain silent, outstepped into the dullnight, and the air was dry and brittle like the bones on the floor of some dustish valley, and there was not even a single lilt of wind, let alone three or four, what could breathe life into the slain what sang their songs into the skykill river of stars. There was only a jewbird flown from the dustvillage, what had been pulled from a pile of people what included his family, what had done no more or less than overlive in every year and every moment since, yoh, but what had now walked alone into the ocean what is inside philadelphiye, had walked directly into one doctorly house, had passed through the shadow of amerike itself, had gathered help as he did so from so many helpful animals, what waved now with tiny paws and antennae goodbye to Leyb'ele, yoh, to Leyb, yoh, to the Lion of Zatelsk, what held in his arms one stolenest, sleepingest bundle.

All the World

tuk tuk tuk.

Opened the door Charles, and there stood Leyb, and in his eyes was an animal electricity and in his arms was a sleepingest bundle, and Gittl stood from the bed and moved toward Leyb, yoh, almost she ran, but she could not then run, so she began to stumble, but the apartment was so small that it took Charles very few paces to reach her, and he reached her, and he grasped her shoulder, and yoh, Gittl Khayeles did not then fall, yoh, only she stood, and then she walked toward Leyb Mireles, and she took from him the bundle, the child of Zatelsk, her child, her Reyza, and everything was still.

Reyza awoke and started wailing and Gittl sat with help from Charles and from Leyb on the springish couch what perched before the bookshelf, and she opened the shirt what Charles had given her to wear and she brought the child to her breast, and her child's lips searched amidst her wailing and then, o wa, onlatched, and at first this was like a firefinger instabbing into Gittl, yoh, but then it became as a heat spreading through her, and Gittl downlooked at the face of her child, Reyza, and Leyb then was only quiet, and Charles was only laughing and weeping.

Might I hold her? Charles said, after Reyza had finished and backfallen into halfsleep.

And Gittl strained to let go from Reyza, but she nodded, and she passed to Charles his child, and Reyza woke from the movement, but settled into Charles's arms, yoh, without again wailing.

Hello, Reyza.

The next moment was a moment what should be outstretched over time, but what cannot be, for it was made only of light and longing and belonged even as it started to the kingdom of before, and some time passed in this way, as it must, yoh, always there is after, and Charles kissed his child, Reyza, on her tiny forehead, and then handed her back to Gittl.

Leyb was now crying, rivers slipping down his face, waters rising around his feet, upfloating from the earth all the creatures what had againgathered there.

Gittl, what had not cried since one of the later days in the forest in what she placed under the earth everyone what she knew on earth, and also her siblings, did not now cry, she only stood, holding her child in one arm, and she placed her other hand on the back of Leyb's neck, and all the remnants of Zatelsk stood, then, under the lintel of the doorway, and the wind, then, gentled opened the door with its six hundred hands and it entered the apartment, yoh, and also the faintmost strumming did.

And then, only then, did the walls of Goldfarb's building begin to crumble into dust.

You'll write, yes? Charles said to Gittl.

I will write, Gittl said. And you will?

Charles nodded, and he forwardleaned and kissed again the forehead of his child, and then backleaned to keep hold of his balance as his apartment disconnected fully from the rest of the building. The air around them grew colder, and the city's sounds inflew from each direction, and Leyb and Gittl and Reyza were backpulled from the edge by the wind, and they stood in the doorway to Charles's home, and Gittl downlooked onto the ceiling of the apartment below.

You'll be alright, Lion, Charles said. If they do come, just tell them you're the tateh.

Charles turned. Give them all hell, Gitt.

And Charles looked once more at Reyza, and then closed his eyes.[102]

---

102 Reyza.

If you are reading this, know only that the moment in which I first held and beheld you was among the finest and most agonizing of my life. Know that I thought to say, "Come with me, all three of you," but did not do so, aware that there are only so many impossible maysehs a person can speak out loud before their tongue turns to ash. Know that this translation was done with you in mind and heart: not that I think for a moment that Child Gittls will need any american assistance, Marx forbid, in understanding the original Yiddish of Gittl Khayeles's mayseh, but there is, contained here, I hope, I trust, something more than just an approximate regurgitation. That woven together, perhaps, the two might even tug one another toward something of an emesdike mayseh, toward some disheveled version of a truthsome story.

A package containing Gittl's mayseh arrived in Moscow, in the spring of 1935, shortly after I did, along with a letter saying that Comrade Anna Trunksboym had helped arrange for publication later that year through Khvalyes, a new Yiddish press in Philadelphia, and that Gittl wondered if perhaps, after all, I might consider working on a translation. In this same letter was a postscript that told how she and Lion had taken you to meet your grandmother, and that everyone agreed that you have your Grandma Rose's smile.

And so, after, I set to translating these pages, hoping that one day you will read them, and trusting that one day, I will get to see your smile, to talk with you about all of this, and more, and longing that until then, the forest, which is after all everywhere—here, too, one can feel it closing in these days—will stay forever far away from you, my child.

And before?

Before that, Reyza, one last mayseh, about how, from the corner of Seventeenth and Lombard, Charles's apartment would break away from the rest of Goldfarb's building, exactly as Gittl wrote it, and would be carried by the rising waters filling the city, first toward a river, and from that river, toward another, and from that other river, toward the ocean, and when Charles reached the ocean, he would wonder for a moment or two about stepping out into it, and finding stillness there, but he found instead that he was held up, moving across the surface of the water, by a collection of words and memories and a few hopes, even, for the next day, and the one after that, and he'd have with him his books, and plenty of ink, and some eggs, and some blank pages, and the moments passed, as they did, as they must, until, from the bowels of the Atlantic Ocean, Charles arrived finally on a distant shore, and there, three men in furry hats with magenta tusks sprouting beneath their fine, thick mustaches—can you imagine it, Reyza?—would barrel toward Charles, and the tallest among them would snarl for Charles to state his business, live-bait fingers drumming frantically on one of the tusks, and he'd inquire as to who exactly was this Charles, indeed, and Charles would tell him that he was Charles Du Bois, nephew of, but that he'd prefer to use the revolutionary moniker C. Roses, and that he was here to work on a book adaptation of Tovarisch L. Hughes's unfinished mezhrabpom film, and before he could even finish his sentence, the three men's tusks would soften with comradely feeling until they all but melted and their mustaches would perk up over victorious smiles and C. Roses would be guided into the heart of Moscow with somber yet enthusiastic celebration regarding this Tovarisch's defection from the so-called land of the free, and he would not protest as he was paraded about, for as the old Bolshevik saying goes, better a bauble than not breathing, and good old Pushkin would wink at him as he passed by, and there would be something to the Ya ne rab, ya chelovik feeling after all, but in the meantime, before any of this, Charles simply closed his eyes, and then opened his eyes again, and looked toward the crowd of Zatelsker Jews gathered under the lintel of a home which was once his, in a sense, in the heart of a city which he sensed he would likely never see again, and he felt, then, a sadness, and a smallness, and the presence of death, and the pull of away, and agony, and the swollen fullness of evening, and the rising waters lapping at the building, and something akin to stillness before it all.

Reyza, here's to a good life, and to peace.

And then Charles said, Reyza, mir gleybn nit az di gantze velt iz kheyshekh, yoh?

And then Gittl said it also, and Leyb said omeyn.

and we said it
we all said it
we all did
o wa

yoh, we do not believe that all the world is darkness.

Acknowledgments

o wa.

The idea of condensing five years of gratitude into a handful of pages is daunting, dizzying. It cannot be done, and I cannot but try. Here goes, then.

A beautiful thanks: To my truly extraordinary editor, Jenna Johnson, for her vision, patience, rigor, and brilliance; it is difficult to overstate how much this book owes to her wisdom and insight. To my friend and teacher Rob Adler Peckerar, with whom I consulted over our Yiddish "red phone" constantly, agonizing over and delighting in questions of dialect, history, idiom, and transliteration. To my agent, Julia Kardon, who believed in this novel from its strange, meandersome beginnings. To everyone at MacDowell, where the first sparks of this book took form in the winter of early 2017, and where later stages of this book took wing in the winter of early 2020. To Yiddishkayt's Wallis Annenberg Helix Fellowship, and to everyone from the 2018–2019 cohort who traipsed with me around the fields and forests of Belarus and Lithuania. To my first Yiddish teacher, Esther Rollansky, who, at the end of our 2017 course through Tel Aviv University's Naomi Prawer Kadar summer program, reminded me, in her Argentinian-inflected Hebrew, that we'd barely scratched the surface, and said, in so many words, that the real magic of Yiddish is found in its combinationwords. To my dear friend, the novelist and playwright Kia Corthron, who read an early version of this novel, and whose suggestions and reflections on Augusto Boal's teachings about hope, ethics, art, and endings deeply influenced subsequent versions of this book.

To the incredible team at Farrar, Straus and Giroux, who took such magnificent care with and of this book, especially Lianna Culp, Julia Judge, Logan Hill (who took my seven-page letter of made-up grammar rules in brilliant stride), NaNá Stoelzle, Brock Foreman, Bri Panzica, Nina Frieman, Rebecca Caine, Debra Helfand, Daniel del Valle, Sara Hayet, Caitlin O'Beirne, Sheila O'Shea, Nick Stewart, Hillary Tisman, Amber Williams, Gretchen Achilles, Na Kim, and Pauline Post; and to Lauren Peters-Collaer, for the beautiful jacket design. To Hannah Popal, Soumeya Bendimerad Roberts, and everyone else at HG Literary. To those institutions that provided financial support in the form of emergency writers grants during the early months of the pandemic: PEN America Writers Emergency Fund, the Authors League Fund, the Carnegie Fund for Authors, and the Jewish Book Council (JBC) × CANVAS Emergency Authors Fund.

To Bert Struewing, to Nicole and Brian Gay of the Open Air Village School, and to Ann Guthrie and Athena Potter and everyone at the Antioch School, for their generous and wondrous childcare over the years in which I worked on this novel.

To other early readers of this book in its various forms. To Itamar Manoff. To Kirstin Allio. To Josh Weiner. To Jacob Udell. To Eimear McBride. To Marci Calabretta Cancio-Bello. To Colm Tóibín. To Nguyễn Phan Quế Mai. To Sarah Castleton, and everyone at Corsair Books.

To my beloved family members. To Randi Land Rothman and to Jay Rothman. To Jesse Rothman (who was also, as always, an early reader of multiple drafts) and to Chloe Zelkha. To Liana

Rothman. To Susan Elster and to Steve Zecher. To Ari Zecher and to Aurora Zecher, and to Chai and Eden. To Chana Kranzler and to Yannai Kranzler, and to Netta and Tidhar and Noam Lev. To Angie Hsu-Mazur and to Matan Hsu-Mazur, and to Kailin and Miko.

And to my friends, colleagues, and companions whose influence and presence shaped and guided these pages. To Lila Rose Clark and Cassidy Clark and to Evadene and Maeve. To Kumar Jensen. To Nick Eastman. To Andrew Forsthoefel. To Abeo Miller. To Lynn, Tim, and Andy Sontag, and to Sol. To Niquelle Orr and to Locksley Orr. To Jay Smithberger and to Tom Oktavec. To Noa Yammer. To Hamutal Blanc. To Uri Agnon. To Joshua Mabra, and to Ellery and Cecil. To Avner Gvaryahu. To Jonah Fisher. To Jasmine Amussen. To Jerry Lieblich. To Keelay Gipson. To Ayelet Waldman and to Michael Chabon. To Adina Marx-Arpadi. To Rhiya Trivedi. To Madeleine Thien. To Jacqueline Woodson and to Juliet Widoff. To Mutasim Ali. To Sara Shaw and to Avromi Kanal. To Daniel May. To Clare Fester. To Christa Whitney. To Zoë Aqua. To Brian Getnick. To Lisa Grissom. To Julie Weitz. To Sarah Nahar. To Abe Katz. To Heather Christle and to Chris DeWeese, and to Harriet. To Karen Isaacs and to Daniel Roth, and to Lev. To Gus (who may or may not be able to read this, given that he is a dog). And to so many others, comrades, acquaintances, interlocutors, and near strangers, whose kindness, weirdness, intelligence, humor, decency, creativity, and spirit also impacted this novel in innumerable ways.

In memory of Silly, beloved companion, dear friend. In memory of Esther Steinberg Rothman and Philip Rothman, and of Myra Rudick Land and Morton Land, and of Simon and Anna of Uzlyany, and of my other ancestors, too. In memory of Eric Friedland.

In memory of Karen McKee, Moya Shea, and Lauren Heaton. In memory of David Shneer, zol er hobn a likhtikn gan eydn; some of the final words of this book reference a correspondence we had about the Russian language and about Langston Hughes's time in Moscow. I think often of David's smile, and of his bright red shoes flashing over the pavement as we ran together through the Gorky parks of Grondo and Baranovich.

This book is dedicated to the memory of my grandmother's youngest sibling, Leonore, or Lee, and is also dedicated to her child, whom I'd so like to meet someday.

To Kayla—this book would not be what it is without your unparalleled, transformative readings; I would not be who I am without you. Thank you for everything, Kay. I can't wait for your change-the-whole-story notes on the next book, and on all the ones after that, too.

And to Nahar, little lightbeam—I love you more than all the words and all the pages in the world can contain.

Notes

yoh, and then come the books.

The following is a very partial list of the novels, political texts, history books, plays, essays, poems, articles, and translations that were central to this book's formation: *An Anthology of Modern Yiddish Poetry*, edited and translated by Ruth Whitman (particularly the work of Yankev Glatshteyn and Anna Margolin); *Gay New York: Gender, Urban Culture, and the Marking of the Gay Male World, 1890–1940*, by George Chauncey; *Stories and Pictures*, by I. L. Peretz, translated by Helena Frank; *An Anthology of American Yiddish Poetry: A Bilingual Anthology*, edited and translated by Benjamin and Barbara Harshav; "Talking About Feygelekh: A Queer Male Representation in Jewish American Speech," by Michael J. Sweet, from the anthology *Queerly Phrased: Language, Gender, and Sexuality*; "Negroes in Moscow: In a Land Where There Is No Jim Crow," by Langston Hughes (special thanks to the archivists at Central State University); *The Gay Metropolis: The Landmark History of Gay Life in America*, by Charles Kaiser; "If We Must Die," by Claude McKay; *Ulysses*, by James Joyce; *Mr Norris Changes Trains*, by Christopher Isherwood; *Selected Poems*, by Langston Hughes; *Pogromchik: The Assassination of Simon Petlura*, by Saul S. Friedman; *The Lesser Bohemians*, by Eimear McBride; *Kinus Dumiot* (Hebrew), by

Avrom Sutzkever; *Gavoha Min HaPakhad Ashir* (Hebrew), edited by Velvl Chernin, Yael Levi, and Yoram Nisinovich; the play *rozhinkes mit mandlen*, by Peretz Hirschbein; *Black Deutschland*, by Darryl Pinckney; *This Little Art*, by Kate Briggs; "The Task of the Translator," by Walter Benjamin, translated by Steven Rendall; *The Life and Struggles of Negro Toilers*, by George Padmore; *Lonely Crusade*, by Chester Himes; *Envy, or Yiddish in America*, by Cynthia Ozick; *Better Angel*, by Forman Brown, *Her First American*, by Lore Segal; *Wayward Lives, Beautiful Experiments: Intimate Histories of Riotous Black Girls, Troublesome Women, and Queer Radicals*, by Saidiya Hartman; *Songs in Dark Times: Yiddish Poetry of Struggle from Scottsboro to Palestine*, by Amelia M. Glaser, and especially the work of Esther Shumiatcher highlighted and translated therein; *The Romance of American Communism*, by Vivian Gornick; *Speaking Truth to Power: Essays on Race, Resistance, and Radicalism*, by Manning Marable; *Going to Meet the Man* and *Another Country*, by James Baldwin; *Jewish Radicals: A Documentary History*, edited by Tony Michels; "The Problem Negro and Other Tales," by Joe Wood; "Keeping a Legacy of Shared Struggle," by bell hooks; "Negroes Are Anti-Semitic Because They Are Anti-White," by James Baldwin; *Philadelphia Divided: Race and Politics in the City of Brotherly Love*, by James Wolfinger; *Jewish Personal Names: Their Origin, Derivation and Diminutive Forms*, by Rabbi Shmuel Gorr; the Vitosk yizker bukh; the Rozhnyatov yizker bukh; the YIVO encyclopedia page on pogroms; *In geveb*'s special issue entitled "Race in America, *af yidish*"; *Beyond the Color Line and the Iron Curtain: Reading Encounters Between Black and Red, 1922–1963*, by Kate A. Baldwin; "The Pattersons: Expatriate and Native Sons," by Rimgaila Salys; "The Harlem Renaissance at 100: As Black as it was Gay," by Rob Perrée; *The Portable Nietzsche*, edited and translated by Walter Kaufmann; Rudolf Rocker's 1919 Yiddish translation, *azoy hot geredt Tsarathustra*, accessed through the

Yiddish Book Center's digital archives; *Pogrom: Kishinev and the Tilt of History*, by Steven J. Zipperstein; *The Second Coming of the KKK: The Ku Klux Klan of the 1920s and the American Political Tradition*, by Linda Gordon; *The Joys of Yiddish*, by Leo Rosten; "On Yiddish Poetry and Translation of Yiddish Poetry," by Kathryn Hellerstein, in *Radical Poetics and Secular Jewish Culture*; *Imagining Each Other: Blacks and Jews in Contemporary American Literature*, by Ethan Goffman; *The Philadelphia State Hospital at Byberry: A History of Misery and Medicine*, by J. P. Webster; "The Yiddish Conundrum," by Dovid Katz; *The Book of Enoch*, by god in himl (jk); *Leaves of Grass*, by Walt Whitman; Alexander Harkavy's 1928 Yiddish-English Dictionary; the University of Kentucky's online Yiddish dictionary; Columbia University's "Mendele: Yiddish Literature and Language Forum"; and some aid, too, from reb google; the Jewish Museum of Philadelphia; "der goylem," by H. Leivick; "mayn umru fin a volf," by Moyshe-Leyb Halpern; "'Community On Trial': The Coatesville Lynching of 1911," by William Ziegler; *The Zelmenyaners*, by Meyshe Kulbak, translated by Hillel Halkin; *Gay and Lesbian Philadelphia*, by Thom Nickels; *Anarchism: What It Really Stands For*, by Emma Goldman; "'I Shall Speak in Philadelphia': Emma Goldman and the Free Speech League," by Bill Lynskey; "Black and White: The Story of a Failed Film Project," by Galina Lapina; *in amerika*, by Sholom Aleichem; "Narrating Nationalisms: Black Marxism and Jewish Communists Through the Eyes of Harold Cruse," by Alan Wald; "Race, Politics and US Students in 1930s Soviet Russia," by Meredith L. Roman; "When the Harlem Renaissance Went to Communist Moscow," by Jennifer Wilson; a conversation between Minkah Makalani, Meredith Roman, and Steven Zipperstein on the *SRB Podcast*; editorials from various issues of *The Crisis* and *Young Spartacus* from the 1920s and early 1930s, accessed through Marxists.org; additional interviews and conversations I had with Noyma Appelbaum about Jewish communist Philly, and with Hershl Hartman about communist New York, and with Tony Michels about the CP and Jews, and with Paul Buhle about C. L. R. James and Paul Robeson, and with Meredith Roman about pseudonyms and Soviet show trials, and with Dovid Katz about dialectal borders and naming traditions in Yiddishland, and with Steven Zipperstein about the geopolitical history of pogroms, and with Dylan Kaufman-Obstler about the Workers University; the films *Der Dybbuk* (1937) and *Hester Street* (1975); and the Stonehill Yiddish Song Collective's archives, where I first heard the song "tuk tuk tuk."

The chapter title "Coffinbird" is drawn from a line from Yankev Glatshteyn's poem "The Poet Lives": "di yiddishe levaye-feygl shnapn," or, in Ruth Whitman's translation, "The Jewish coffin-birds snap." The reference to the Kuren Smerti, or the Clan of Death, is drawn from the book *Slaughter of the Jews of the Ukraine in 1919*, by Elias Heifetz (1921). The Bird-Jew story that Charles tells Leyb in the "Tormenta" chapter is an approximate retelling of a story from Sholom Aleichem's memoir, *The Great Fair: Scenes from my Childhood*, translated by Tamara Kahana. The story of George Queen's assault and trial is based on a footnote in W. E. B. Du Bois's *The Philadelphia Negro*. Sections of Charles's speech delivered by Weissberger at the CP meeting include references to C. L. R. James's speech "The Two Sides of Abraham Lincoln"; the phrase "reject the shibboleth of bourgeois democracy" used by Charles in footnote 76, as well as the argument made in this footnote, are both drawn from James's speech "The Revolutionary Answer to the Negro Problem in United States." The detail in this speech about George Washington's teeth is drawn from Professor Hasan Kwame Jeffries's 2019 *New York Times* interview with Nikita Stewart. Footnote 23 ("They want to go to the commune! They want to make boots with their hands!") is a reference to a line from the popular 1931 Soviet film *Road to Life,* directed by Nikolai Ekk. The phrase "the pineapple of politeness" in footnote 73 is drawn from a line by the character Mrs. Malaprop in Richard Brinsley Sheridan's 1775 play *The Rivals.* Footnote 85 is a quote from Richard Bruce Nugent's "Smoke, Lilies and Jade," which was first published in the 1926 issue of *Fire!!.* Footnote 100 is a compressed quote from W. E. B. Du Bois's *The Souls of Black Folk;* the reference to the "dark and pierced Jew" in footnote 49 is drawn from the same book. I learned the parable of Moses and the lost sheep from my dear friend Josh Weiner. Angela Brentlinger and David Shneer both helped out with the fragments of Russian interspersed throughout the novel. Some of the weirder 1930s slang ("rhino suds," e.g.) came from the "Slang of the 30s" page on a site called Paper Dragon. The detail about boiled puffins in Iceland was drawn from Leni Zumas's marvelous novel *Red Clocks.* The scene in which the women of Zatelsk "let dance in the pan just a few pinches of sorrel and a snippet of thyme or two" is a tribute to a detail in a short story in which the contemporary protagonist does something similar with onions, but—Marx in himl forgive me—I cannot remember which story it is, or by whom, or when I read it, even; I am indebted to that author and text. Part of the Phonye's monologue in the early parts of the "philadelphiye" section is one of a few instances of deliberate anachronism, and is based on the transcript of an interview Claude Lanzmann did with the former first lieutenant of Einsatzgruppe C, Karl Kretschmer, for the film *Shoah.* Parts of this section (and others) reference the story of Sholem Schwartzbard's 1926 assassination of Simon Petlura. The phrase "o wa" was drawn from I. L. Peretz's *Stories and Pictures,* and from David Pinski's *Yiddish Tales,* also translated by Helena Frank. Comrade Bear-Meerkat's recitation at the CP meeting is a partial amalgamation of the poem "Lynching," by Barysh Vaynshteyn, and the poem "Strange Fruit," by Abel Meeropol. Charles's poem, "america," contains references to Osip Mandelstam's poem "The Stalin Epigram," also known as "The Kremlin Highlander," and to Anna Margolin's poem "langzam un likhtik," or "Unhurried and Radiant" in Ruth Whitman's translation, which is referenced a few other times throughout this novel. The character of Anna Trunksboym is a tribute to three Annas: the poet Anna Margolin (Clara Lebensboym), the writer and political activist Anna Strunsky, and my great-great-grandmother Anna Land. The phrase "Here goes, then" is a tribute to Etty Hillesum and her collected writings, published as *An Interrupted Life* and translated by Arnold J. Pomerans, which begins with the same phrase.

Zatelsk is a fictional village, but it is firmly located in the Volhynia region of northeastern Ukraine, somewhere near the center of a triangle formed by Lutsk, a midpoint between Rivne and Zhytomyr, and Pinsk, Belarus. Its location is significant in terms of both its geopolitical history and its dialectal nuances, and was determined in consultation with Rob Adler Peckerar, who also helped me come up with its name, which is an amalgam of Slavic and Yiddish, and which means something along the lines of beyond (Ukrainian/Slavic preface "za") catastrophe (Hebrew/Yiddish "tel"). Other physical and spiritual features of Zatelsk are based on the shtetl of Uzlyany, in central Belarus, where my great-great-grandparents were born, and where I was lucky to spend a time-bending, heart-changing morning, alongside folks from the Helix Fellowship in the summer of 2019. The trees on the cover of this book are based on a stand of trees in Uzlyany.